DEATH IN A SUMMER COLONY

AARON STANDER

WRITERS & EDITORS
INTERLOCHEN, MICHIGAN

ISBN: 978-0-9785732-9-4

Printed and bound in the United States of America

FOR BEACHWALKER

WHO HELPS THIS ALL HAPPEN

1
~

The blast from an assault rifle, intensified by the heavy overcast, reverberated through the valley, and bounced off the steep, heavily wooded hillsides. As the blare faded away, Ray Elkins, the Sheriff of Cedar County, lying behind an embankment of sand and second growth hardwoods, glanced up. He became aware again of the pounding rain on the newly emerged foliage overhead and the distant thunder as the storm continued to roll off Lake Michigan.

The clothing beneath his body armor had soaked through hours before, and he shivered as he and the other members of the SWAT team held their positions surrounding the cottage.

An early morning confrontation in the Mission Point Summer Colony had turned into a daylong standoff. The shooter had holed up in an old cottage of the still-deserted colony, a collection of more than 250 small seasonal dwellings built on the shore and through the valleys of an old Indian mission. Most of the structures in the colony dated back to a period near the turn of the twentieth century.

Ray lifted his head above the ridge, looked toward the white-framed building, and glanced at his watch. It was only a few minutes after four. Even with the dreary weather, there were still hours of light. And if the situation continued into darkness, banks of spotlights were already in position to illuminate the area.

In the early hours of the confrontation, Ray had tried to establish communication with the shooter, Garrick "Garr" Zwilling. First he had attempted to use a landline, then a cell—the numbers provided by the manager of the colony. Both were out of service.

Next, he had tried a bullhorn. Each attempt was met with gunfire, not necessarily in Ray's direction. Most of the action seemed to be directed toward a nearby cottage, the windows and doors the focus of the shooter's fury.

In the earliest stages of the faceoff, trying to avoid a "suicide by police" scenario, Ray quickly moved to contain the scene. SWAT team members surrounded the cottage from protected positions behind rolling dunes, preventing any possible escape. Other officers, some from neighboring jurisdictions, helped seal off the site from a hoard of curious onlookers drawn to the area as rumors of confrontation spread through the nearby communities.

Ray had hoped that Zwilling would eventually run out of bullets, rage, or both and come out with his hands in the air. These always end badly, he thought. He reflected on the all too familiar patterns. The shooters, always male and usually young, with histories of depression, conditions often exacerbated by alcohol and drugs, would force a deadly showdown.

A prolonged break in gunfire prompted Ray to move to a better vantage point. He slowly surveyed the scene as he reviewed his options. The exterior of the century old cottage was covered with lap siding, the multiple coats of white paint peeling in places. The trim around the windows and porch were a forest green, as was the lettering of the name, Ravenswood Cottage.

The glass in most of the windows facing Ray was now cracked or broken. Heavy shutters still covered the windows on the second story.

Using binoculars, Ray tried to peer into the dark interior through the heavy gloom. He could see no light or movement, just indistinct shadows. Then his focus shifted to the sound of breaking glass, followed by the shutters on a second story window being pushed open. He anticipated another volley of gunfire, but only silence followed.

Several minutes later a tiny flicker of light appeared on the left side of the ground floor. A flash followed. Windows and doors exploded outwards, waves of flame propelling the fragments of wood and glass. Then the walls buckled out, fracturing in the middle. The roof and second story seemed to be suspended midair for a second or two before collapsing into a roaring inferno. Ray could see a figure moving among the debris that was thrown from the structure, the man's hair and clothing aflame.

Before he could move from his position, other team members were already running toward the figure. By the time Ray reached the man, two EMTs had smothered the burning clothing with blankets and pulled him a safe distance from the roaring pillar of flames. "Still alive," said one of them, in answer to Ray's questioning expression. Then the victim was quickly loaded on a stretcher and carried away.

Firefighters and their equipment moved forward from a staging area a few hundred yards away and began to pour water on the flames. Within minutes, all that remained were the blackened remnants of the cottage. The cement block pillars of the foundation, only four courses high, now rose above the debris.

2
~

The next morning Ray stood on the promontory that had been his command post the day before with Richard Grubbs, the manager of the Mission Point Summer Colony. In the dappled light—the brilliant sun streaming through the dense foliage of the hardwood forest—firemen shifted through the charred debris.

"Building was there for close to a hundred years," said Grubbs. "Made it through lots of storms, winters, generations of families, gone in what...?"

"Fifteen minutes," answered Ray. "Actually, it was gone in a few seconds, fifteen minutes more for the fire to destroy what was left." He looked over at his companion. Grubbs was tall, thin, and slightly stooped. A blue cotton, button-down shirt extended beyond the neck of a sweatshirt and khaki pants hung on his aging body. His feet disappeared into a worn pair of Bean camp moccasins.

"Well, there wasn't much there, just framing, no drywall or plaster. It was one of the few cottages that hadn't changed much over the years."

"The explosion reduced it to kindling. What was left was quickly consumed by fire," said Ray. He turned to Grubbs. "Sounds like you were familiar with the place."

"I was in there many times over the years. In fact, I stopped by a couple of days ago to talk to Garr. One of our maintenance guys had reported that Zwilling was in residence. Normally we open the grounds for the summer residents the last weekend in April, but this year we moved it to the middle of May. That last ice storm in March, the one that knocked out the power for four or five days, caused a huge amount of destruction here. We still have roads blocked by fallen trees. Power hasn't been fully restored to all the cottages. We notified all the owners of the delay, but somehow Zwilling didn't seem to get the word. I went over to ask him to leave the area."

"His response?"

"It was clear that the man had been drinking…probably for days. He was wild, unshaven, and belligerent. In fact, I was thinking about calling your department for assistance. That said, we try to keep things in the family. Yesterday morning I asked one of our guys to check and see if Zwilling had left as he'd promised. Five minutes later Ted was back, saying that Zwilling was on his front porch, gun in hand. I walked back with Ted. I had some silly notion that I could talk him down. As we approached, he started shooting the windows out of the neighboring cottage. That's when we crawled behind this hill, and I dialed 911."

The men stood in silence for a long moment and watched the activity below.

"What's Zwilling's condition?" asked Grubbs. "Is he in Traverse City?"

"No. He was transported to the burn center in Ann Arbor as soon as he was stabilized. When I checked earlier this morning, he was still in critical condition. Have you had other encounters with him over the years?"

"I can't say that I have. In a place like this you get to know people over many decades and generations. Granted, it's only two months of the year, just a slice of their lives. I remember Garr's grandparents, lovely people. His grandfather was a psychiatrist, a very quiet, thoughtful man. By default, he was our resident physician during the summer, first aid kind of things, cuts, bruises, the occasional stitch or two. Garr's grandmother was always in the choir, a soprano. She also worked in the costume shop for our annual play and did the flowers for the chapel. They were lovely people. They had children late, after Dr. Zwilling returned from service in WWII.

"But their three kids were rounders of the worst sort. Remember, it was the 60s when they came of age, but they were all about drugs, sex, and rock 'n' roll to the exclusion of everything else. Garr is the child of the second son, Jeff, and his hippy girlfriend. As I remember it she went by the name Moonbeam. That first summer they carried him around in a cardboard box with Tide printed on the sides. Then they sort of disappeared. Word was they were living in a commune in California or Arizona. Next time I saw the kid he was in his teens, sent to spend the summers here with his aunt, Regina. She ended up inheriting the cottage after Dr. Zwilling and his wife had passed on. She was the only one of the three children who turned out okay."

"And she still owns the place?"

"As far as I know. I haven't seen her around here in years. In fact, the cottage has been standing empty for a number of seasons. That happens sometimes. People vacation in other places, get sick, and sometimes end up in nursing homes or die. No one uses the cottage. So I was surprised when Garr showed up. I hadn't seen him for years, but he looked just like his dad, long hair and all. Impossible not to recognize."

"Did you contact Regina about the fire and her nephew?"

"I tried to call her yesterday. The number I had was out of service, and I don't have an email address for her. We have lots of people dropping their landlines, and they just don't notify us. Then when there's a problem, or I need to talk to…."

"Well, I'd like to have any information that you can provide about Regina. We will try to find her. Also, Zwilling's car, I didn't see one near the cottage."

"No," said Grubbs, "there wasn't one. He knew he shouldn't be in here. So if he came by car, he deserted it somewhere in the woods or maybe left it in town and hitched a ride out here. If you follow me down to the office, I'll give you all the info I have on Regina. And how about some coffee? It will take the chill off."

3

Richard Grubbs placed two books in front of Ray, black plastic bindings holding the 8 x 11 pages together. Ray looked at the titles, each from the imprint of a woodblock—The History of Mission Point Summer Colony and The Cottages of Mission Point Summer Colony.

Grubbs pulled the second book back to his side of the desk, briefly looked at the index, thumbed through the large pages for a few moments, and then pushed it back toward Ray. "There's the Ravenswood Cottage. There are several photos on that page and the next. As you can see, other than the trees getting bigger, not much changed over the years. How do you want your coffee?"

"Black, please."

Ray studied the photos and the text carefully, then turned to the next page. The pictures appeared to be at least thirty or forty years old. He quickly paged through the book. The snapshots, grainy and indistinct, were all in black and white. Turning back to Ravenswood Cottage, he looked at the building and the children who had been assembled in front of it, three boys and two girls holding towels and smiling in beachwear from the early part of another century. A United States flag hung from a pole at one end of the porch. Ray looked at it closely, wondering about how many "stars" were included in the folds.

Grubbs set a heavy, thick-walled coffee mug in front of Ray, its ceramic finish dulled by decades of use. He peered over at the page with the Ravenswood Cottage. "Looks about the same."

"Yes," said Ray. "I'm guessing from the names listed that four families owned it over the last hundred years."

"Yes. That's probably sort of average. I've never looked at things quite that way. Maybe this summer I can get one of the kids to make a database for me. I'd like to do that kind of analysis."

"Pretty easy to set up a…."

"For you, perhaps. My computer skills are limited to hunt and peck typing. I can sort of do e-mail, too. Don't plan to learn anything else. People will expect me to do things I don't want to waste time on."

"As you can see," Grubbs continued, "some of the places are still in the hands of the original families, passed down from one generation to the next. If the kids don't want the cottage, it often goes to a niece or nephew, or sometimes cousins who summered here. Mission Point Summer Colony is magical. Lots of people with rich childhood memories hope to come back and recapture that magic every summer for the rest of their lives."

"And I see here that Regina Zwilling is the owner of record. I need her contact information."

"I haven't forgotten." Grubbs pulled open a battered wooden file box and flipped through the 5 by 8 cards. "I must not have put it back." He crossed the room to another desk, one with a computer and phone. "Here it is."

Sliding it across the desk to Ray, he said, "Sorry I can't make you a copy. The toner cartridge died last week, and I haven't had time to run to town and get a replacement."

Ray opened a small notebook and copied the information, then took a picture of the card with his iPhone. "Just in case I can't read my writing," he explained. "I need to go over some of the things you told me earlier. First, this is the number you called?"

"Yes. I dialed it, and I got one of those out of service recordings."

"When was the last time you had contact with Regina Zwilling?"

Grubbs looked thoughtful and pulled at the skin on his Adam's apple. "I'm not quite sure. People come and go all summer. Some are very social, stopping when they arrive for the summer, taking part in the colony's activities, visiting me here in the office for coffee and conversation, and always coming in at the end of the season to say goodbye. Then there are others. If I see them at all, it's just a chance event."

"But how about Regina?" Ray pressed.

"Like I said, I'm not sure. I don't think I saw her last summer, perhaps the summer before."

"And the nephew?"

"Garr, I haven't seen him in years, not until yesterday, or I guess it was the day before wasn't it. Hard not to recognize him, though. As I think I told you, he looks just like his father. And I'm about his father's age, a few years older. We were teenagers here at the same time."

"Were you friends?"

"No," said Grubbs. "We were just different enough in age that we didn't hang out together. You remember how much two or three years seems to matter when you're fourteen or fifteen. I do remember he was wild, even in high school. Like I was telling you before, Jeff became a real hippie his freshman year in Ann Arbor. Next time I saw him he was in bells, with beads, long hair, and tie-dyed shirts. He and his girlfriend were around for a year or two, Garr arriving along the way, and then they headed west."

"Have you seen Jeff in recent years?"

"No. I don't know anything about him. The only member of the family that I've had contact with over the years is Regina."

"For the record, what is your title here?"

"I'm the Executive Director for the Mission Point Summer Colony. That's a new position. We never had anything like that before. But after I retired from my college teaching position, the board members decided to get this place more organized. So they created this position. They also wanted me to write a history of the colony. They tied those two things together, paying me a pretty good salary and turning the old caretaker's cottage into a year-round residence so I would have easy access to the county road. Before that, I had been the mayor of the summer colony."

"Mayor?" said Ray, some amusement in his voice.

"The summer colony has been run as a cooperative corporation through the years. There were no officials, policy was set by an elected board. But about 30 years ago major serious rifts began to develop between some of the summer residents."

"Over what?"

"In a nutshell, one group was against any changes in the colony. The other group was interested in modernizing things a bit. Like we had that big incident over cutting some trees a while back. We had to call your department to keep people from coming to blows."

"When was that?"

"Oh, maybe 20 years ago, perhaps a little longer."

"Before my tenure. What was going on?"

"The township fire department came in with their new pumper truck. They wanted to make sure that they could get it through the colony roads and down to the lake. There were several places where trees had to be removed to make the road wide enough for the truck. We had some people who surrounded the trees with their bodies, the human chain thing. We had other people who stood around and heckled them. It got pretty nasty. Finally, we had a meeting and talked the whole thing through. Calmer heads prevailed, and trees were removed with the stipulation that the road would be widened with extraordinary care taken to avoid any unnecessary cutting or trimming. After that incident someone suggested that I serve as the mediator when there were major disputes between members of the colony. Someone gave me the title of mayor, in jest at first, but it sort of stuck. Then the board formalized the title, making it an appointed position."

"And this book," said Ray, "is the history that you wrote?"

"Yes, that's the current working draft. I've made draft copies available to members of the colony since late last summer, hoping to get corrections and additions before we do our first edition. Then it will look like a real book. It will be in hardcover with high-quality paper and lots of photographs, some of them in color. I've spent years on it. I'm looking forward to holding the finished product."

He pushed the book in Ray's direction. "You're welcome to take this with you. It will give you a complete background about the colony."

"I would like that, thank you. I have become a student of the history of this region. My memory is that this was first an Indian mission."

"That's correct. The first few chapters of the book cover that period, and to my way of thinking, probably as a historian, they are the most interesting chapters in the book. Geoffrey Mather came out from New England in the 1830s to minister to the Indians. His first mission was south of here down around Saugatuck. Apparently he made a poor choice of terrain, the mosquitoes drove them out by the end of his first summer."

"How do you know this?"

"Fortunately, Mather kept a detailed diary, day by day, of his adventures from the time he left Vermont until almost the day he died. So to continue my story, he loaded his wife and two small children and all their possessions in a small sailing craft and they headed north. Some of his Indian converts followed along with their families in canoes. There is a shoal just off the end of the colony's beach area, not much really, just some big boulders one of the glaciers dropped off on its way north. Mather was coming up the coast close to shore with a good wind at his back. He managed to hit the rocks at a good clip and take the bottom out of his little boat. The family made it to shore, their meager possessions floating in after them. Mather records in his diary that his wife thought this was a message from God directing them to build the mission here. In the next sentence he opines that their landing at that location had more to do with his lack of seamanship than any message from the Almighty." Grubbs chuckled, then continued, "Having studied Mather's diary closely over several years, I think he was very much a believer, but there was always a bit of skepticism over what was God's will and what should be attributed to human error or incompetence."

"So how long did the mission continue?"

"Mather was able to buy a large tract of land, the money coming from a missionary organization back east. And he spent decades ministering to and looking after the spiritual and political interests of native people. Over the course of several decades Mather could see that the federal government was routinely robbing the Indians of the property and rights that had been promised to them in a number of treaties. He did his best to protect them, but his diary suggests that he could see it was a lost cause. While his faith in the Almighty remained steadfast to the end of his life, he totally lost faith in the federal government.

"His eldest son, John, followed him into the ministry and kept the mission going after Geoffrey's death in 1881. By 1900 the area had been lumbered and settlers were building farms on the best land. Most of the Indians, the ones who survived smallpox and measles and the other diseases brought by the white settlers, had moved from the region.

"John Mather was rather entrepreneurial, but he still had his father's sense of a Christian mission. By then the resorters, the first wave of summer people, had started to arrive from Chicago and St. Louis and points south and east, initially by lake steamer, and then increasingly by rail. So John created a Protestant resort without the strict denominational ties found in summer colonies like Bayview and Epworth. He did follow the Chautauqua model, creating a summer community for interfaith worship, recreational activities, cultural activities, and intellectual engagement. In the last years of his life he turned the whole enterprise over to a public corporation so it would continue on in perpetuity." He pushed the book toward Ray. "It's all here, and I think it's a pretty good read."

The sound of heavy footfalls pulled Grubbs' gaze toward the screen door, interrupting the conversation. Ray watched a tall, stout, red-faced man march into the room, his voice thundering in Grubbs' direction as soon as he crossed the threshold.

"I want you to get a contractor in here today, Grubby. I want that site bulldozed and cleaned up. Get the landscape restored, make it look like the building never existed. I don't want a trace left, not a goddam trace. You hear."

Without responding directly, Grubbs said, "This is Sheriff Ray Elkins. And Malcolm, I don't think we can go forward until his people have completed their investigation."

"What's to investigate," said the man in a scoffing tone.

"It's a crime scene," answered Ray, coming to his feet and looking directly into the eyes of the intruder.

"Crime scene my ass, there's nothing there."

"Sheriff, this is Malcolm Wudbine, he is the president of the board of the Mission Point Summer Colony," said Grubbs, now standing also.

"Well, get your people to chop-chop," Wudbine said directing his comments to Grubbs. "I know we are up north, and these folks have a way of doing everything in their time, but this needs to be done now. Don't go native on us, Grubby. The property owners will start arriving in a week or so, and they expect to have things ready."

"When can we have access to the area?" asked Grubbs, looking over at Ray.

"Right now we're waiting for the state police arson investigator. He's working on a case in Mecosta County. He hopes to be here sometime late this afternoon." Ray remembered seeing Wudbine before. He was trying to remember where.

"Again, I ask, what's to investigate?" said Wudbine, his words now directed at Ray. "Known crazy shows up, shoots up his place and one that I own, also. Then he blows himself up. And now that indigent SOB is in the hospital at taxpayers' expense. I told him yesterday morning that he didn't belong here. Too bad I didn't grab him by the scruff of the neck and toss his sorry ass off the property."

"About what time did you have this conversation with Mr. Zwilling?" asked Ray.

A look of surprise crossed Wudbine's face. It took him several seconds to adjust to the fact that he was being questioned. "I think it was about nine. I had gone over to Dune Side Cottage with one of my workmen. I wanted to give him precise instructions on how the job was to be done. Zwilling was on his front porch smoking. I went over to talk to him. He looked drunk, probably doped up, too. I told him I was interested in buying the place. Told him I wanted to contact the current owner. That's when he started swearing at me. Foul stuff, an unending stream of obscenities."

"How did you respond?" asked Ray.

"Can't remember exactly. I probably told him he was just a piece of garbage. It seems to run in the family. They were all trash, the lot of them."

"You said he was out on the porch smoking?"

"Yes."

"Did you see a weapon?"

"No."

"Was that the end of your conversation?"

"Yes. That was it. I didn't want to waste time talking to that idiot. I'm not surprised an hour or so later he went totally postal. Apparently my cottage was the target of much of Zwilling's rage. Guess I was lucky to be out of the area when the shooting started."

"And you're pretty sure of the time," said Ray.

"Sheriff, that's my best guess, but don't involve me in your investigation."

"Mr. Wudbine, I'm trying to piece together what happened. Zwilling committed multiple felonies. Anyone who was a witness or has information about this incident is of interest to me."

"Whatever. So back to my initial question, when can we get that mess cleaned up, and when can I have my people assess the damage and get started on repairs?"

Ray took his time answering. "It all depends when the state police arson investigator completes his work. We need to know if this was a natural gas explosion, or something else. We also need to make sure that no explosive materials are in the wreckage. Then the utilities have to sign off that the gas and electricity have been turned off. We don't want anyone hurt in the process of clearing this site."

"Specifically, what does that mean, Sheriff?"

"It means a day or two more, whatever it takes to do a thorough job. I will inform Mr. Grubbs when we are done with our investigation. I suggest you contact him in a few days."

Wudbine directed his attention to Grubbs, "As soon as they are done let me know. We'll get this mess cleaned up." Then he spun on the heels of his spit polished boots. The screen door on the old colony office building slammed hard after he departed.

Grubbs looked over at Ray, a faint smile played across his face. "If you ever get a phone call from the Mission Point Summer Colony saying that there's been a murder, I'd be willing to bet Malcolm Wudbine will be the victim. And you will have great difficulty finding the murderer."

"Why's that?" asked Ray.

"There would be so many suspects, so many people with a motive. Almost everyone here has been abused by that odious man over the last 40 or so years."

"Didn't you say he was president of your board? It is an elected position?"

"It's an interesting story, Sheriff. Can I get you another cup of coffee?"

4
~

"Was this your first introduction to Malcolm Wudbine?" asked Grubbs, refilling Ray's coffee mug, then his own.

"In the formal sense, yes. But I have seen him before. It took me a moment to make the connection. I was seated near him in a restaurant sometime last summer."

"And he was part of a large group?"

"Yes, that's my memory."

"Let me guess, he was louder than anyone else, not only in his party, but in the whole place, making decrees rather than conversation and being surly to the wait staff at every opportunity?"

"Exactly," said Ray. "At the time I wondered if the man had a hearing problem."

Grubbs chuckled at Ray's response. "No hearing problem, at least none that I know of. Although at his age it's possible, but the loud voice and dominating presence is not new. It has been his modus operandi for as long as I've known him."

"You said the board presidency was an elected position. If he is as disliked as you suggested, how does he...?"

"It's quite simple," explained Grubbs. "He continues to rescue Mission Point Summer Colony financially. When our recreation building burned down, he paid for the rebuilding. Not only did he rebuild it, but he made sure that the job was done on a timely basis. The fire was in late

February. The new building was ready for use in early June. And that's just one example. When our sewage system was starting to fail and the health department was barking at our heels, his foundation spent millions building a new system. At the same time he had a modern water system installed, complete with high-pressure hydrant lines for firefighting. We've all learned to put up with Malcolm because this place would fall apart without his money."

"The building that Zwilling was firing at, I assume that was Wudbine's cottage?"

"It's one of Malcolm's many properties in the colony. He purchased one for his son and daughter-in-law. Dune Side Cottage is for his aircrew. And he owns several more that are used by guests or other employees."

"So he doesn't live in the colony."

"Correct. His cottage is just north of our property. And it is not a cottage. It's a mansion on more than a thousand feet of lakefront," Grubbs looked over at Ray and chuckled. "I see I'm completely confusing you. All of us locals, and I mean locals in the sense of long-term summer colony residents—not to be confused with real locals like you—all of us locals know the backstory."

"Which is?" ask Ray.

"Malcolm was first married to Verity Wudbine-Merone. Her maiden name was Behrens, German stock who settled in Illinois in the 1850s. She was a descendant of several of the earliest members of the colony. Her family was from a farming community west of Chicago, her father was a local banker. She met Malcolm in college, Champaign, I think, or perhaps Northwestern. The father took him into the business after Malcolm and Verity were married. It's the old story; a lad from a modest background is brought into the family business and later walks with a fortune. When his marriage to Verity was coming apart, he sold his interest in the family bank and bought a seat on the Chicago Mercantile exchange."

"How do you know all of this?" asked Ray.

"Verity is my age. I was quite taken with her when we were 15, or 16, or 17. Summer romance and all that." He paused for a moment, looked away and then back at Ray. "That's not quite true," he said, repeatedly tapping two fingers on the table. "It was a teenage boy's silent infatuation. I'm not sure she ever knew, but I was a great admirer. And over the years she told me bits and pieces of her story. I think that's one of the things we do here, especially when we get old. We tell our stories. Let's see, where was I?"

"The Chicago Mercantile Exchange."

"Yes. Verity told me he made a fortune in pickles futures. I don't know if there's such a thing. She's very sarcastic and quite bitter. From pickles or whatever it was, he moved onto gold, at first losing most of his fortune, but then learning how the market worked. He was already enormously successful when he moved into stocks and bonds. But, by all accounts that wealth pales when compared to what he's done in the last decade or so. Reports are that he's made billions in things like derivatives and currency trading. I don't understand any of that. Not part of my world."

"You said his property is outside of the colony."

"Let me explain," said Grubbs. "When they were divorced there was a major fight over the family cottage. Verity prevailed. So then he buys this big place just on the beach. And he does it in such a way that she can't look north from her place without seeing his. I'm sure he did it out of spite. And then he started buying up cottages in the colony."

"Does Mr. Wudbine participate in your activities?"

"Absolutely. He thinks of himself as quite the thespian. Malcolm always has a part in the annual summer play. And he always participates in the fathers and sons baseball game—I think he played college ball. After the baseball game, we all wander down the beach to his manse for a New England lobster boil and clambake with several kegs of beer. We have a no-alcohol clause in the colony covenant. Somehow it's okay if we're on his land. I wonder what our founder would think of this."

"He preached abstinence?" asked Ray.

"Yes, but I think Mather's avoidance of alcohol was driven by his concern for native people. He saw traders cheat them with cheap whiskey and politicians manipulate them with free drinks on election day. And I suspect this place was pretty much alcohol-free in the early years, but who knows what happened behind closed doors. After the war, I'm talking about WWII and my parents' generation, the cocktail hour became the norm. But again, it was never done in public places.

"But to go back to Malcolm," Grubbs continued, "even though I am the executive director of the summer colony, when he's in residence he's always about telling people what to do. Like I said, we've all learned to put up with Malcolm. His money has kept us going at critical times. And we all pray that the good Lord will accept him with open arms, the sooner better than later. That said, it would be good of him to leave the colony a generous legacy."

Ray closed the top of his laptop and pushed himself from his chair.

"Is there anything else, Sheriff?"

"No, I think that's about it. Here's my card if anything occurs to you that you think I should know."

"You'll let me know when we can begin the cleanup?"

"Absolutely."

"There's one more thing," said Grubbs.

"Yes?"

"Well, it can wait a few days. Please keep me informed about Garr Zwilling's condition. In spite of the unfortunate events, he's part of our family, part of our history."

5

The next morning Ray Elkins was up, dressed, and out of the house before 6:00 A.M. Gale force winds had been advised the evening before, and he wanted to walk the beach early and watch the pounding surf. He did a couple of miles on an out-and-back hike, stopping occasionally to watch the waves and listen to the howling wind. Ray needed time to absorb the beauty and power of this special landscape.

By the time he arrived at his office a little after 8:00, Detective Sergeant Sue Lawrence, in her usual highly organized manner, had laid out two piles of documents on the conference table in Ray's office and was working on her laptop as she waited for him. Simone, a cairn terrier Sue and Ray co-parented since rescuing her from a crime scene in the late winter, was curled up in an overstuffed chair in the corner of the office. Ray sat on the edge of the chair and scratched Simone's ears for a few moments before joining Sue at the table.

"How was your walk on the beach?" she asked.

"It was great. Some big wave sets, huge breaking surf. It almost looked like November."

"I'm surprised you didn't go paddling."

"Not this morning. Not today. The winds were too high. It would be impossible to launch without getting broached. Some days you just have to walk on the beach." Sliding into his chair, he said, "Looks like you've been busy. What's happening with Zwilling? Any news?"

"I talked to one of the doctors at the burn center in Ann Arbor before I went home last night."

"What time was that? I think our no extraordinary hours we've got to have a life pledge is starting to break down."

"It was okay, Ray. Simone was with me."

"And?"

"The doctor, I didn't get her name, said the first 72 hours are the most critical. She also indicated that the prognosis was rather bleak. In addition to the extensive burns, they suspect lung damage, but have not been able to assess how extensive. About all I came away with was that he was lucky to be alive, and it's extremely difficult to estimate the viability of a patient with his injuries."

Sue gave Ray a few moments to absorb the information before bringing his attention to the material on the table. "On the top sheet," she motioned with an index finger, "is a list of everything contained in that pile. The first item under that sheet is a summary of my conversation with Mike Ogden."

"I thought he was tied up...?"

"He was, a suspicious warehouse fire in Gaylord. He arrived about four. We still had plenty of light to pick through the ruins. Before we started I showed him the video of the explosion—we've got it from two directions. His immediate response was that it looked like natural gas, the way the building came apart, the appearance of the flames. Mike did take samples for analysis, but he was pretty certain that Zwilling had turned on all the burners on the stove or opened a gas line. The remains of the water heater and stove were down in what was once the crawlspace. There's a connection from the gas line to the water heater, he had a name for it."

"Coupling?"

"That sounds right. How do you know that?"

"Remember, my father was a jack-of-all trades, and I spent much of my childhood and teenage years following him around as his assistant."

"Okay," she continued, "it appeared that the coupling had been disconnected. He suggested that Zwilling was doing his best to blow the place up."

"Anything else?"

"You were worried about a large stash of ammo. It wasn't there. Zwilling must have run through most of it before the explosion."

"And the weapon?"

"It turned up in the bottom of the debris. It was pretty grimy. Ogden said it looked like a Chinese knockoff of an AR 15, something about the machining being crude and the serial number looked like it had been done by junior high shop kids. He's going to run it through the ATF tracking system, but didn't think they'd get a hit."

"Probably a gun show special," said Ray.

"His words, exactly. We also had a run-in with a citizen."

"What was that all about?"

"This obnoxious ass comes marching right into the site, tells us he's the president of the place, and demands to know when we're going to be finished. Ogden explains to him that this is a crime scene and politely asks him to leave. The guy just continues ranting at us. Ogden asks him to leave a second time. This time he's much more direct. The man's unfazed. So Ogden tells him if he doesn't leave immediately, he's going to be arrested and put in jail. Just about that time Richard Grubbs shows up in a golf cart and hustles the man away."

Ray chuckled, "You met Malcolm Wudbine. He's a piece of work, isn't he?"

"I can think of a few other ways of describing him. Not long after that Grubbs came back. We were just finishing up about that time. He said he thought he found the car."

"Zwilling's?"

"You got it. It's an older Chrysler 300 with Arizona tags. It had been tucked behind one of the cottages close to the highway. I ran the plates. It was registered to a Garrick Zwilling in Tucson. I made a call to their PD, ended up getting a chatty detective on the line. Mr. Zwilling is known to the department, lots of problems with alcohol, lots of mental health issues. He's one of those guys who goes out of control, gets taken to the hospital, three days later he's back on the street. Occasionally he ends up in front of a judge, promises to stay on his meds, and in a few weeks or months, the whole cycle starts again."

"It's a familiar pattern. You got all that accomplished before the end of the workday?"

"No, I did that in the evening before going home."

"I thought as part of our plan to have lives outside of work we...."

"That was a good thought. But neither one of us is going to be able to do that. It was okay, Ray. I went to dinner with Mike Ogden. I always thought he was very married, turns out he's not anymore. I guess he wanted me to know. It was a little bit awkward. It's not like he asked me out or anything, or even asked if I was involved with anyone. But it was clumsy." She paused for a few moments. "I've got one more thing. You sent me an e-mail with the out-of-date contact info on the owner of the cottage, Regina Zwilling-Glidden."

"Yes,"

"I ran that by the detective in Tucson. Seems she's well known to the PD, also."

"How so?"

"I guess she's been an assistant prosecutor there for years. She was incapacitated by a stroke sometime in the recent past. I explained to him the reason for my call, and he said he would check on her and get back to me."

"Sometimes life is a train wreck," said Ray.

"So the rest of the materials there are first drafts of evidence to take to the prosecutor. I've also asked for a search warrant of Zwilling's car. If he survives there will be a whole list of charges."

"And," said Ray, "the issue of whether or not he is competent to stand trial."

6

~

After Ray delivered his line on Zwilling's competence to stand trial, they sat in silence, each reflecting on the horror of the scene.

"Is there anything else?" asked Ray.

"Simone, she has a vet appointment late this afternoon. She needs a heartworm check and a Lyme disease vaccination. And Ray," she gave him her wry smile, "we don't have an arrangement in our joint custody agreement for Simone's veterinary bills, but if you would cover this I'd really appreciate it. I'm sort of short this month."

"No problem. And I apologize for not having thought about that earlier. In fact, from this point forward I'll look after the vet bills, you do more than your share with her other expenses."

"And after the vet, would you take her for the evening. I'm going to dinner and a movie in town with the girls. I'd like to not be in a rush to get home."

"No problem," said Ray. "She's always good company."

"And you have no other plans? I guess I should have asked that first."

"No. She will be the center of my universe."

"That's true. Whether you want her to be or not." Sue retrieved a brown paper bag and set it on the table. "Here's Simone's overnight bag. There's a can of her special food, her favorite tennis ball, and some treats, to be doled out judiciously when she sits to have her leash taken off."

Many hours later, after the trip to the veterinary hospital, Ray took Simone home. As he started supper for himself, he opened her bag of supplies and pulled out the can of food. He eyed the label carefully and looked over at Simone. "Do you know what's in here? Let me give you the highlights. Pork by-products. Simone, I can't imagine what that would be. The stuff they can't put in hotdogs because it's too disgusting. How about powdered cellulose? That's sawdust, kid. Then there's marigold extract." He paused and returned her intense look. "No, I'm not making this up. But wait, there's more. Dried beet pulp, and guar gum—always one of my favorites. Then there's a whole list of multisyllabic, chemical sounding stuff with the monos and tris, the sulfates and phosphates. Do you really want to eat this?" He held out the can, turning the ingredients list in her direction.

Simone, looking up at Ray, continued to hang on every word.

"How about a couple of lamb chops? You can have them with rice or whole wheat couscous."

Simone woofed, a command bark.

"Okay, I take that to mean the whole wheat couscous. And we have to do something with this first." Ray carried the offending can to the garbage. He dropped it in and then pulled paper over the top of it. "Simone, this is called destruction of evidence. In certain circumstances, this is a felony. However, extreme times require extreme measures. So don't rat us out."

After dinner and a long walk, Ray and Simone settled in for a quiet evening—Ray in his favorite chair reading the New Yorker, Simone straddling the top of a couch near a window guarding against marauding squirrels and killer rabbits. She soon nodded off.

Eventually, Ray moved to the bedroom and went through his journal writing ritual, filling a favorite fountain pen and reading over his most recent entries. Then over the next several pages, brown ink on ivory paper, he reviewed the tragic encounter with Garr Zwilling. He speculated on other ways he might have handled the confrontation, concluding that there were few alternatives. At the end he gave Malcolm Wudbine a few paragraphs, trying to capture his mannerisms and the way he treated Richard Grubbs. He wondered if he'd ever encounter Wudbine again.

Ray's journal entry was cut short by a command bark. Simone was at the door awaiting a second evening walk.

7

Ray sat in the passenger seat of Sue's Jeep, Simone standing in his lap looking out of the windshield. A golf cart piloted by Richard Grubbs led the way along the narrow, curvy main road of the Mission Point Summer Colony.

"So what's this all about?" asked Sue.

"Grubbs wouldn't tell me on the phone. Weeks ago, after the Zwilling incident, he said there was something he needed to talk to me about. Then he just dropped it. Late yesterday afternoon he called me and said there's this police matter he needs help with. Would I please come by and could I bring an evidence technician. When I pushed him as to what was going on, he said he couldn't talk about it on the phone; it had to be face-to-face. It's all very mysterious."

Grubbs slowed and pulled off the road. Sue parked behind him. They followed him to the bluff overlooking what had once been the site of Ravenswood Cottage. Several pickup trucks were clustered around a new building that closely resembled the original.

"A lot can happen in a short time," said Grubbs.

Ray and Sue stood in silence taking in the scene.

"How many weeks has it been since the fire?" asked Ray.

Grubbs looked thoughtful. "I think four. This is the start of the fifth week."

"How did this happen so quickly?" asked Ray.

"Well, even before that unfortunate incident, there were a lot of things going on. Mr. Wudbine, in his role as president of the board, is always doing his best to micromanage both me and everything that happens in this organization. On the other hand, he's not very good at communicating what he's up to. Anyway, Malcolm had been negotiating for the purchase of Ravenswood Cottage, something he never mentioned to me until after that whole unfortunate affair.

"As you will remember, the owner of the cottage was Regina Zwilling-Glidden, Garr's aunt. When her nephew found out about the sale, he came up here to see if he could disrupt things. Apparently he has a long history of mental illness."

"How did you learn this?"

"Well, once you sent me word that we could go forward with the site cleanup, Wudbine wanted to have his own people do the work. When I challenged him on the legality of that, he told me he'd purchased the property. Then he told me he wanted to get started on the new building as quickly as possible. We have this process here and a whole series of guidelines that any remodels or new buildings have to conform to. We're trying to preserve the character of the place. He told me to make sure that process happened instantly, his favorite phrase 'chop-chop.'

"Like I said, we have this process here. We have a committee. We ask for architectural drawings. Our goal is not speed. Our goal is continuity. Malcolm doesn't think any of that applies to him. And he pushed his contractor the same way he pushed us. The contractor pulled a building permit, and the first time the inspector showed up, he put a cease-and-desist order on the job because walls were going up before the footings had been checked. I was impressed by that guy, whoever he is. He refused to be cowed. Malcolm was yelling and screaming at him, and he was totally unmoved. Luckily for Malcolm, the contractor was able to smooth things over with the inspector and a day or two later they were back at work."

"So how about this building, does it conform with your colony standards?" ask Ray.

"Absolutely. As you can see, it's a beautifully built replica of what was originally there. But the point is that we have this process, and Malcolm goes out of his way not to cooperate." Grubbs looked over at Ray and Sue. "So a lot happened in a few weeks. We had a very dangerous confrontation. A man has died from horrific burns. It was a death of his own making, but still he's gone and with him a hundred-year-old building with all of its memories and all of its history. The debris has been carefully removed from the site, the earth sanitized, and a new structure erected. That's a lot of change in a place where change takes place very slowly. It's something this old historian is having difficulty comprehending. But that's not why I called you here. There's another matter that needs attending to. Malcolm said I shouldn't involve the police, but I think it's something that should be investigated."

"What's going on?"

"We had a robbery of sorts. Actually, I think we've had many of them. I can only verify one, and I think that's a good starting place. This whole thing is rather embarrassing, and I hope we can handle this discreetly."

"What do you mean?" said Ray.

"We have our traditions. I wouldn't want to read about this problem in the local paper. Follow me down to Verity Wudbine-Merone's cottage, and I'll explain the whole thing."

"Sounds like trouble in paradise," said Sue as she followed the slow-moving golf cart past the dozens of cottages that lined the sandy trail, some clinging to hillsides, some—like Ravenswood Cottage—clustered in two or three building cul-de-sacs.

"Yes," agreed Ray.

Grubbs parked behind one of about a dozen cottages that were built on a bluff overlooking Lake Michigan.

Ray and Sue joined him, leaving Simone in the Jeep. The door of the cottage opened as they approached the building. A small, wiry woman came out to greet them. Ray guessed her to be in her late 60s or early 70s.

"This is Verity Wudbine-Merone," said Grubbs, "her ancestors were among the first families to build in the Colony. Sheriff Elkins, Detective Sergeant Lawrence."

"Come in, please," she said, after shaking each of their hands.

"I've made some coffee, I hope you will have some." She quickly filled a cup, placed it on a saucer, and handed one to Sue before any of them could respond. "Please, sit." She directed them toward a table at the front of the cottage. "There's sugar and cream, please help yourself to the cookies."

A series of casement windows, each with a latticework of framing holding small panes, provided a panoramic view of the lake.

Once they were seated, Ray asked, "What seems to be the problem?"

"What have you told them?" Verity looked at Grubbs.

"Nothing, Verity."

Ray and Sue sat and waited, finally Verity said, "I've been robbed."

"What was taken and when did this happen?" asked Sue.

"I can't say for sure when it happened. I was here in late April just to drop off some supplies and then came back a week ago and noticed things were missing."

"What kinds of things?" asked Ray.

A long silence followed, Grubbs and Verity looked at each other. Finally Grubbs said, "A large quantity of alcohol."

"Could you be more specific, please?"

"Well, I always restock the cottage in the spring. On my first trip up here I stop in Chicago and buy enough liquor to last the summer. We have cocktail parties every evening, us old timers. I sort of know what everyone drinks, that's what I stock up on."

"So how many bottles were taken?" asked Ray.

Another long silence followed. Then Verity answered, "I'm afraid it was more than bottles. It was cases, five cases. Five cases," she repeated. "It was all the top notch. All of it. Single malt scotch, Irish whiskey, some bourbon, some very good vodka and gin. I lugged them up here and with Richard's help got everything discreetly stored away."

Verity got up from the table and crossed the room and opened the pantry door. "It was all here on the floor. The cases were on their sides so I could get to the bottles without having to do any lifting."

She returned to the table and looked at Sue and then Ray before continuing. "We do more than just give lip service to the temperance roots of this colony. If you go into the cottages, you won't see liquor bottles out in the open or any other drink making paraphernalia. And no one consumes alcohol out in the open. With the exception, of course, of Malcolm's damn clambake, but that's off the property. Even when I go to someone's cottage for dinner, I always carry the wine in a basket."

"What was the value of the stolen property?" asked Sue.

"Well it was a lot, yes indeed. I can't quite say for sure. You know how it goes, they ring it up and you just give them your card. I'd have to try and find my MasterCard bill. But I'm sure it was $1000 or more. And there was also some wine on that bill, the brands and vintages that are hard to find up here. And the wine is all here. They didn't touch that. Just the liquor, the hard stuff."

"And you have no idea when it was stolen?"

"Well, yes. It happened some time during the weeks I wasn't here."

Ray looked at Sue, then looked out at the rolling surf.

"How did the thieves gain entrance to your cottage?" asked Sue. "Was there damage to a door or window?"

"No, nothing that I noticed. I'm not even sure the doors were locked. As you can see, there's nothing really worth stealing here. It's just old stuff. Old China, old flatware, the furniture is mostly castoffs from other homes. That little flat screen I bring with me at the beginning of the season and take it home in the fall. Electronics don't make it through the winter here. It's too moist.

"And the doors and windows hardly fit in the frames anymore. One of my little grandsons takes great delight in the fact that he can jiggle the locks open on either door." She pointed with her thumbs, one toward the lakeside door, the other toward the inland door.

"So there were no signs of forced entry, but maybe no force would have been necessary, and you can't pinpoint when the theft may have happened?"

"Correct. That's why I told Grubby that it wasn't necessary to call the police."

"And other than the missing cases of liquor, there is no evidence that a robbery took place," said Ray.

"True," she responded.

"We can take a report. It would help if you could get a receipt for the stolen alcohol. I would like to know exactly what was taken by brand and quantity. Also, I'd like to know the exact dollar value of this property. You can probably get all of that information by calling your credit card company. You will need that if you are intending to file a claim with your insurance company."

"Insurance, I hadn't thought about that. But I wouldn't want them to know about this."

"Like I said, we can take a report, but there's not much for us to go on. Any chance some of your neighbors might have seen something?"

"No one has said anything, and they certainly would have."

"Well, we could canvass the neighborhood. Ask if anyone has...."

"I wouldn't want that. First, almost no one has been around yet. And this would be very upsetting. I don't want to ruin anyone's summer."

Richard Grubbs cut her short. "Sheriff, I asked you to bring your evidence tech because I thought maybe you could find a fingerprint or something."

"That would be very unlikely given the time that's passed," said Sue. "Any chance the thief left something behind like a hat, gloves?"

"Nothing of the sort. And I didn't even notice that the boxes were gone for several days. Not until Grubby stopped off for a drink, and I went to get a fresh bottle of Scotch.

"I'm really afraid, Sheriff, we're wasting time," said Verity. "What's lost is lost. It's never happened before, and it will probably never happen again. Let's just get on with our lives, Grubby. That's what Malcolm wanted you to do, and it's probably the first, last, and only time I've ever agreed with that SOB."

Verity stood, "Thank you for coming, Sheriff. And you, also, Detective. I think this matter will take care of itself without any outside help. But, again, my thanks. Would either of you like a cookie for the road?"

8

~

"If he would move over a little, we could get out of here," said Sue as they followed Richard Grubbs in his golf cart two-track.

"You're showing remarkable patience," observed Ray. "A few years ago you would have been laying on the horn."

"Yup. Yoga. Deep breathing. I keep telling you to show up. The women would like you. And you'd like the view, fit women in Spandex. And there's never a man there. You would be a cherished minority."

As they got close to the colony office, Grubbs waved them over. "Would you come in for a couple of minutes, I have a few more things to tell you? Bring the dog."

Sue looked over at Ray and smiled. "Deep breathing, Ray. Pretend that you're listening as you focus on your mantra slowly running through your brain. Nod occasionally, like you're attending to his every word."

"I don't have a mantra."

"Then think about lunch, have food fantasies."

They followed Grubbs into his office, settling into chairs, Simone in Ray's lap.

"I'm sorry to have wasted your time, Sheriff. But I thought that Verity would be more helpful, especially after Malcolm told her to let it go. She usually does the opposite of what he tells her. You see they were once married."

"Yes, you've told me about that."

Grubbs cocked his head and looked at Ray. "I guess I did, didn't I. Sorry, I'm afraid I'm starting to do that. Where was I?"

"You were saying that Verity usually does the opposite of Malcolm Wudbine...."

"Yes, of course. So the fact that she mentioned him is a surprise. They don't talk much, not since their son grew up. I mean, occasionally they're in the same place at a colony gathering, but she seems to keep her distance from him as much as possible."

"So there are no grandchildren?" asked Sue.

"None from that marriage. And I know Verity remains close to her son and tries to protect him from Malcolm. Wudbine is extremely hard on Elliott. He's got him running the business, but he micromanages the hell out of him. Elliott is the COO of Wudbine Financial, Malcom continues on as the CEO. Around here people make a comparison to old Henry Ford and his alleged mistreatment of his son, Edsel."

"You said you had a few more things to tell us," said Ray, trying to get the conversation back on track.

"Yes, this burglary. It's not the first. There were a few last winter. And it's not every cottage that's getting hit."

"So what are you telling us?" probed Sue.

"Well, as I think about this. Let's say teenagers from around here, some of the locals, were looking for booze in the winter when the colony is unoccupied. They'd probably just go down the line, wouldn't they? That's not what's happening here. It's only selected cottages, places with lots of alcohol, that are getting hit. Whoever is behind this is one of ours. They know where to find the booze."

"And in Verity's case, it didn't happen in the dead of winter," added Sue.

"Exactly. When it happened before in the past, I was thinking, you know, January or February, something like that."

"But no one has ever contacted us before? What's going on?" asked Ray.

"People are very protective of this place. They don't want outsiders in here doing an investigation, and they certainly don't want to read in the local paper about break-ins and the theft of alcohol. I can imagine we would be the butt of lots of jokes in the greater community. And we all live with the memory of the last time we had something like this happen. It just pulled this place apart."

"What was that?"

"Arson. As I remember it, two cottages the first year, three the next, and then it stopped."

"When was…?"

"Oh, let me think, late 70s, no, it was the 80s. It was the time of, what did they call that? You know, the big ugly piercings, nails through noses and ears, people dressing in black."

"Punk?" offered Sue.

"Yes, that might have been it. Well, our young people, they follow the fashions or movements, whatever those things are. We had a few kids, maybe a dozen, who, for a number of summers, just dressed like bums. First, there were stories about the kids, like they were into devil worship. Then the fires started. Vacant buildings, no one ever hurt. The township fire chief said the fires were of suspicious origin, all of them. But if there was an arson, well."

"Well, what?"

"There was never an investigation or anything, but kids, the punk ones, they were the prime suspects. And it was like a Hawthorne story. There were secret meetings, vigilante patrols, rumors, anger, and weird prejudices. An unusual number of cottages went on the market. But by the third summer nothing happened. Some of the kids were still around, most had moved on or grown out of that mode of dress. And I don't think anyone quite noticed them anymore. People just wanted to get things back to what they had been before. And that sort of happened.

"I'm telling you this because I think that's what may be going on here. No one wants to talk about this. If anyone would have been willing to file a police report, it was Verity. And Malcolm turned her. So, as the chief administrator of the area, I've got this problem. I've had a string of robberies, and people, especially our board president, want to keep it quiet. What is your counsel?"

Ray passed Simone to Sue and took a while to consider his response. "If no one is willing to document the fact that a crime has taken place, our hands are tied. If what you say is true, clearly there is criminal activity taking place here. So far it's just about theft, no one has been harmed. That could change. Keep us in the loop. Our job is protecting and serving you and your community."

Ray stood, setting his card on the desk facing Grubbs. "Please don't hesitate to call."

Back in the Jeep, just before starting the engine, Sue said, "A tradition of temperance, and a tradition of summer cocktail parties. What am I missing?"

Ray laughed, "Traditions are sort of funny that way. They are hard to understand unless you're a member of the group. You've got to be part of the system, native to the culture. Outsiders always find them silly, even branding long-held traditions as little more than superstitions."

"Well, Margaret Mead, where do you want to go for lunch, the Tiki Café? You can get the vegetarian Samoan Samosa."

"I think you're mixing cultures and cuisines."

"It's all about fusion, Ray. The wave of the future."

9
~

Over two months passed before Ray returned to Mission Point Summer Colony. In the intervening time there had been no further calls from Richard Grubbs about break-ins, missing cases of liquor, or anything else. And with the coming of warm weather and the influx of tourists and summer residents—doubling the area's population—the day-to-day demands on the Cedar County Sheriff Department had doubled as well. Ray had only thought about the Colony as he occasionally rolled past the front entrance—two tall, widely spaced telephone poles with a sign reading Mission Point suspended by ropes high above an open gate—when he was in the area on some other business.

In mid-July an invitation, the address hand-written by a skilled calligrapher and sealed with wax, beckoned Ray back to the colony for a gala cocktail party and buffet, performance of the annual summer play, and an afterglow the first week of August. Richard Grubbs, who signed the invitation, added that he hoped Detective Sergeant Lawrence would come also. The R.S.V.P. card had Ray and Sue's names already penned in. There were two blanks for the names of their guests. When Ray first floated the invitation past Sue there was a lack of enthusiasm on her part, but a few days later she asked if he had sent back the response card. Ray shifted through the pile of mail in the wire bin on his desk and handed her the envelope.

"What's this about a play?" she asked, toying with the invitation.

"Every summer they do a play. It's one of their annual activities. They have sporting events, concerts, lectures, and all sorts of classes and special celebrations."

"And the play, Murder at the Vicarage? What's that about? Am I going to be bored to tears?"

"It's based on Agatha Christie's book by the same name. I read it years ago when I was working my way through Christie. It's an engaging story. I suspect it's great fun to act and to watch."

"I've never read Christie," said Sue. "Is she as good as Sara Paretsky or Dennis Lehane?"

"Not as edgy. It was a different time. She challenges you to figure out who did it before the end. And there's usually this wonderful concluding scene where all the suspects are gathered in the drawing room, and Miss Marple or Hercule Piorot goes through them one at a time, finally naming the killer. The suspense goes to the last page, or in this case, the final curtain."

"Real life isn't quite like that, is it. But I guess the play could be fun." She looked at the invitation again. "Are you going?"

"Is this a double dare?" asked Ray.

"Yes, I'll go if you go."

"You're on."

"I'll get this in the mail," she said. "Harry will be here that weekend. Actually he will be around for the rest of the week. I'll be able to show him a little local color."

A few weeks later, standing at the far end of Verity Wudbine-Merone's deck, Ray looked at the crowd.

"We're bringing down the average age by twenty or thirty years," observed Hanna Jeffers, the woman he had been seeing for a number of months, someone who shared his passion for kayaking and big, empty spaces. She pointed toward the beach and Lake Michigan stretching out at the base of the bluff. "I think I'd rather be out there."

Ray smiled and nodded in agreement.

"It's been a long time since I've seen so many women in dresses and men in sport coats and ties. I didn't know seersucker and madras were still in. Hawaiian shirts, too. Looks to me like most of these folks have been wearing the same party clothes for quite a number of decades."

"Maybe generations," retorted Ray.

Richard Grubbs came to Ray's side carrying two glasses of sparkling wine. "There wasn't any chardonnay, but I thought this Mawby...."

"Perfect," said Ray.

"We don't get much call for wine," explained Grubbs. "This is a martini and Manhattan crowd." He moved closer to Hanna, tipping his head in her direction. "I'm sorry I didn't quite get your name, Miss, when you came in. I have trouble hearing when there's a lot of background noise."

"Hanna Jeffers," she responded.

"And what do you do?"

"I'm a cardiologist."

"Well, welcome. It's good to have a doctor in the house, or on the deck in this case. Especially given the age of this crowd. Maybe you can tell me what's current medical theory," he said with a twinkle in his eyes. "Most of us here believe that having a few drinks before dinner is enormously heart healthy."

Hanna considered his statement and caught herself just before she launched into a discussion of diet and exercise, her usual mantra with heart patients.

"I think we're pretty health-conscious as a group," said Grubbs. He turned his attention to Ray, "That young assistant of yours, what's her name again?"

"Sue Lawrence. She's going to be here before the curtain goes up."

"I'll entrust the tickets to you, then," said Grubbs, fishing them out of an inside pocket. "They're center seats ten rows back from the front." Grubbs' final words were almost drowned out by a helicopter coming straight in from the lake, slowing and banking in the direction of the cottage, and then disappearing over a neighboring dune.

Grubbs, his eyes turned toward the craft, mouthed what appeared to be a short string of obscenities, his words drowned out by the scream of the jet engine and low, percussive pounding of the whirling blades.

"Malcolm always makes a dramatic entrance, doesn't he," said a short, portly man coming to Grubbs' side, "even if he's not invited. What do you think, Grubby, was he really coming this direction or did he have his pilot do a flyover to remind us of his importance."

"Well, at least you know your leading man has returned to the area in time for the performance." He gestured toward Ray and Hanna. "I'd like to introduce our local Sheriff, Ray Elkins and his guest, Dr. Hanna Jeffers.

And this is Sterling Shevlin, who has directed our annual summer colony play for what…?"

"This is my thirty-third year," answered Shevlin. "My grandparents had a place in the colony, and my first stage experience was here in the children's drama program. I made a trip back here in my thirties as a one-summer replacement for the long-time director, and the rest is…"

"And a very good history it has been," interrupted Grubbs. "You see, Sheriff, and Dr. Hanna, the summer play pulls together so many talents from our group. Costumes get made, sets get built—and then we have actors, light people, properties—the whole community gets involved, more so than anything else. And then we have this cocktail party and dinner, followed by the grand performance."

"How do you decide what play to produce?" Ray asked Shevlin.

"I look for something that's fairly light. I want a play with lots of parts, both genders, and a big age span. In this one we've got a range from teenagers to people in their eighties. Fifteen years ago we did a Christie play, and it was hugely popular. People have been pestering me to do another. So I looked at her other plays and selected Murder at the Vicarage."

"He's just wicked," said Grubbs. "He's got Malcolm Wudbine cast as Colonel Protheroe, a man loathed by everyone in St. Mary Mead."

"Wicked, no," said Shevlin. "He told me he had to have a part, but he didn't want to learn any lines this year. So I accommodated him, like we always accommodate Malcolm. He gets to wear a period costume, and all he has to do is slump over a desk and try not to move too much for a few minutes. It's just a perfect part for him. And a great plot. Everyone in the village wanted old Protheroe dead, and the audience gets to try to solve that mystery before dear Miss Marple sorts it all out just before the final curtain." Shevlin made a modest bow to Ray and Hanna. "Nice meeting you both. I must run. The director can't get smashed before the show. Hopefully, I'll see you at the afterglow. We'll have a big bonfire on the beach."

"Since you're our special guests, I want to get you two in the front of the buffet line," said Grubbs, as he led Ray and Hanna through the crowd.

10

~~

After the buffet dinner, Ray and Hanna, accompanied by Richard Grubbs made their way to the Assembly Hall where the play was being staged. They waited for Sue Lawrence and her date, Harry Hawkins, and then found their seats, assisted by one of the teenage ushers. They had just settled in when a flash of lightening shot through the building from the windows that lined the walls, followed immediately by a roar of thunder. The ground shook, the lights flickered, dimmed, went out momentarily, and then came back on.

"Perfect," said Grubbs, sitting next to Hanna and directing his comments to Ray. "Don't you think that sets the tone for something sinister."

"What would happen if the lights stayed out?" asked Ray.

"I think we would sit quietly for five or ten minutes, then Sterling Shevlin would slowly make his way to the center of the stage, carrying one candle that would illuminate just his face. He'd wait until he had absolute silence, and then in his rich baritone voice he'd announce that the play would resume tomorrow evening, and that the ushers—equipped for the event with, he'd probably say torches rather than flashlights, will help with a row by row exit, just like our Sunday services. We are a very disciplined group, Sheriff. The building would be emptied expeditiously and the afterglow would start, this time by candlelight in cottages all across the colony. And tomorrow we'd all be back. That's why this place is so magical.

A little bad weather or most calamities in the outside world don't affect us. We have this wonderful respite here for a few months each year that's quite disconnected from our usual lives."

Another peal of thunder rocked the building and reverberated through the rolling terrain. Ray looked up at the elaborate framing overhead, huge timbers notched and fitted and pegged in place, carried by massive hand-hewn beams that rested on fieldstone pillars. Between the roar of each thunderclap, the room was alive with voices, voices that were suddenly subdued by the flood of rain cascading off of the long eaves and slamming into the ground.

Ray squirmed in his seat, trying to get comfortable on the hard plywood surface.

"How was dinner?" asked Sue. "Up to your standards?"

"Unusually good. A friend of the host is a Cordon Bleu-trained chef. These people are serious about their eating and drinking."

The lights flashed on and off three times, alerting the few stragglers that the show was about to begin. A hush fell over the audience as the curtain slowly opened on the interior of a large room. On the left facing the audience was a sofa. Behind it French doors opened to a brightly lit garden. The dinner table stood on the right near the front of the stage. The surrounding chairs, two at the back and one on each side, faced the audience. At the back right of the set was a desk and chair. The walls in this area were surrounded by bookshelves. An old typewriter sat at one corner of the desk and a dial phone at the other, giving the dimly lit area the appearance of an office. Four characters, three men and a woman, came on stage and took chairs at the table. The eldest man, graying at the temples and wearing a clerical collar, sat at the head of the table. A woman, much younger than the man, took the chair at the opposite end of the table. Between them were a teenage boy and a thirty-something man, who was also wearing a clerical collar. The man at the head of the table started a prayer, "For what we are about to receive, may the Lord make us truly thankful. Amen."

A young woman, plump and in an ill-fitting cotton dress, entered with a tray and began placing heavy china serving dishes on the table.

Ray looked down at his program studying the list of characters and then reading the synopsis of the first act from the glow coming off the brightly lit stage. He looked back at the scene unfolding in front of him, identifying characters and beginning to follow the narrative, at times struggling to hear the lines as the rain and thunder still reverberated through the building.

As various new characters were introduced, Ray noticed that Colonel Protheroe was part of every conversation. He could see that Agatha Christie wanted the audience to know that almost everyone in St. Mary Mead had a reason to dislike Protheroe.

Ray was on his feet as soon as the curtain closed on the first scene, stretching and trying to extend his back. Sue was at his side. "That was just the opening scene. Are you going to be able to make it?"

Before he could answer, Richard Grubbs, leaning past Hana, said, "I'll be back in a minute, I need to check on things."

Ray dropped back into his chair. Hanna said to Sue, "Notice he hasn't checked his phone for email."

"That's not good. Does he have a pulse, Doctor?"

"Are you enjoying the show," Ray asked Harry Hawkins, not commenting on the repartee.

"The costuming is good," Hawkins responded with a wry smile. "And the woman playing Griselda is very attractive. I wonder what she is doing after the show."

"You've already got plans," retorted Sue.

A flash of blue-white shot through the building, followed instantly by the roar of thunder as the building went dark. The screen on Ray's phone came to life. "You two are lucky I have this. I'll be able to light your way out of here if necessary."

The light from other phones began to illuminate the dull interior. Low conversations filled the room for several minutes before the lights came on.

Ray watched as Richard Grubbs, red-faced and agitated, entered the side door of the auditorium, pointed to him and made a beckoning gesture with his hand. Ray pointed to his chest with his fingers. Grubbs made an affirmative nod.

11

〰️

"What's happened?" asked Ray.

"Please follow. Something dreadful."

Ray trailed Grubbs out of the auditorium through an exit door near the front of the stage. They stayed close to the exterior wall of the building, avoiding the torrent pouring off the long overhangs and ducked back in through a rear entrance, double doors, both propped open. Another set of doors took them into the back of the auditorium. They skirted the rear of the set and entered the room through the door at stage left, the right side of the set as viewed from the audience. The curtain separating the audience from the stage remained closed. Bare bulbs suspended above in the fly space cast an eerie, dull light over the interior.

Ray carefully palpated the neck of a man sprawled over a desk at the rear of the set.

"Who is this?" he asked.

"Malcolm Wudbine. This is where he is supposed to be at the beginning of the second scene, but...."

"Get Dr. Jeffers and Sergeant Lawrence," he said, looking at Grubbs.

"Oh, my God. What's happened?" asked Sterling Shevlin, coming close. "Is he...?"

"I need you to get everyone backstage in one place," ordered Ray. "Everyone! And make sure no one leaves until I tell you otherwise. No one, absolutely no one is allowed to leave. Do you hear me?"

"Yes, of course."

Ray watched as Shevlin herded a few onlookers through the French doors at the rear of the set. A few moments later Hanna and Sue were at his side, with Grubbs peering over them and Harry Hawkins just behind.

"I couldn't find a pulse," said Ray looking at Hanna.

Hanna reached into the soft tissue of the man's neck with her left hand. Then she went to the other side with her right hand. She pulled her hand back and looked at her fingertips, now red with blood.

"I need some light," she ordered.

Grubbs switched on the flashlight he was carrying.

"Bring the beam over here," she instructed.

Ray hovered at her left side. Impatiently, she grabbed the light from Grubbs and ran the icy LED beam along Wudbine's skull. She looked at Ray.

"What?"

"It looks like there are two wounds, one real, the other…looks like a combination of rubber and makeup. I shouldn't do anything more. Get the ME here. Let him figure it out."

"What kind of wound?"

"The real one, something sharp was driven between the vertebrae at the base of his skull. It severed the spinal column. The victim died instantly. But it would take a lot of force."

"Weapon?"

"I don't know. I'm way out of my field. The pathologist will be the best…." Her voice trailed off as she continued to inspect the head with the light. Finally she looked up and said, "There's a third wound here, an exit wound under his forehead. I think that's fake, too."

"How would you like to proceed?" asked Sue, standing at Ray's side.

"We need to get Dr. Dyskin here."

"I've already made the call."

"Secure this area so you can start working the scene. Given the noise out there, the audience is getting restless. Richard, we need to empty the auditorium."

"What do I say?"

"Tell them…tell them that something has happened to one of the cast members. Ask them to please leave the area so emergency vehicles can get in here. And say that you will have full details as soon as you have more information."

Ray's eyes followed Grubbs as he slid through the curtains to the center of the stage. The hum coming from the audience fell away as Grubbs started to talk. His comments were brief, the voices returned as people began to leave the auditorium.

Ray looked at Sue. "What do you want to do first?"

"I'd like to get everything photographed before anyone else is in here. And then I'd like to work the area as soon as Dr. Dyskin is done and the body is removed. At that point we have to secure the area so I can come back tomorrow and take another look when I have daylight. Unless it's someplace obvious, we're going to have to tear this place apart to find the murder weapon."

"Staffing?" asked Ray.

"Let's bring people in on overtime. And Ben Reilly said he'd like to work occasionally, get him."

"Okay. I will talk to the cast members and everyone else who was backstage. I'll let them know what's happened. I'm sure there's been a lot of speculation by now. I will get a list of their names, contact information, and where they were at the end of the first act. I'll try to find out if anyone saw anything suspicious." Ray, using his phone, checked the time. "Given the hour, unless someone has evidence that would take us to the killer, we should organize an interview process and have people lined up to talk to tomorrow morning. We'll have Grubbs get us a place to do the interviews and have Shevlin identify everyone backstage at the time of the murder. Is your Jeep close?"

"Near the entrance. I'll have Harry bring it up here. I'll be able to start taking photos before Dyskin arrives. After the body is removed, I'll take some more pictures and start working the scene."

"What kind of help do you want?"

"Just secure the building. I need to get a sense of this place. It's not like any scene I've ever worked."

"There's a wife out there," said Ray. "I'll have Grubbs help me locate her and other family members."

"How about the family?" asked Ray when he next encountered Grubbs standing with Sterling Shevlin in the hallway outside the green room.

"His daughter-in-law, she's in the cast...well they all knew...she was very upset. Her husband, Elliot, Malcolm's son, he came back here, and

she told him. Elliot took her out of here. There was nothing I could do."
He gave Ray a helpless look.

"How about Wudbine's wife?"

"I think I've told you already, she never comes to colony events."

Ray stood for a moment, collecting his thoughts. "Where do you think
they went?"

"Probably to Malcolm's place, Gull Cottage, unless they went to their
own cottage."

"I want you to go with me. We'll start at Gull Cottage."

"Let's take my golf cart," suggested Grubbs. "There's a paved path."

"Have you seen Gull Cottage?" asked Grubbs, as they slowly rolled
along a macadam ribbon through the woods, the dense fog that was
blowing off the lake limiting the beam of the headlights.

"No," responded Ray. He was working to control anger, trying to focus
on the crime.

"After his divorce from Verity, he bought this big old cottage, gray-
weathered-shake shingle siding, very New England. It was a beautiful
place. He modernized and expanded it, ruined the proportions. Then ten
or fifteen years ago, he had it leveled. Rumor has it that he was celebrating
his first billion. Malcolm loved gulls, he wanted to capture their energy
and freedom in a building. Hired a disciple of Saarinan—concrete, cables,
titanium, and glass, sort of like the Dulles airport, only more delicate and
flight-like. They did a prototype in canvas, making changes along the way.
Malcolm wanted it large. The architect convinced him to build smaller, in
scale with the landscape and then add guest cottages and other structures
away from the shore so nothing would distract from Gull Cottage."

Ray could see the glow as they approached through the mist, the
features becoming clearer as they neared the edifice. One of the twin
entrance doors swung open before they had alighted from the cart.

"Hello, Pepper," said Richard.

"Everyone is gathered in the great room," the young woman announced,
then led the way.

Ray stood for a moment and observed the family and friends scattered
across the room on large, carefully arranged groupings of couches and
chairs. The room was brilliantly illuminated by the beams of dozens of
small lights mounted in the high, sloping ceiling. Everything was in white,
the carpeting, the fabric on the furniture, the vaulted plaster arching above.
The only exception was an ebony grand piano at the rear of the room, its

relative size providing a scale to the dimensions of space. It appeared to Ray to be a mise en scene, the curtain had just gone up and all the actors were in place, silent, holding drinks in delicately shaped martini glasses, looking very composed.

Grubbs provided the opening line to put the scene in motion. "This is the Sheriff of Cedar County, Ray Elkins. Sheriff, this is Mr. Wudbine's wife, Brenda, his son, Elliott, and Jill, his daughter-in-law."

Finally Brenda Wudbine looked up at Ray, her manner unsteady, "Elliott told me what happened. Is it true? Is Malcolm really dead?"

"Yes, I'm sorry to tell you that it is true."

"And that he was murdered?"

"Yes, that appears to be the case."

"How, how was he killed?"

"We will know more after the autopsy."

"Sterling said he was stabbed," said Jill.

Everyone in the room looked at Ray. "It appears that he died of a puncture wound. Like I said, we will have a precise cause of death after the postmortem examination."

"And when will that happen? When will the body be returned to us?" Jill asked. "We need to begin planning his funeral. My father-in-law was a very important public personality. We need to plan an event that's befitting his many life accomplishments."

"I will know more by Monday. In the meantime I will need to talk with each of you and the members of your staff."

"What on earth for? How would I know anything about this?" asked the new widow, pique in her tone.

"Sheriff," said Jill Wudbine, "we need time to adjust to this. I think we need to be alone."

"I plan on beginning these interviews tomorrow."

"Sheriff, I was Malcolm's personal attorney for the last two decades. From this point forward I will act as the family's legal counsel in this matter," her tone flat and businesslike. "I will facilitate scheduling these interviews at a time that's convenient to family members and not disruptive to work schedules of our employees. You must understand that Mr. Wudbine's death comes as a great shock to all of us. If you provide a phone number, I will be in contact. Now please leave us to our grief."

Ray handed her a business card. "I will begin the interviews tomorrow afternoon. Memories fade quickly. I need your cooperation in finding the killer." He spoke directly to Jill Wudbine, then slowly made eye contact with the other people in the room.

Jill rose, she appeared to Ray to be a bit unsteady. "Ms. Markley will escort you out, Sheriff. I will be in contact with you relative to the interviews in the morning."

Once outside, Ray walked across the drive and then turned back toward the structure. He wanted to get a sense of the building, and he needed a few moments alone to reflect on what had just happened.

"She has a heart of ice, doesn't she?" said Grubbs as Ray slid onto the seat of the golf cart.

"Who is that?"

"Jill, the family attorney. No emotion with that woman, ever. She's totally cognitive. I hope she doesn't get in your way too much. She's probably more into protecting the family than finding out who killed her employer, father-in-law, whatever."

12

~

Ray was leaning against his car stretching his back when Sue's Jeep came creeping up the narrow road. She parked next to him.

"Short night," he said, lifting his vacuum coffee mug.

"Too short, way too short." She took a long moment to stretch, leaning against her Jeep and rotating from side to side, extending her back. Then reached back into her vehicle and retrieved a tall cardboard coffee container.

"What did you learn from Dr. Dyskin?"

"Not much more than Hanna told me. The victim died from the wound near the base of his skull. Dyskin said that it appeared to have been made by an extremely sharp instrument. The skin was cut rather than torn. He also said that a lot of force would be needed to drive the weapon through the spine. And he went on to say that in his long tenure in Wayne County looking at hundreds and hundreds of murder victims, he'd never seen anyone killed in quite this way."

"Anything else?"

"Well, you know Dr. Dyskin is usually so dour. He almost seemed jolly last night. He was intrigued by the other wounds, the rubber and greasepaint ones. He made some comment about never seeing a murder victim with fatal fake wounds before."

"You seem to be tolerating Dr. Dyskin much better these days."

"I'm getting used to him. And now that he doesn't reek of cigar smoke anymore...."

"He didn't get any more specific about the murder weapon?" pursued Ray.

"He said the forensic pathologist should be able to give us a description of the cutting part of the weapon, that it almost looked like a chisel or push dagger. He also went through a whole array of other kinds of weapons with sharp edges, said he'd seen them all in Detroit and Wayne County."

"You're done photographing the scene?"

"Yes," said Sue. "I need to go through the pictures again, and perhaps I'll shoot more today. But nothing jumped out at me."

"And the weapon?"

"You would've known last night," said Sue, taking a yogic lunge pose and holding it for a number of seconds before continuing. "I did look around the stage area and the offstage wings. I need to do that again today. We've got to get some light in there. The place is just filled with dark corners and nooks and crannies where you can get rid of something." She paused and looked at Ray. "What's the plan?"

"Tell me what you think about this. You start with the stage area, then move on to the dressing rooms, greenroom, costume loft, carpentry shop…everything backstage. Then do the front of the Assembly Hall and the outside grounds. We'll get the whole place taped off. I've got Ben Reilly, Brett Carty, and our summer intern Barbara Sinclair scheduled to come in and help you today and tomorrow. We will add days as necessary."

"And what did you learn last night?" asked Sue.

"I talked to the whole group. They were all in shock, or at least appeared to be. No one had seen anything unusual, and no one remembers seeing anyone in the theater who shouldn't have been. The crew and cast members were mostly in the green room before the beginning of the second scene."

"Why the long scene break?" asked Sue. "They were really taking their time. It was like the end of an act."

"My question also. As Grubbs explained that, people had been eating and drinking for quite some time, and then went off to the performance. And that most of the audience is of an age where…."

"You don't have to explain, Ray."

"But there's more. The restrooms are in two buildings adjacent to the Assembly Hall, women's on one side and the men's on the other. It takes some time to negotiate back and forth."

"But it was pouring rain. That would make people go faster."

"Yes," said Ray, "but the weather wasn't a factor in the original thinking. The director said the opening scene was overly long and did what the first act usually does, so he decided to treat it like an act and put a break there."

"Okay, so while I'm finishing up the scene and searching for the weapon, you'll start the interview process?"

"Yes," said Ray. "And as soon as you're done I need major help. Richard Grubbs has given us the use of the colony library." Ray pointed off at a building nestled in the woods about 50 yards south of the Assembly Hall.

"This is going to take a lot of time. There are 12 cast members and 10 or more members of the crew. And then there are the young women who worked as ushers, a custodian, and several maintenance men. And that's probably only part of the iceberg. We've never had anything like this before."

"So give me the rest of the iceberg."

"Based on what Grubbs said in a previous conversation, a lot of people in the colony hated Wudbine."

"What was the basis for their enmity?"

"He didn't go into the specifics. There's a long history here that we are going to have to probe. And in addition to the colony people, Wudbine has a personal staff and assorted family members living with him in his compound and in several cottages in the colony. We have to find out about those people, too."

"So where do you start?"

"Cast and crew. I scheduled them last night, and I'll start talking to people one at a time. I'm starting with Grubbs at ten o'clock, there are things I need to go over again, background info. Then it's every half hour. Will you help me set up the audio equipment right now? It's in the trunk."

"Sure. Let's get it done. I'm eager to get started in there," Sue pointed toward the Assembly Hall.

13

Ray pushed the oak table against the timeworn umber wainscoting that covered the lower half of the wall in the colony library building. He placed a recorder near the paneling, turning it on, repeating, "testing," several times, and then playing his voice back. His distrust of recording equipment went back to an incident early in his career, and the new digital devices—without any overt sign that anything is going on within, no turning of the cassette reels, just the bouncing of small bars on a miniscule screen and one small glowing red diode—did little to reassure him.

He looked up from his seat facing the door as Richard Grubbs entered and collapsed in the chair across from him. He studied Grubbs' face. The margins of his pale blues eyes were bloodshot. The gray-black stubble of a day-old beard covered his face. Ray noted how much older this Richard Grubbs looked from the gregarious, energetic man he had met a few months earlier.

"I will be recording our interview," he said, hitting the red button and reading a boilerplate intro as he turned his head toward the machine.

"How are you today?"

"Stunned, still stunned. Nothing really bad has ever happened here before. Well, that's not quite true. That incident in May, that was almost beyond the realm of possibility." He pulled himself up in his chair, leaned back and inhaled deeply. "Unbelievable…that kind of savagery…here. It's a violation of this sacred land. I never even imagined the possibility…."

"Didn't you tell me that you had several cases of suspected arson?"

"Well, yes, but that was years ago and doesn't compare. I mean, they were old cottages, unoccupied, probably just bad wiring. This…murder… right here. And on our stage. Why not…if they wanted Malcolm dead… kill him up in that big house of his. Sabotage his helicopter. Put a bomb in his car. But not here, not where we worship. Why do this to the colony? Why make us victims, too? I mean, there were children out there, teenagers, too."

"Did you get any sleep last night?"

"Very little. Everyone wanted to talk to me. Or maybe, more correctly, people wanted to talk, needed to talk. People of my generation and near generations, we have so much history, so many years here. We're struggling with the shock and horror of this event, and yet I feel there is kind of a shared shame and guilt."

"How so?"

"I need to think about that a bit. A big part of it is that we didn't like Malcolm, none of us. We tolerated him. He was sort of a boogeyman. It was safe to make jokes about him because everyone felt the same way. Even this play was sort of a joke. Colonel Protheroe, the most disliked man in the village gets murdered."

"I've been wondering about that," said Ray. "I can't imagine that Malcolm Wudbine wouldn't have noticed the nature of the character he was playing."

"Yes, I'm sure he noticed. I kind of think he would relish that. Colonel Protheroe gets murdered during the course of play, but Malcolm gets to go to the cast party. And even though lots of people won't be too sad to see his passing, no one would have wanted it to happen this way."

"Well, Mr. Grubbs, someone obviously did. Do you have any idea who might have been angry enough to kill him?"

"That question kept running through my head when I was trying to sleep. First I thought about the people who had the longest history with him, especially his first wife. You've met Verity. You've talked with her on two occasions. Can you imagine her as a murderer?"

"No. But I know nothing of her relationship with her ex-husband. She was in the building at the time of the murder…."

"Yes, but you'd be wasting your time on her."

"Let's leave Verity for the moment. At the end of the first scene, you got up and left us and exited through the west entrance almost before anyone else was out of their seats. I can't remember exactly what you said at that moment. I need to know where you went and what you saw. And where were you when the lights went off? Please, step by step, from the time you left us until you were beckoning me to follow you backstage. Take your time."

"There is some history here. I sort of freak out during thunderstorms. We did have someone killed by lightning here when I was eight or ten. The victim was a teenager, not that much older than me. Like I said, lightening unhinges me a little bit. And I was concerned about the electrical system in the building, especially with all the stage lights on. I needed to make sure that everything was okay, that's what I do around here. So I went out through that nearest exit and then back into the building through the nearest stage door. As soon as I got into the hallway there was that huge crash, the flash of lightening followed instantly by the thunder. The building shook. The lights flickered and went out. I stood and waited for a few moments, you know how the power goes out and then comes back on. When it didn't, I used my phone to light the way. I popped into the green room and people were using their phones.

"Everyone in the green room seemed to be chatting away, not bothered by the dark. They were joking and laughing. I, of course, was worried about what would happen if the power was not quickly restored. How long should we wait for clearing the auditorium? When would we reschedule to play? Would some of the actors be leaving at the end of the weekend for work or other commitments? That's what was running through my head.

"Sterling was in the green room near the door. By the light of our phones we discussed our options if this turned out to be a long-term blackout. When the lights went back on David Johnson, he's our lighting guy, comes in from outside by the east stage door soaking wet. He's looking very upset. I ask him if everything's okay. He says we need to talk after the show. He heads off toward his lighting loft. Sterling and I follow him through the east door into the backstage area. We're discussing if the break should be extended a few more minutes. The stage manager, Tony Grattan, was right behind us, intending to check the set. I don't know quite who noticed Malcolm first. His head was down on the desk, not moving, just like he was supposed to be at the opening of the second scene. I went over to him and said something, but he didn't move. I put my hand on his shoulder to shake him. Then I saw the blood. For a few seconds I dismissed it as makeup. Then it struck me. This guy is dead. I told Tony and David to keep everyone away. That's when I ran to get you."

Ray looked down at the notes he'd been making on a legal pad. Finishing a sentence, he looked back up at Grubbs. "So once you went backstage, you only encountered three people. First you saw Sterling Shevlin."

"That's right."

"Where was he?"

"Like I said, he was in the green room. He was standing just inside the door that opens to the main hall."

"You're sure of that."

"Absolutely."

"And then the lights came back on. You started down the hallway going to the stage area. At that point you were with the director, Sterling Shevlin, and the stage manager, Tony Grattan."

"Correct."

"And that's when you encountered…?"

"David Johnson."

"And he was coming from…?"

"The outside, the east stage door. "

"And he said he had to talk to you after the performance."

"Something to that effect."

"What was that about? Have you had a chance to talk to him?"

"No, not yet. But I assume he wanted to talk about electrical problems and what needs to be done. We have this conversation every year. Things are not up to modern standards. And when the stage lights are on, we're just about at capacity. We've blown the main fuses even without an electrical storm." Grubbs paused briefly, then he explained, "The fuse boxes, breaker panels, and shut offs are on the exterior of the building. They're in a protected enclosure. I assume that he'd gone out there to see what had happened."

"Besides Malcolm, who else would have been onstage during the break?"

"I'm not sure. Maybe some crew members."

"I notice that the emergency egress lights didn't come on when the power failed," said Ray.

Richard Grubbs squirmed in his chair. "Yes, that's a problem. One of the units was shorting out and had to be disconnected. I thought I could buy one unit, but the owner of the fire safety company we contract with counseled against that, saying that given the age of the system all the units should be replaced. I gave him the go ahead. They will be installed early this week."

Ray looked at Grubbs for a long moment.

"Yes, I know, Sheriff. I'm sure I broke the law or violated some building code. The units had been in place thirty or forty years. I can't remember a single instance when they were ever needed. It never occurred to me…well in the end they weren't needed…and…"

"Did anyone else know about this problem?"

"No…well…maybe…yes. I told the girls, the ushers, that there was a problem. I gave them each a new flashlight just in case."

"When did you do that?"

"Friday. I found out about the problem on Thursday. Friday morning I went down to the hardware for the flashlights."

"How secure is the Assembly Hall when it's not in use?"

"During the summer it's unlocked. That's the way it has always been, and that's true of most of the colony buildings. People come and go. At the end of the season we get everything secured to guard against possible vandalism during the winter."

"So if someone wanted to come in and tamper with something…?"

"The building is open 24-7 in June, July, and August. There are constantly things going on. We have our nondenominational worship services, our summer chorus, children's theater, band concerts, chamber music, rehearsals of all kinds, and the summer play. There are always people around."

"How about 3:00 A.M.?"

"Well, not then, but…."

"And you have no security personnel, no one walking or driving around?"

"There's never been a need." Grubbs sagged in his chair. "What's going to happen now?"

Ray looked across the table. "We will be figuring that out as we go along. The first step is to completely process the crime scene."

"When can we get in there? The Assembly Hall is the center of much of what happens here."

"I don't know how to answer your question. It will take us a while to finish up. We are still looking for the murder weapon. I think you can probably have the building on Wednesday or Thursday, perhaps a day or two later."

"And when will you be done and out of here?" Grubbs pressed. "When can we start rebuilding our summer, what's left of it?"

"We will try to finish up our interviews in the next few days. The investigation will continue until we find the killer."

14

Ray walked Richard Grubbs to the door and then returned to his notes, scanning the contents and making a few additions. While Grubbs' story was completely plausible, he had the knowledge and easy access to commit the murder. If Grubbs was the perpetrator, Ray wondered where he would have stashed the weapon.

Ray's consideration of Grubbs as a suspect was interrupted by a gentle rapping at the door. He stood and greeted David Johnson, the lighting technician. Once Johnson was seated across from him, Ray studied his face. He guessed Johnson to be about Grubbs' age, late 60s or early 70s. He turned on the recorder and read Johnson the boilerplate.

"Have you been a colony resident long?" Ray asked.

"There are pictures of me in diapers here. Born in January, I would have been six months old that first summer."

"And you've been a summer resident ever since?"

"More or less. During college I had jobs downstate, and the summer I graduated I did the grand tour of Europe. Pretty common back then. And then during medical school and my residency, I didn't make it here for more than a weekend or two most years. But after I was in practice and married, we bought a cottage near my parents and started spending much of the summer here. After the kids arrived, my wife would be here for the whole summer, and I'd come up most weekends and spend the month of August. Since I've retired, we're here for the season."

"Medicine. What was your specialty?"

"I was a general surgeon."

"How long have you been involved with the summer play?"

"I started acting here as a kid. I was fascinated by this magical world of grease paint, costumes, lights…everything about it. I had a part in the children's play every summer growing up. And I also liked the technical aspects, especially the lighting. And in the winter, downstate, I was involved with the community theatre and school plays. I really thought that's what I'd do with my life."

"Tell me about last night. Take your time. Give me a chronology of what happened," coached Ray.

Johnson rubbed his stubble-covered chin, then looked at Ray. "Give me a moment, I need to collect my thoughts." He peered over Ray's shoulder—his head cocked to the right—toward the back of the building. Then he straightened and looked directly at Ray. "I was at the party at Verity's and saw you there. I had no idea who you were, but outsiders are rare at these events. After the wife and I got through the buffet, I sort of wolfed my food and got over to the Assembly Hall. This is old equipment. I always want to check things before anyone else is around. That gives me the time to bring out a ladder and replace a bulb or do any other wiring change without having to hurry or have people in my way. So that's what I did. Then I went into the green room and chatted with people until about ten minutes before the performance when I climbed back up to the light box. Not much to do up there in this play. After the first scene ends, I have to adjust the lighting on the exterior of the set. The first scene takes place at mid-day. The second scene takes place the next day in the early evening. I was in the process of making the changes when we had that incredible lightning and thunder. Everything went black. I held tight for a bit, then I climbed down and headed out to the electrical services out back."

"Let me stop you for a bit. From your position in the…?"

"Light box."

"What can you see? Was there anyone onstage when the lights went out?"

"With this set, I can pretty much see everything onstage. I can also see what's happening on the off-stage wing on my side. The other side is hidden by the set. So I have to separate what I know about who needed to be there with what I can remember. The properties person would have come through to make sure everything was in place, and I think I saw her. And then there was Malcolm coming through, being attended to by Florence Carlotta, our makeup person. Malcolm had a ghastly wound on his forehead. It was huge, like something you'd see at a Halloween party. I couldn't quite figure out what was going on."

"I'm not following," said Ray.

"In this scene, Malcolm plays—not really plays, he's just a prop—a body. We could have stuffed a suit and it would have worked as well. The character just fills a chair. I couldn't figure out why he had that elaborate makeup on."

"Then what?"

"They went over to the table where Protheroe's body is found sprawled across the Vicar's desk at the beginning of the scene. Malcolm sat down and Florence helped position him. It seemed to me that they were going to a lot of trouble for nothing. When she left, he just stayed in that position, like he was taking a nap."

"And no one else was onstage or in the wings on your side when the lights when out?"

"Correct, that's my memory."

"Okay, the lights go out, then what do you do?"

"Like I was saying before, I waited for a little bit to see if the power was going to come back on, then I killed the power to the dimmers, climbed down the ladder, and headed outside to the electrical panels."

"What were you using for light?"

"I've got one of those headlamps with the six or eight little bulbs. I keep it there just for this kind of emergency. This is not the first time we've been in darkness, the problem is more common than it should be. We've been overloading the system for years."

"Did you see anyone on your way out, and what door did you use?"

"Strange, I didn't see a soul. Guess they were all in the green room. I went out the east stage door. The electrical panels are in a utility cabinet on the back wall of that side of the building. When I got there the cabinet doors were open. They should have been closed. And then I noticed some of the lights downstream from the Assembly Hall were coming back on, but we were still in darkness. So I started looking around and saw that someone had turned off the main disconnect for the building. I pushed it on and went back inside. I wanted to get up to the booth and get the lights on so we could start the next scene."

"Did you see anyone on your way?"

"I saw Grubby. He was heading toward the stage area."

"Did you talk to him?"

"Let me think. At that moment I was fairly agitated. It looked like a stupid act of vandalism had created a potentially dangerous situation. I may have said something. Obviously, that was not the time to discuss the matter. I climbed up to the booth and did a quick check of the lights and then noticed what was happening down on stage. I watched for a minute or so, and then started down. You arrived about that time."

"What happened next?"

"I was herded into the green room and sat there and waited until you came to talk to us."

"Tell me about the green room. What was happening there?"

"People were sitting in groups talking. When I walked in everyone was still in the dark," he stopped briefly, "well, you know what I mean, in the dark as to what had happened. But I think they could tell something was very wrong. And then you came in and told us that Wudbine was dead. And when someone asked you if it was a stroke or heart attack, you didn't equivocate. You said he was murdered."

"And what happened when I left?"

"First there was stunned silence. Then I think people started thinking about what they should do, who would need support. Verity went to her daughter-in-law's side, some other people as well. Then people seemed to cluster in small groups. There was some sobbing. Lots of hushed conversations. I think we were all bowled over by your announcement."

"Did you see anyone out of place, anyone backstage or in the green room who shouldn't have been there?"

"Not that I can remember."

"What was your relationship with Malcolm Wudbine?"

Johnson looked off to some point beyond Ray, then back. "He was a real pain in the ass. Obnoxious and controlling. I learned years ago whenever possible to stay away from difficult people. This is a big area and our cottage is in a remote corner of the property, very private. The only time I saw Malcolm most summers was connected with the play, and I didn't have any face-to-face dealings with the man. So while he was enormously vexatious to some people here, Malcolm was never more than a faint blip on my radar. And I worked to keep it that way."

"You talked about electrical problems?"

"Yes, like I was telling you. All the equipment is old and should have been replaced decades ago. But it has been hard to make a case for stage lighting against the other needs of the colony. The whole infrastructure of Mission Point is crumbling. Everyone is sentimental about this place, but few are ready to put up some real cash. In fact, every time there's been a major crisis—like our treatment plant dying and pouring raw sewage into the lake—Malcolm and his millions have come to the rescue. I think we all started to believe that we didn't have to attend to these problems because at the end of the day Malcolm would come in and take care of them."

"Motives for murder, do you know anyone who wanted Malcolm dead?"

"No. He was enormously unpleasant. But murder, that's a whole different story."

"And you've never had any personal or financial dealings with Wudbine?"

"Like I suggested, my motto is to avoid skunks. I always tried to stay upwind of Malcolm."

15

Ray's conversation with David Johnson was just winding down when he noticed Richard Grubbs standing outside the screen door peering in, looking agitated and weary. As Johnson walked away, Ray ushered Grubbs in.

"What's the problem?" he asked.

"I thought you should know, Sheriff, there's a panic going on. I mean, now that people are awake and drinking coffee, and…well…people are thinking of going home. What they're saying is that there was one murder, there could be more. They want to get away from this place, take their families somewhere safe."

Ray didn't respond for a long moment, then said, "I can understand their fears. I think you need to be out there helping people vent their feelings. You might want to consider bringing in a crisis response team. That said, you probably have trained mental health workers in the colony. Pull them together and get their guidance."

"People are demanding that I hire a security service and get streetlights installed immediately." Grubbs' face was flush, his hand trembling as he gesticulated his points.

"I was just chatting with you twenty or thirty minutes ago. How many people are we talking about?

"Well, a few, but they were very upset."

"You need to be calm, Richard. Think about this crime. Does this look like a random event?"

"Well, no. Someone clearly wanted Malcolm dead. This murder was, what do you people say, premeditated. But why here, why onstage?"

"That's a very interesting question. How often is Malcolm alone? How easy would it be to get to him?"

"Malcolm was seldom alone. He always had his people around him. The 'people' thing, that's his phrase, not mine. He was always saying 'I'll have my people take care of it,' or 'I'll have my people look into it.' Phrases like that."

"Did he have a security detail?"

"Personal assistants, I think that's what he called them. I never paid close attention. But now that I think of it, yes, they could have been security people. If rock stars and politicians all have security details, why shouldn't Malcolm?" He paused for a moment, then pointed at his chest, "This old college professor, there's this big world out there that I don't understand." He paused again, "Come to think of it, that new person, Alyson Mickels, his personal trainer and helicopter pilot, could be a security type. He bragged that Alyson was a former special ops officer. She's quite attractive and clearly a jock."

"Was she in the audience last night, or backstage, or when we went up to the Gull House?"

"No, I didn't see her, and she's hard to miss. Tall, very blond with long, thick hair like a Norse goddess. And the way she fills her clothes, I don't think she means to be provocative, but boy."

"There was another Wudbine in the cast."

"Yes, his daughter-in-law, Jill. She had the part of Anne Protheroe."

"Was his wife in the audience?"

"No. To my memory Brenda has never stepped foot in the Assembly Hall. She figured out the chemistry of this place the first summer Malcolm showed up with her. What you have to know is everyone was on Verity's side when the big breakup took place. And to give you a little background, years before they split there were rumors of physical abuse and infidelity on Malcolm's part.

"Brenda never became part of the colony. When she's here in the summer, she doesn't participate in any of our events. She just stays up there in that enormous house. I have heard that she has a group of women friends who come and visit. Rumor has it that she's an alcoholic. I guess that's one way you could endure living with Malcolm, but one should not speak ill of the dead."

Ray listened to Grubbs closely. He wondered what was really going on in the man's mind.

"Well, I better get back," said Grubbs. "I imagine my office is probably filling up again. And your advice was good. I'll get some people organized to help me deal with this."

"Events like this generate enormous stress. Like I said, people need to vent their feelings and fears. If you can get that process going, I think you will see things start to calm down."

After Grubbs hurried away, Ray thought about the cast and crew in the green room when he went in to talk to them. He was starting to put faces with names, starting to see relationships. He wandered outside, seeking the warmth of the sunshine.

"I was hoping to catch you between interviews," said Sue Lawrence coming down the sand trail, a well-worn path bordered on each side by moss-covered stones. The path snaked through the second-growth hardwoods.

"What's going on?"

"There's not much more to do there, other than tear the place apart looking for the weapon. Brett and I went out to take a break, and he called my attention to the four dumpsters sitting at the base of the hill. We went down and took a look. And while we were there one of the residents drove up with a couple of garbage bags. Here's the deal, that's where everyone drops their garbage. It's all got to be bagged. Pickups are on Monday and Friday."

"I think I know where you're going."

"Do I need to get a search warrant?"

Ray took a long time to answer. "Let's be on the safe side. And get some hazmat suits. I'll come and help you when I'm done. That Brett, he's too observant for his own good."

16

Florence Carlotta arrived like a small tornado, breathless and animated, dragging two huffing Scottie dogs, rotund mops of black hair pulling in opposite directions at right angles to her intended course. A pair of vintage Birkenstocks, peaking from beneath a large floral skirt, provided the platform for Florence's ample figure.

Ray started to bend to pet the Scotties.

"I wouldn't do that," Carlotta warned sternly. "Una doesn't fancy men much. Araballa, she's the younger one, doesn't either, but she's less of a biter. They have nailed the phone man, the UPS driver, the plumber, and the painter. I'm sure they would have gotten the butcher, the baker and candlestick maker, too, if they were still around. Equal opportunity biters who don't discriminate."

"Seems to me their targets are very gender specific," observed Ray.

"Yes, that's true, but it doesn't necessarily represent the views of the management, as they say on TV. Nature over nurture, genes over environment. The girls have their own take on the world.

"I know I'm a half-an-hour early. Tony Grattan is supposed to be here, but I've traded time-slots with him. You see, I have to be on the road by noon. Want to be downstate before the southbound rush begins. I'm sure you don't mind. Tony will be here in thirty minutes just like I was supposed to be. That man is totally dependable. A real gem."

"I was trying to interview people in order...."

"Yes, you said that last night when you were setting up your schedule. But it hardly matters, does it? I mean, since we don't really know when Malcolm was killed, at best it's a guess who saw him last. Well, of course, in truth the killer was the last one to see him alive, but he or she was hardly going to admit their guilt so you could have your little arrangement in proper order. Too bad, isn't it? We could get this whole untidy incident over with. So you have some questions for me?"

"Tell me about last night. What time did Malcolm arrive? What kind of makeup did you apply, and why did you walk him onstage?"

"Malcolm arrived late. I mean later than anyone else...."

"Let me interrupt you for a minute. When he came in, was he alone or was someone with him?"

"What do you mean, like with him?"

"Was he with other cast members, or one of his employees, or...?" Ray let the question hang.

"When I saw him he was alone. I mean, most of us came together or almost together. People had been at Verity's. And Tony Grattan, being the good stage manager that he is, got us moving toward the Assembly Hall with enough time to get everyone costumed and in makeup. I mean, it's a lot like herding cats, these people, especially after a few drinks, but that man has so much grace and skill. I could never figure out why he and Mrs. Grattan didn't make it. Some people thought perhaps he was gay, or perhaps she was gay. I thought she was just a floozy, and he couldn't stand it anymore. I mean, some people look so good when you are in college, but when you get out there, jobs, kids, that's when the rubber slams the road. All those good looks don't amount to much when there's work to be done.

"So what I was telling you is that Malcolm came in alone. Most of the other people in the cast took care of themselves, put their make-up on, got into their costumes. Not Malcolm, he insisted upon being attended to. I mean, he's used to that kind of thing, having people scurrying around. And other than getting into that vintage suit, there was no need for make-up. I mean, he was just going to put his head down on a desk and try to look dead. But he wanted makeup and wounds, bullet wounds. Like I said, he didn't need them for the play, but he wanted them for the cast party. So I did that for him, two big wounds, an entry and an exit. It took awhile to get everything right. I had to glue them in place, and then I had to apply makeup to his forehead and neck to make everything match. Then he walked around the green room and asked everyone how he looked. Got lots of comments. That man always needed attention. I mean, not that most men don't, but Malcolm was especially needy."

"Okay, so once the makeup was on, and he had an opportunity to show it around, what happened?"

"Tony Grattan popped in to make sure people were ready for the next scene. At which point I got Malcolm queued up. As soon as the curtain was down on the first scene, I walked Malcolm onstage. Once he was seated, I helped him situate his head just so. He didn't want to mess up his makeup. I mean, he wanted it perfect for the cast party. I told him I'd repair any damage, but he…."

"And when did the lights go off."

"Well, I left him there. Told him sweet dreams and went back to the dressing room to see if anyone else needed help. I was floating around checking on people when it went dark. Right away people were using their phones for light. I found a chair and decided to stay put till the lights came back on. I mean, I wouldn't want to break a hip or anything. This lighting thing is such a problem. David does his best to hold things together. Every year we hear the rewiring is high priority, and then there's a major crisis and…."

"So to the best of your knowledge, Malcolm never left the chair after you walked him there."

"Correct. He wasn't planning to move till the scene was over."

"Was there anyone else on stage or in the wings."

"Not that I saw."

"How about David Johnson?"

"I don't recall. He might have been up in his crow's nest."

"Was there anyone around that shouldn't have been there, someone who wasn't an actor or crew member?"

"I don't recall that. There's often family around, I mean, like kids. Or sometimes a spouse pops in. But not on show night. Then it's real business."

"Wudbine, how long have you known him?"

"Well, we're contemporaries. I've known him thirty or forty summers, on and off. And I've been friends with Verity, summer friends, most of my life. But even at the time of the great breakup, I wasn't totally on her side. Verity could be very selfish and self-centered. I've noticed especially pretty women are like that. They can get away with it. I think Malcolm got tired of being little more than an adornment to the perfect family."

Ray waited, assuming more was coming. When it didn't, he asked. "What was your relationship with Wudbine?"

"I would see him a few times over the summer. He was pretty much excluded from the private parties after the divorce. But he'd always come by my cottage early in the season and have a drink. Did the same before the end of the summer, too. He also gave me some investment advice. Helped me with my inheritance. He made some good money for me, and fortunately, I got out early. Never lost a dime in the dotcom or the Bush crash. I've heard some people didn't do as well. There are some jokes circulating about "Malcolm" Madoff. But that wasn't my experience."

"Would you give me…."

"I mean, people were just joking. It was something I overheard. People were jealous that he seemed unscathed, while lots of the older folks here lost a big part of their retirement. I don't know if any of them had anything invested with Malcolm. In recent years he became too big time for us."

"So you were positively disposed toward Malcolm Wudbine?"

"Absolutely. He had his moments and could be horribly obnoxious. But that was just a cover. I mean, in truth, Malcolm was a black hole of insecurities. All the puffery was just a cover.

"And I'll tell you something else. In spite of what you may hear, he will be greatly missed. Whenever there was a crisis, the powers that be would run around like a bunch of chickens with their heads cut off. Eventually they would get around to asking Malcolm what to do, and he'd tell them. And often he'd even put up the cash to make it happen. Most of these guys couldn't organize a…well, you get my drift. They are good at goal setting and visioning, but as I said, when it comes to the rubber smacking the road, they can't get it done. Malcolm was a doer, a damn efficient one."

She looked at her watch. "Now, Sheriff, you really have to excuse me, but I've got to get on the road."

"What's the purpose of your trip?"

"The girls, they need grooming."

"And you're driving downstate for that?"

"No one up here knows how to cut Scotties. And Stephanie is the only one who can groom them without being bitten. She majored in psychology at Michigan State, and boy does she know how to use it. Few people ever use what they learn in college. She sure does."

"When do you plan on returning?" asked Ray.

"Tuesday morning. I don't want to waste any of this beautiful weather."

"I've heard some people are considering leaving…."

"Pure silliness. Let me tell you, lots of people have died here over the years, heart attacks, strokes, and drownings. And, yes, this is a murder and that's different, but…you know what I mean. I can't imagine packing up and going home over something like this. If you have any more questions, I shall return by midafternoon on Tuesday."

17

After watching Florence Carlotta and her pack depart, Ray sat for a long moment and enjoyed the quiet. He listened to the wind in the tall trees and the distant echo of waves against the beach, perhaps more imagined than real. He turned his attention to his notes, highlighting Carlotta's comments about Malcolm Wudbine looking after her investments. He wondered how many other colony members had had financial dealings with Wudbine over the years. Clearly, Florence Carlotta, given some careful planning, was in a position to kill Wudbine. Would she have been able to shut off the power, or would she have needed a collaborator? His musings were interrupted by a gentle rapping at the screen door.

At Ray's beckoning, Tony Grattan walked into the building. After shaking hands, Grattan settled into the chair across from him, shifting from side to side, using the armrests to aid in positioning his narrow frame. He sat ramrod straight, his nose, chin, and shoulders in perfect alignment.

"I trust it's okay that Flossy and I made the trade. She was most insistent. Quite formidable, that woman. It's hardly worth the psychic energy to oppose her on issues that are less than of life-shaking importance."

Ray's only response was a bemused smile. "Walk me through everything that happened last evening. I would like you to start at the cocktail party. Or even before if something comes to mind that you think might shed light on this crime."

"Well, I can't imagine that I have anything more to tell you that you didn't hear from Flossy. My comments will be skeletal by comparison. She's probably blended every rumor and innuendo from the last 40 years into her account of last night's tragic events. That woman has a memory like an elephant, and she holds nothing back."

Ray noted both the words and tone in which they were delivered. "A chronology without extra elaboration would be perfectly acceptable," Ray responded. "Just the facts."

"Well, like you said, I started moving the actors and crew toward the theatre an hour before the performance. I had two motives. First, I wanted to get the characters there and in costume and makeup well before curtain time. I wanted people there early so they would have some quiet time to get into character. And the second motive, which probably should have been the first motive if I was really thinking about this chronologically, was to get people out of there so they wouldn't have too much to drink. Let someone have two, three, or more drinks and their lines get muddled or disappear by the time they walk on stage."

"And you were able to succeed…."

"Remarkably well. Good group this year. No unpleasantness or friction. No surly drunks. I circulated through the crowd, pointing to my watch, and everyone got the message. Everyone but Malcolm, of course, because he wasn't at the party. Arriving late is his modus operandi, always the grand entrance, usually with his entourage in tow."

"How late was he?"

"We were getting ready for the opening curtain. When he came in, I pointed to Flossy and said, 'You're in charge. Get him ready.' She's the only one in the colony he couldn't buffalo. I knew he'd be in place and ready for the second scene."

"You mentioned his entourage. Who was with Wudbine?"

"Interesting enough, no one that I remember. He might have been accompanied as far as the stage door, but I wouldn't have seen that."

"So continue."

"Well, I knew that Malcolm was under control, and we managed to get through the first scene without any lost lines or other problems. I was worried about the lights. That's been a problem for years, but now it's worse than ever. People just keep plugging more stuff in. And with all the thunder and lightning…well."

"So if something went wrong with the electrical system, do you know your way around the collection of electrical boxes?" asked Ray.

"Oh, absolutely. Not all of them, grant you. But I know the main shutoff. David has always said that if something goes horribly wrong, and he's getting fried, turn off the master switch first. Don't touch him or try to remove his body. Turn off the master switch and then attend to him."

"How many other people know about this?"

"Lots. We have this whole safety procedure, and we go through it every summer during our opening orientation. We show crewmembers where the main electrical shutoff is located, just like we show them the locations of the fire extinguishers and how they work. But some of the old-timers have heard this spiel so often, I'm not sure they bother to listen. They just stand there and nod their heads. But in a real emergency, hopefully someone would remember."

"Where were you when the lights went off?"

"I was in the green room checking that people were ready to go onstage. I was near the door that opens into the main hall. There was lightning and thunder, the lights blinked and then went out. I just sort of held my position waiting for them to come back on, that's the way it usually happens. Only this time it didn't. Then people started using their phones for light. I asked everyone to stay put. Eventually, everything came back on."

"Give me your best estimate of how long the lights were off?"

"Hard to say, really. Two minutes, maybe more. I was trying to keep people calm. Lots of questions were coming my way. People wanted to know how we were going to handle the situation. That kind of thing."

"Then what happened?"

"I asked everyone to remain in the green room until I checked with David that it was safe to go onstage. I left the green room and walked backstage to talk to him. I could see that something was terribly wrong. I just stayed in the background. A few minutes later you arrived. I was ordered back to the green room."

"Before and after the lights went off, were you blocking the green room door?"

"I wouldn't say blocking. And it's a big door, two doors, actually. I was off to the left on the inside."

"When the lights were out, could someone have entered or left without your knowing?"

Grattan's answer was slow in coming. "I don't know. But if truth be told, I might not notice comings and goings even if the lights were on. My former wife used to say that I had no sense of what was happening around me. And she would have been right on that. If someone is talking to me, that's where my focus is. I don't know if it is a problem of peripheral vision, or something cognitive."

"So you have no memory of anyone entering or leaving the green room when the lights were out, or immediately before or after?"

"Correct. I do remember David saying that someone had pulled the main disconnect."

"Has that ever happened before?"

"No, not in my memory. That's the curious thing. Having the lights go off—some of them—that's no big thing, a common occurrence. But having someone pull the main switch, that's a big thing."

"Have there been other acts like this? Maybe one or more individuals, perhaps teenagers, who have been engaged in some mischief or shenanigans?"

"Through the years I can think of cases, even name names of the parties thought to be the troublemakers. We haven't had those problems in awhile. The population here is getting older. There are almost no young families, not like when I was a kid. And teenagers are few and far between. This event, this messing with the power, is outside the realm of what happens here. Water balloons and toilet paper, maybe, but nothing like this. To my way of thinking, it's directly connected with Wudbine's murder." Grattan paused for a minute. "And you know it's not rocket science."

"You've lost me," said Ray.

"All those panels back there. Anyone with limited knowledge of how things work could figure it out. That switch is clearly marked. I think it's done that way for firefighters. What I'm trying to say is that you shouldn't just be looking at colony people. If some outsiders were looking to kill Malcolm, they could figure this out."

"Wouldn't you notice strangers hanging around?"

"That is pretty much a public building. People take tours. We're used to having visitors around. It's not unusual to have people standing in the back of the auditorium during rehearsals. They are not disruptive, and we pretend they're not there."

"Malcolm Wudbine, how long have you known him?"

"Maybe thirty years off and on, he's a bit older than me. I worked in the auto industry and got moved around the country a lot. After my parents passed, I shared our cottage with my sister and her family, but there were periods where we didn't make it here for several seasons. For many decades I knew who he was, but little more. When I got involved in the theatre again, after I got pushed into early retirement, that's when I had more contact with him."

"How did you find him, Wudbine?"

"My dealings with him were very limited. He didn't bother me."

"Did you have any business or financial dealings with him?"

"No," Grattan answered. "My contact was here."

"Do you know anyone who might have a motive to cause him harm?"

"All I know are the rumors and stories, and I don't even know those very well. I live on my own. I listen to music, read books, walk the shore, and enjoy this place. I do my best to keep away from the noise of other people's lives."

18

～

"Some people thought it was a cruel trick," said Sterling Shevlin, "casting Malcolm Wudbine as Colonel Protheroe, the most disliked man in St. Mary Mead. And while it is easy to make comparisons between the two, it was no trick, indeed. Malcolm, like he always does, showed up one evening in early June at my cottage with a couple of bottles of Bombay Sapphire. And you see, that's just the essential Malcolm, far too busy and important to show up and read for a part, but having the time to spend an evening sitting around and talking. And, as usual, before departing, asking if there was a role for him this season."

Ray looked across at Shevlin as he listened.

"I told him there wasn't much in Murder at the Vicarage for someone his age. If the people who dramatized the story had stayed closer to Agatha Christie's book, I would have the perfect part, but as it was in the play, Colonel Protheroe was only a cadaver, and I was planning to use a dummy in the part.

"You can imagine my surprise when he expressed interest in the role. He said it was just perfect. He wouldn't have to learn any lines, said that was getting harder every year. Malcolm told me he liked being part of the play every year because of the energy he absorbed from other cast members. He liked the tension and excitement and spending time with some of the younger actors. There was also something about that being a replacement for the grandchildren he never had. Malcolm, he was such a bundle of contradictions. There were so many things I liked about him, yet at times over the years, I was the target of his prejudices."

"Could you elaborate?"

"I used to bring my then companion, Ellis, with me. Malcolm seemed very offended by that. At the time I heard he had started a whispering campaign. He reportedly feared that the colony would become a second Saugatuck. So I confronted Malcolm directly. Ellis and I marched up to his house, the old place before he flattened it and built Gull House. We demanded to talk to him. At first one of his employees said he wasn't available. I told the young woman that we weren't going to leave until we had a conversation with Malcolm. She disappeared in sort of a panic. Eventually we were escorted into the library. You can always tell a library created by an interior decorator. None of the books look read, they are just adornments. Eventually Malcolm arrived. I told him what I had been hearing and how offended I was. Well, of course, he denied the whole thing. He was at his most charming, served us sherry, a very good sherry, and told us how much he hated bigotry of any kind. He's a real chameleon, a lying SOB. But I have to say that after that confrontation, I didn't hear anything more."

"Let's talk about last night," said Ray. "Were you part of the group that accompanied Tony Grattan down to the theater from the cocktail party?"

"No, I was ahead of the group by 10 or 15 minutes."

"What were you doing?"

"I have a pre-performance ritual. I love being in an empty theater. I like walking around with just the working lights on. I try to envision how the show should go, and I make a little list of final instructions. I think about each of the main characters and what they have to do to create the necessary tension. Actually, I've been doing this from the first rehearsal, but this is my last chance to help people focus. Once you get a cast beyond learning their lines and blocking, it's all about tone and nuance. Right before they go onstage, I try to remind each of them of one or two things that will make their character more believable."

"Who else was in the building?"

"Well, I don't think anyone was. I didn't see anyone, but this is a big rambling place. It supposedly has a history of being one of the favorite places for teens to have assignations, probably some of their parents, too. In the costume shop and the property area, there are lots of places one, or shall I say two, can disappear. And then there's the ghost." Shevlin looked at Ray. "I can tell, Sheriff, you don't believe in ghosts, but there is one here. I've been in this building for years, sometimes alone, at times in the company of others, when I, we, have heard her laughter. It's never from the same place. I don't know how to explain it, eerie, almost hysterical, and definitely sexual. Earlier this summer we had a heating and cooling guy working on the ventilators. He was here and heard it several times. He told me he'd never work here again."

"To the best of your knowledge, no one else was in the building?"

"As far as I know, no one of a non-spectral nature. I think I heard the ghost, but I don't pay any attention to her anymore."

"And then the cast arrived?"

"They all came in together. They were noisy and in high spirits. I think alcohol and the kind of weather we were having last evening played into it. Most of us resonate with violent weather. It causes a kind of madness. Of course, I was immediately concerned about their behavior. When you talk to the cast members, some will tell you I was cross with them, a misinterpretation on their part. I needed them to quiet themselves and start getting into character."

"Two questions. First, was there anyone missing who should have been here? Second, was there anyone around who shouldn't have been here? And was there anything out of place, anything that seemed wrong or unnatural?"

Shevlin rubbed his balding pate with his right hand, fingers spread like he might be running them through hair. Then he pulled off his glasses, the heavy horn-rimmed frames, and wiped his eyes, first the left then the right, with a rumpled handkerchief.

"I hear your questions, but other things are bouncing around in my brain. Something is wrong, unnatural. Did I see anything? Let me ponder that for a moment. I don't think so. But something was completely wrong. We do a play about murder. We wrap the scariest piece of the human experience with the cozy atmosphere of an English village. People drink tea and eat biscuits as they try to puzzle out the real killer from the many possibilities. And so no one in the audience has to work too hard, Miss Marple, with her unerring logic and amazing memory for detail, eventually identifies the killer. It's a comfortable evening of theatre—dinner and drinks before, dessert and drinks after, and some light mental gymnastics in the middle. What took place last night is completely unnatural. I am struggling to believe this really happened. Murder, it's not part of my experience. It's not part of the experience of anyone here. It's the stuff of theatre, film, and TV."

"But it is real," said Ray. "It was carefully planned and skillfully executed. Again, was there anyone backstage who shouldn't have been there?"

"No one that I saw. It was just the cast and the crew. Malcolm was late, that was his custom. There was the usual anticipatory buzz, the kind of energy that gets everyone prepared for the opening curtain."

Shevlin looked at Ray, "The first scene went very well, don't you think?"

"Yes. Where were you?"

"I usually try to go around the outside of the auditorium and sneak in a back door to watch, but with the rain starting to fall, I just stayed in the wings and listened. Then at the end of the scene, actually it was a bit before the end, I slipped out the stage door and headed for the john. I knew there would be a line, and I was …."

"I understand."

"Then I came right back. I was in the green room giving positive strokes and waiting for the next scene. We made this an extra long break in consideration of our…"

"Yes, that's been explained to me. So you were in the green room the whole time after you returned to the building."

"Yes, until I walked backstage with Grubbs. That was after the lights came back on."

"And at that time was the whole cast in the green room?"

"To the best of my knowledge. People were spread out through the adjoining areas, the dressing rooms and makeup area. So if you're asking who was there and who wasn't, I can't answer that. I remember a conversation with Tony Grattan and an overlong exchange with Florence Carlotta. It's not a static situation with people sitting around in assigned seats."

"Do you know anyone who would want Malcolm Wudbine dead?"

"I know scores of people who have been pissed at Malcolm over the years, myself included. But dead, that's a different story. For example, you have Verity, his first wife, Miss Marple in the play. I guess it was a bloody divorce, theirs. That was years and years ago. In spite of that they successfully reared a son. And here in the theatre, this year, as in years past, I won't say that they were excessively fond of one another, but they were able to get along without any overt enmity.

"What I've heard many times over the years, Sheriff, is people saying something like, 'I wish Malcolm would just go away.' Then people end up adding, 'Of course, he should be good enough to leave a big stack of money in our care.' Malcolm had us all hooked. He was the goose that laid the golden egg. His fortune kept this place going, not that we couldn't have figured it out on our own if there had been no Malcolm. He just made it so easy. His money would fix any problem, and we didn't have to dig into our own pockets. It was like having someone around who was always good enough to pay the mortgage and the taxes. That's real addictive."

"Did you ever have any financial dealings with Malcolm Wudbine?"

"Oh heavens, no. The first step to investing is having something to invest. I've never been there. The fluctuations of the market, up or down, have never affected me, not one bit."

"Is there anything else about Wudbine or the events of last night that…?"

"I didn't sleep last night, not much. I've always kidded myself into believing that I had a unique ability to see into the human heart. As a writer and actor, I've often run the scripts of those around me in my own head. I thought I could tell what others were thinking. I don't want you to believe that I'm completely delusional, but now it's clear…that…well…I don't know where I was quite going. What I'm trying to say is that there is a killer in our midst, and I don't have any idea who that might be. This morning in the hours before dawn I worked through the cast and crew, their appearance, language, gestures, moods, even their unique odors. I thought about every nuance. I can't make it work. I can't see any of them as killers. I can't think of anyone who would have a motive, or anger, or passion to do anything like that."

19

As Ray looked across the desk, Verity Wudbine-Merone didn't appear quite the same as he had remembered her. Her sprightliness, so evident the evening before at the colony cocktail party was gone. She seemed weary and dispirited, her Lord and Taylor resort-wear replaced by a shapeless sweatshirt and jeans.

"Hard night," he said.

"Very. People needed to gather. People needed to talk. And somehow, I don't quite understand their thinking, many felt compelled to express their sympathies to me, like I was the widow. I know it's not possible to march up to the big house on the hill and see the real Mrs. Wudbine, but...."

"I don't understand?"

"Brenda Wudbine, my successor, has never been part of the community. Most people here don't know her. Most have never seen her. I know Brenda from weddings, graduations, and funerals. Other than guilt by association, I bear the woman no ill. But I don't know anyone who would be comfortable going up to Malcolm's palace. It's foreign territory, by invitation only. I don't think anyone just dropped by. And from what I've heard, by evening Brenda is too smashed to make any sense."

Ray noted her last response before asking, "Did you see your son?"

"I did. I slipped away at one point and went over to his cottage. Elliott and I sat on his porch and drank champagne and smoked. I haven't had a cigarette in years. We had a good talk, then he went to be with his wife."

"Champagne?"

"Hardly an appropriate choice, but it was cold, had alcohol, and was there in my fridge, part of what we'd staged for the afterglow party. I've read that the bubbles make the alcohol go to your head quickly. That's what I wanted. I'm struggling with this. Not so much his death, but the fact that he was murdered, an affront to the sanctity of our community. Even his last act around here was offensive."

They sat in silence for several minutes as Verity sipped from a tall paper container of coffee. "Miss Marple, the character I was playing, would tell you that I'm the natural suspect. I had the motive—albeit of ancient malice at this point—the means and the opportunity."

"And would Miss Marple name you the killer in the final scene?"

"I think not. She would know that I don't waste time on old grievances. Malcolm and I went our separate ways thirty-some years ago. He hurt me greatly, but I did my best to shed that as quickly as I could. I wasn't going to be continually poisoned by his evil."

"So tell me about your relationship with Malcolm Wudbine."

"Where should I begin?" she asked.

"In the beginning, and only a summary, please."

"We met in college. Malcolm was a big, handsome farm boy with broad shoulders and wonderful curly brown hair. He had a great smile and was the life of the party, every party. He had a wonderful singing voice, and could sit down at a piano and belt out romantic ballads. He was loved by everyone: women, men, and dogs. People just followed him around.

"We fell in love our junior year and as was the custom in those days, we married after graduation—without ever living together, imagine that. I taught math, and he went to graduate school, Northwestern, MBA. Eventually he was brought into the family business. My father and Uncle Sid ran a small-town bank, a place that catered to farmers and area merchants. Malcolm transformed the place. He had new ideas, was very aggressive. His primary goal was to make a lot of money. Before long he had bought up most of the other small banks in the area. While my father and uncle didn't especially like his business methods, they were delighted with all the cash he generated. For the first time in their lives, they were suddenly wealthy, modestly so, but in the chips. I think it was about this time that Malcolm decided that if he wanted to make some real money, he had to move on. It was, perhaps not too coincidentally, about the time our marriage ended."

"Your differences were…?"

"Other women, right from the start, actually, before the start. I heard years later that the night before our wedding he had a tryst with one of his former flames, and his groomsmen had to drag him out of bed and get him showered and sober before they brought him to church. I learned to overlook his dalliances for years, but when he told me we were moving to Chicago, that gave me an exit ramp. He was generous in the divorce, and the size of my later inheritance from my father was directly tied to Malcolm's time at the family bank.

"And it all worked out, Sheriff. Two years after Malcolm left, I married a very nice man. We had a child together, a daughter. John was a great stepfather to Elliott during his growing up. While pretty much an absentee father, Malcolm seemed to be around for all the important events, didn't interfere in between, and always met his financial obligations to Elliott and me."

"Was Malcolm up here in the summer during those years?" probed Ray.

"That was the peculiar thing. I got the summer cottage in the divorce. Of course, I should have. By that time Malcolm could have bought a resort home almost anywhere in the country, but for some perverse reason he wanted a place up here. And it worked out because Elliott got to see his father more often, and Malcolm really didn't intrude on my life."

"The hyphenated name, Wudbine-Merone?"

"I did that for my children. Elliott had a mother who was a Wudbine, and Jenny, my daughter, had a mother who was a Merone. In our small town people got used to our hyphenated name."

"From your description, the relationship with Malcolm remained amicable?"

"More or less. In recent years I've been concerned about how hard Malcolm worked Elliott. And I'm not always sure he was very nice to him. I sense he treated his son like just another member of his staff, someone at his beck and call 24-7. Then I would think I needed to back off. Elliott is an adult. He needed to fight his own battles. And I think the same goes for his wife, my daughter-in-law."

"She's the other Wudbine in the playbill…"

"Yes, Jill. She and Elliott married after she graduated from law school. Shortly thereafter she became Malcolm's personal lawyer. I think these days most of her time and energy is devoted to looking after his foundation. You know she's Richard Grubbs' daughter?"

"No, he didn't mention that."

"Not surprising. They are not close. After Jill and Elliott were married, she bonded to Malcolm. In the beginning they seemed to have a father and daughter bond, later he seemed to treat her like a loyal servant. Strange marriage, Jill and Elliott, but I keep out of it."

"Strange, how?"

"I don't know how to explain it. She has no affect, like she has Asperger's or something close to that." She paused, glanced out the window, and looked back at Ray. "There's another part of the story you should know."

"What's that?"

"Malcolm, the womanizer, the consummate Lothario. In the early days, after our divorce and before he remarried...how do I explain this... Malcolm just had a way with women. He would manage to seduce someone new every summer, mostly colony women. In addition to his wonderful cottage—the first building, not that cement bird—he always had a big boat, a cabin cruiser. And before the helicopter, he kept an airplane here...you know...with pontoons. He'd land on the lake and drive it right up on the beach. He did a lot of entertaining. I think that's how he isolated his prey. Taking people out on the boat or for airplane rides. Veronica Grubbs—Richard's wife, Jill's mother, pretty woman—she was one of them. Richard seemed quite crushed, but somehow they got through it. And a year or two later she was dead, breast cancer. Very sad. I don't know if Jill is aware...well, she must at least have heard rumors.

"I was surprised when Jill showed up to read for the play. She's never done that before. I couldn't imagine her acting. Like I said, the woman is without affect. But Sterling saw something that I certainly didn't see. I must say, freed from who she is in real life, Jill is quite remarkable. On stage she is alive with warmth and emotion. I've never seen that before, never. It's totally foreign to the Jill I've known for...well...since the time she was a little girl."

"Could Richard or someone else who was cuckolded by Malcolm...?"

"I've wondered about that. But I don't think so. That was so long ago. When he started bringing his own retinue of pretty women, he stopped hitting on colony wives. Now what he does around Chicago, that's another story.

"Sheriff, we're not killers, not here in the colony. That said, few tears will be shed as the result of his passing. If Malcolm's demise had only happened some other way. A heart attack would have been perfectly acceptable. Or, perhaps, crashing in his beloved helicopter, taking that Amazon personal trainer and pilot with him. But murder, I can't think of anyone who would commit murder."

"When did you arrive at the theatre last night?"

"Just about everyone in the cast came together. I had to change into my costume and do makeup. I was in the first scene, so I wanted some time to settle into my role and go over my lines."

"And after the first scene?"

"I checked my makeup and was sitting in the back corner of the green room. I was going over lines again. I have a big part in the second scene. I like to act out the part in my head before I go onstage. Although I've never had this happen, I'm so afraid of going blank. Maybe that's a false fear, part of being 70."

"That's where you were when the lights went out?"

"Yes, I just stayed put."

"Last night in the backstage area, was there anyone around who wasn't a member of the cast or crew?"

"I don't think so."

"How about in the last few weeks. Anyone unfamiliar to you, not part of the colony?"

"I don't think so, but it's hard to say. There's a lot of coming and going. People have guests and visitors. And there're tradesmen in and out, carpenters, and whatever. But the people I know, I can't see any of these people as killers. It doesn't fit. I believe it's got to be someone from the outside, maybe a team of people. Professionals. People who were trying to get even with Malcolm. God only knows how many people he's screwed along the way: other billionaires, the Mafia, foreign potentates…."

"Why here, why during the play?"

"I thought about that. Usually Malcolm has one or more of his security people lurking about. It's only up here that he feels comfortable enough not to have someone around all the time. Elliott says, though, that up at his father's place," she pointed in the general direction of Malcolm's property, "he's got all types of cameras, motion detectors, and what not. Looks like Fort Knox or the White House."

"It has been alleged that Malcolm provided investment services to some of the residents of the colony. Do you know anything about that?"

"I've heard that over the years. What you need to know is I did everything in my power not to have conversations about Malcolm. My only connection to him for decades was about matters that concerned Elliott. People learned long ago not to talk about him in front of me.

"So, Sheriff, if I can go back to playing Miss Marple again, I don't think you're going to catch the killer by looking at the cast or crew, or anyone else in the colony. Like I said, I'd bet he'd made some big-time enemies. When it came to money, he'd be ruthless. And it's public knowledge that he'd made billions, especially in the last ten years. He was frequently mentioned in Forbes and Bloomberg. Chicago Magazine did a big profile on him a few years back.

"I think you're looking for some highly skilled professional killers. And they didn't fly commercial. Send one of your minions over to the airport to check the log of private jets that have arrived and departed the last few days. I bet the killer is long gone. You're spinning your wheels here. I don't mean to be dismissive, but finding Malcolm's killer is probably beyond the reach of a local sheriff. It's going to take the FBI or Interpol to figure this one out."

20

After Verity Wudbine-Merone departed, Ray looked over his notes, adding a few more observations. The things Verity had worked into the interview intrigued him. Although not happy about being trapped inside a musty old building for so many hours, he was fascinated by how Verity and the other people he interviewed before her represented themselves. Everyone's story always puts them in the best light, he thought. Ray had seen this so many times over his career, whether he was dealing with a minor infraction of the law or a major felony.

"Lunch?" asked Sue, standing outside the screen door.

"Sure," he answered, looking up. "Want to run into town?"

"I've got a cooler of food, things you'll approve of. I was planning a romantic picnic with Harry."

"Can't you use them…?"

"Not tonight. Harry is going up to Fishtown for some fresh lake trout. He wants to show off his skill at the grill. It's a guy thing."

"Obviously, you didn't find anything in the trash, or I would be hearing about it," observed Ray.

"We found many things, but nothing that could pass for a possible murder weapon. I can tell you this much, these people eat way too much pizza. I don't think they do much cooking."

"I've never known you to comment on other people's eating habits."

"I've spent too much time with you."

"Where do you want to eat?" asked Ray.

"On the beach, looking out at Lake Michigan. See, your influence continues."

Sue drove them to the colony's beach in her gear-laden Jeep, and they carried the two coolers to the top of a small dune overlooking the shore. She unfolded a large blanket and carefully arranged the contents from the coolers in the center: a loaf of peasant bread, cheese, olives, grapes, apricots, and chocolate. "You can have mineral water or sparkling wine," she teased.

"Sorry to mess up a romantic weekend."

"It's okay. He's getting an idea of what I do, and who I am. How's the interviewing going?"

"I'm pretty much through the cast and crew."

"And?"

"Means and opportunity, everyone. Motive, that varies. It seems that Malcolm Wudbine had, at a minimum, annoyed most of the colony members in one way or another over the years."

"And at a maximum?" asked Sue.

"Look," said Ray, motioning toward a small group of gulls floating peacefully in the wind. An eagle, wings partially folded, talons extended, dropped out of the noonday sun, grabbing one of the gulls, then opening its wings, and carrying its prey inland. A single feather, a piece of downy fluff, marked the spot of the kill for a brief moment, then was carried toward shore in the breeze.

"How did you know that was going to happen?"

"I didn't. I've never seen an eagle go after a gull before. I wouldn't have thought it would be worth the trouble. Gulls weigh next to nothing. Can't be much meat there."

"The killing was so fast."

"A fraction of a second."

"Means and motive, a quick lunch. A target of opportunity."

"Motives for killing Wudbine are starting to emerge. I keep pushing the financial question, but no one is accusing Wudbine of leaving their retirement in ruins. He wasn't a Madoff. It's been intimated that several decades ago he seduced a number of the colony wives. Passions cool over the years, but who knows if some long festering wound might have suddenly propelled an assailant to take action."

Sue gripped the round loaf and tore into the bread, handing a chunk to Ray. "So how many suspects are there?"

"I've got to start charting this. With the crew and actors, about twenty. Then there's Richard Grubbs. They would all have had easy access. And that certainly doesn't preclude someone coming from the outside. Then there is also Wudbine's family and various employees. I haven't even factored them in yet."

"One assailant?"

"That's what I fell asleep speculating about. We need to walk through possible scenarios with a stopwatch. My gut feeling is that two people were involved. Too much could go wrong with only one person. With two, the assailant could be at the ready when the power was switched off. Picture this, the killer is offstage, just a few steps from Wudbine. The lights go out and the fatal thrust follows in a few seconds. Then they make their escape back to the green room or out the door into the blackness."

"How do they find Wudbine in the dark?" asked Sue.

"I'm not sure. The assailant would need a few moments for their eyes to adjust. Maybe they had a small light. Night vision glasses—but then that would be one more thing to hide or get rid of. The fatal strike required great precision. I don't have an answer. Our perpetrator, or perpetrators did a lot of careful planning."

"And if the perp was a member of the cast, he or she had to get rid of the weapon and slide back into the green room or dressing rooms without being noticed."

"They could have carried the weapon out with them. We should have sent everyone through a metal detector last night before we let them leave," said Ray. "Verity Wudbine-Merone made a big point of telling me that the crime couldn't have been committed by any colony member, it had to be an outsider, maybe the mafia, foreign agents…."

"Who arrived on the beach during the storm in black helicopters," suggested Sue with a wry smile.

"Actually, she had them flying in on private jets. She also told me that Wudbine's daughter-in-law was Richard Grubbs' daughter. Strange that he never mentioned it."

"Any other major revelations?"

"Yes, for a few minutes the hits just kept coming. According to Verity, years ago Malcolm had a fling with Grubbs' wife. The woman died a few years after their affair."

"Not mentioning the daughter is strange. The affair, probably not something anyone would mention."

"The weapon," said Ray, "you mentioned it earlier. Tell me again what Dyskin said."

"Well, you know how he sort of mutters to himself as he looks things over. He said the weapon might have been a chisel, an extremely sharp one. There was no tearing, just a clean cut. He also mentioned a bayonet or a dagger. I think we have to brush up on knives and other sharps. The important thing he said was that the killing was done with great precision. The assailant knew where to place the blade, and they had the strength to push it through the connective tissue to effectively sever the spine and instantly kill Wudbine. He said the perp was a trained assassin."

"Black helicopters," said Ray, reaching for more bread.

"So where does that leave us?" asked Sue.

"The choice of weapons, the scene of the attack. The whys and wherefores. We're doing our usual early investigation wheel spinning. I need paper or my white board. We have to slow down, but I think that if we don't solve this one quickly, it will slip out of our hands. People will start going away. The trail will cool."

"Lemon Perrier?"

"Sure." Ray leaned back, sipped on the bottled water, and looked out at the lake. "Why there? Why in the theatre? And why the chisel or knife? This whole thing is fairly exotic."

Sue started to giggle. She looked at Ray affectionately.

"Where's the humor in that?"

"I was thinking," Sue responded, "what if someone shot a picture of the two of us right now, think about how that would play before the next election. Put a caption on it like, Sheriff and detective sergeant enjoy a romantic lunch on the beach while killer runs wild in community.

Ray didn't respond, his focus elsewhere. "We're looking for an eccentric, nothing here is conventional."

"Have you interviewed any eccentrics?"

"They're all eccentrics, so I guess I need a better term. An outlier, someone not constrained by conventional patterns of thought. I'm back to the location, weapon choice, motive. Verity, the first Mrs. Wudbine, said Malcolm was usually surrounded by security, that only up here did he move without it. And his position onstage, with his back to an attacker, made him completely vulnerable for a short period of time."

"That sort of limits the suspects. They had to be extremely familiar with the play. You've got the cast and crew," said Sue.

"But there could be others," countered Ray. "Were some of Wudbine's people around? And someone mentioned family members of the cast and crew—it's summer, people dropping by to see Grandma. Then there are people who could have just blended in."

"Like?"

"Custodians, tradespeople, trash collectors, and all the people who come and go in white vans and seldom register on anyone's radar. There are the colony people, with no connection to the play, who drop by and watch the rehearsals. If someone were intent on killing Wudbine, it wouldn't be too difficult to come up with a plan."

"Motive? Your usual list: love, lust, lucre, and loathing."

"All of the above."

"The man is past seventy," said Sue, "can't we dismiss the first two?"

"Sonnet 15, Shakespeare."

"What's that suppose to mean?"

Ray looked over at her and carefully recited four lines from the sonnet.

"When I perceive that men as plants increase,
Cheered and cheque'd even by the self-same sky,
Vaunt in their youthful sap, at height decrease,
And wear their brave state out of memory.

"It's the last line, Sue. And wear their brave state out of memory. Wudbine may have been getting a bit long at the tooth, but that doesn't mean he'd changed much. Verity talked about him as being a womanizer. He was a man of great wealth. He probably had no difficulty attracting younger women. And there are arrays of potent pharmaceuticals to extend his manhood. So don't be too quick to dismiss the love and lust. From what everyone has said in the interviews thus far, there was no lack of loathing for Wudbine. People tolerated him because he was the proverbial goose, and no one wanted the golden egg to go away.

"Lucre is the complicated one," Ray continued. "Who would benefit financially from Wudbine's death. There's so much we don't know."

"Where do we go from here?"

"I would like you to be with me when I interview family members this afternoon. Are you almost done with the trash?"

"We have yet to do the recycling container. I asked Brett and Barbara Sinclair to go through it after lunch. There seems to be some chemistry between those two."

"I thought she had a boyfriend back at college, some big football player."

"Absence makes the heart grow fonder for someone else," said Sue as she started to pack up remainders of the picnic. "What else needs to be done?"

"Until we come up with the weapon, I guess we're not done. It's just a question of how much we want to pull that place apart. We could spend a week or more just in the Assembly Hall, time we should probably use following other leads."

21

Sue parked in the circle near the front door of Gull House. A young woman greeted them at the door.

"Sheriff Elkins, I'm Pepper Markley, a member of Wudbine staff. Ms. Wudbine will be meeting with you in the library. Please follow me." She guided them through a long hall to the library. "Please have a seat. Jill will be with you in a few minutes," she said before she excused herself and left the room, closing the door behind her.

"Quite the joint," said Sue.

"The furniture is beautifully designed and crafted," observed Ray, looking around the room. "There's no clutter, nothing to interrupt the visual impact of each piece. The place has the feel of a sculpture gallery."

"Didn't she say this was the library?" observed Sue, a twinkle in her eye. She had long observed Ray's penchant for carefully looking through the titles of books when trying to get a sense of a victim or suspect.

Ray was already out of his chair by the time she reached the end of her sentence. "Yes, not many books. I don't think it means he wasn't a reader, not anymore. Although most people his age still like paper and ink. I do, also." He carefully surveyed the room, walls and ceiling.

Pepper Markley reentered the room carrying a tray with two glasses of ice tea. "Ms. Wudbine apologizes for the delay, she's on a conference call and will be with you as soon as possible." She set the tray on the small table.

"This room won't do," said Ray.

"I don't understand. Ms. Wudbine specified this room for the interviews."

Ray pointed to one of the small security cameras mounted on the ceiling. "We are going to be interviewing a number of people, including Ms. Wudbine. These are confidential interviews."

"Oh," she said looking up at the camera, "those are just part of the system. It goes on tape somewhere, it's not like anyone is listening."

"I'm sorry, that's not acceptable."

Markley looked stunned. "What are you proposing?"

"Sergeant Lawrence and I are returning to the library building at the colony. That's where we will conduct these interviews. In her last e-mail to me late this morning, Ms. Wudbine stated that the interviews would begin at 1:30 with members of the family and staff scheduled every 30 minutes. Please let her know that we arrived at the specified time. Also, remind her that this is a murder investigation. I will wait for her at the colony library until 2:00. After that time all further interviews will be held at our office in the Cedar County Government Complex. Do you have any questions?"

"No. I will convey your message."

"What was that all about?" asked Sue as they walked toward her Jeep.

"She established the time, then she doesn't show up. And what member of the staff, or the family, for that matter, will be open with a camera running."

"So what now?" asked Sue.

"We go back to the colony and give her until 2:00. If she doesn't show, I'll try to find some way to turn up the heat. These people are going to start slipping away in the next few days. We've got to get this inquiry going. So let's really stay on Jill Wudbine and the others and see what we can squeeze out of them."

Within minutes of their return, Jill Wudbine was standing at the screen door of the library, clearing her throat rather than knocking. Ray motioned with his hand for her to enter.

"This is not good," she said as soon as she was through the door. "Most inconvenient to me, my family, and our staff. I can play hardball, too. None of us need to talk with you."

"Counselor, you've been out of law school a long time, and you've forgotten much of what you might have learned in your criminal procedure course. This is a murder investigation. You've told me that you will be representing the family. In that position you will be held accountable for your actions. Perhaps you should brush up on the obstruction of justice statutes in this state. At this point I am merely conducting interviews. There are currently no suspects or persons of interest. We will be moving this inquiry forward as quickly as possible. You can aid us, or you can get in our way. If you impede the investigation in any manner…." Ray let his comments hang. He carefully took in Jill Wudbine. He knew she had to be near forty, but her perfect complexion showed no signs of impending middle age. She could easily pass for 30 or younger. Her black hair was cut short in a way that added to her youthful appearance.

"Look, Sheriff, I'm just as interested as you are in finding the killer. I apologize for scheduling a meeting and then not being available. As for the choice of room, I just didn't think. The recording part of the security system is archival, no one is monitoring it, but I understand your concern. Now can we get started?"

Once she was seated, Ray turned on the recorder, and established the time, place, and participants in the interview.

"Let's start with your relationship to Malcolm Wudbine, both familial and professional."

"Well, you already know this. I'm Mr. Wudbine's daughter-in-law. I'm married to his only son, Elliott."

"And how long have you been married?"

"We got married after I completed law school and passed the bar exam. I was twenty-four at the time. We've been married for 16 years."

"Children?"

"Unfortunately, no."

"Where did you meet your husband?"

"Up here, years ago, when we were kids. I can't remember not knowing him. I'm told we played in the sand together when we were toddlers. And we hung out during our teen years and started dating occasionally in college. It got serious when I was in law school, and we were both living in Chicago."

"So in addition to being a daughter-in-law to Mr. Wudbine, you've indicated that you also served as his legal counsel. Would you tell us how long you had this position and the nature of your work?"

"As soon as I passed the bar, Malcolm asked me to come work for him. Initially, it was more on the business side. I was a liaison between his investment company and the law firm we had on retainer to look after legal issues. About twelve years ago he launched his philanthropic foundation, and I became the executive administrator of that endeavor while continuing to serve as his personal counsel."

"And what's the focus of the foundation's work?"

"Really, Sheriff, I can't see how this has any bearing on...."

"Ms. Wudbine. We know very little about your father-in-law. We are trying to get a better sense of the man. Hopefully, this will give us some direction as we search for the killer."

"What was your question, again?"

"The foundation, what are your funding priorities?"

"Malcolm Wudbine came from a very hardscrabble background. Through diligence and solid values, he attained a university education and professional success. He was interested in helping others also pull themselves up by their bootstraps. We contributed millions to traditionally black colleges and neighborhood improvement projects. We also have funded scholarship programs to help needy farm kids get a college education. And Malcolm was always very generous with the needs of the summer colony here, too generous perhaps."

"How was he to work for, especially given the...?"

"He was a wonderful man, Sheriff. He never wasted a minute of time. He was always focused on the next project. When he wasn't working on corporate or foundation business, he was in the gym staying fit, or he was busy researching some new passion."

"Did your father-in-law have any enemies?"

"It's hard to be wealthy in this country without enemies. The investment industry is very competitive. He was smart, daring, and a risk taker, albeit a very shrewd, informed one. He seldom lost. I think that did earn him the antipathy of some of his rivals."

"Anyone angry enough to want to kill him?"

"In an abstract way, yes. But I don't think anyone would operationalize their feelings. After all the bravado and chest pounding, they are a pretty meek bunch. If they did want someone dead, they would hire it out."

"Was Mr. Wudbine the subject of any litigation?"

"This is a litigious society, Sheriff. Anyone in business is constantly dealing with this irritation. But to answer your question, nothing of any consequence. And to respond to the follow-up question that you haven't asked yet, he was not subject to any criminal complaints, none, either at the federal or state level."

"How did you get along with your father-in-law?" asked Sue.

"We were," she paused for a long moment and stared past them, "we were great friends. Malcolm was an exceptional man. Why anyone would choose to harm him is beyond comprehension. Once all of this is taken care of, I will allow myself to grieve."

"I'm trying to get a sense of where everyone was Saturday evening. Before going to the Assembly Building, where did you start from, who did you see…would you provide a scenario of everything that happened until I met with you in the green room."

"I was at our cottage waiting for Elliott. He flew commercial to Traverse City, Alyson Mickels and Malcolm picked him up in the Bell. He arrived just about the time I was leaving. On the way I fell in with the group coming from Verity's gala. I don't quite understand the wisdom of drinking before you go onstage. But I am a total neophyte, unaware of the customs and traditions of theatre people."

"So you'd never been in a play before?"

"No, never."

"What prompted you to participate?"

"Forty, suddenly being forty. Realizing my life is half gone. I needed to do something new. I needed to explore. Malcolm encouraged it, said it would be good for me."

"And you enjoyed the experience?"

"Very much so…until…."

"So you joined the group walking to the theater. Continue from that point, please."

"I put on my makeup, got into my costume, and started reviewing the script. I had done well in the rehearsals. In fact, I was often prompting my fellow actors with lines as well as giving my own. I found a quiet corner and tried to filter out the hubbub and concentrate on my part."

"Where were you located at this point?"

"Initially, I was in the green room, but it was too noisy, so I found a place in the women's dressing room. Once the curtain went up, I came back to the green room so I'd be ready to go onstage. I have a brief appearance in the middle of the first scene. After that I went to the green room."

"Did you see Mr. Wudbine at that point or before?"

"I saw him as soon as I returned to the green room. He was in costume and had these dreadfully awful wounds he wanted to show me. There was still a bit of a boy in him, most endearing. I told him to 'break a leg'—that's something theatre people say—and he rushed away. He said he wanted to settle into his part. That was a joke. We both laughed." Jill stopped and gazed around the room, never making eye contact with Ray or Sue. "Then it all sort of gets confused. I was sitting with the playbook, and there was the horrible crash of thunder. Then the lights went out. I don't like darkness. Nyctophobia. I just sat and focused on my breathing, trying to stay calm, trying not to have a panic attack. People were talking, some using the glow of their phones to move around. Eventually the lights came back on, but somehow everything seemed horribly odd. I can't put my finger on exactly what made me think that. Then Sterling came in with Grubbs. I just knew someone was dead, but Malcolm, he never crossed my mind. He was larger than life. I always thought of him as being almost immortal."

"Before the lights went out, was there anyone around who shouldn't have been? Were there any strangers? Did anything seem out of place or amiss?"

Jill's answer was slow in coming. "I don't know. I don't think so. I was into being Anne Protheroe. This acting was not easy for me. It took all of my energy. When I'm focused on something, I'm not very observant of the world around me."

"You mention Richard Grubbs. He's your father, isn't he?"

"My mother, before she died, referred to him as my sperm donor. She was a very hostile woman. I don't understand why she stayed with him. Yes, he's my father, but we don't speak. When I was growing up he wasn't ever there. Physically he was sometimes, but not often. He was off in his world of books and history. He was always with his colleagues, with his graduate students, and never with us. Even up here in the summer, he was busy writing or doing research. He never had time for us." She paused and for the first time during the interview, held eye contact with Ray for several seconds. "He doesn't talk to me now. I don't talk to him. It's better for both of us."

"Can you think of anyone who might have a motive to kill your father-in-law?"

"Absolutely not. His murder is beyond my comprehension."

"You sent me a tentative list for interviews with other members of the family and household this afternoon. We are already running behind. Can we modify that and get this done today?"

"I've started on that already. People are waiting for my call. There will have to be one exception. My mother-in-law is not available. Brenda is physically and psychologically fragile. Her psychiatrist is flying in this afternoon. She may have to be hospitalized again. Is there anything else, Sheriff?"

"As his personal lawyer, you must be familiar with his will. Who would benefit from Mr. Wudbine's death?"

Jill rocked in her chair—a slow, almost imperceptible motion—with her eyes cast down at her hands. Finally she looked up, not at Ray or Sue, just a gaze over their shoulders at some distant point. "Everything has been carefully provided for in an elaborate series of trusts. The majority of the estate goes to the foundation. Controlling interest in the corporation goes to Elliott. Brenda Wudbine is provided for. Most of the money is in trust to protect her financial future. We've had all of this in place for years, modifying the trusts from time to time to adjust to changes in the law."

Jill looked across the table at Ray. "We are in the process of planning a memorial service. When will the body be returned to us?"

"Probably later this week. In all likelihood an autopsy will take place tomorrow. Depending on the findings, they may want to keep it a few more days for further studies. Have you established a tentative time and place…."

"We are just beginning that conversation." Jill looked at her watch. "Sheriff, here's the tentative schedule for the rest of the afternoon. She pulled a folded piece of paper from her shoulder bag, opened it, and pushed it across the desk. "I can have Alyson Mickels, who serves as our concierge, meet you here at 3:00. And I have tentatively scheduled Pepper Markley at 3:30."

"What is her position?"

"She wears a number of hats: personal trainer, pilot, and head of security. She drove Malcolm to the Assembly Hall last evening."

"I have Elliott scheduled at 4:00. Please go easy on him. He's very sensitive and has been completely shattered by these events."

"Are there other people living or working at Gull House?"

"We have a housekeeper, a chef, and a caretaker."

"I would like to talk with them also. Could you schedule that for tomorrow morning?"

"Well, they really don't know anything. They are totally out of the loop, but if you insist. Is there anything else, Sheriff?"

"Thank you for your cooperation. I will undoubtedly need to talk with you again."

Ray signaled the end of the interview by standing, and he and Sue remained silent until Jill exited, settled onto the seat of a golf cart, and rolled out of sight.

"The woman is without affect. Can't make eye contact. Verity mentioned Asperger's," said Ray.

"Not possible."

"Why?" asked Ray.

"Article in the Times last winter. Asperger's is passé. Now it is spectrum disorder."

"Think she's a killer?"

"Don't know. I wonder what's hidden beneath that shell."

22

~~

Ray looked across the table at Alyson Mickels. Her strong shoulders and arms extended from a black tank top, the stretchy material clinging to her toned body. The subtle pink of her lipgloss contrasted against the tight tan skin. Alyson's long blonde hair was pulled into a French twist. She reached up with her left hand to push back a few errant strands.

"How long had you been employed by Mr. Wudbine?"

Mickels held Ray's eyes steady in her gaze. After a few seconds delay, she responded, "It's been about two years."

"What did you do before that?" asked Ray.

"I was a commercial pilot."

"And before that?"

"I was in the military, naval aviation. I graduated from Annapolis and thought I would make my career in the service. But I eventually grew beyond that. I needed some new challenges."

"What was the path that brought you to work for Malcolm Wudbine?"

"Like I said, I had been working as a commercial pilot, and with the slowing of the economy I had been laid off. A friend from the Academy was a principal in an exclusive personal security firm in Chicago. He thought I had the right skill set for his business. The pay was good, and I learned the ins and outs of the profession. The other thing I learned very quickly was that you were mostly sitting around waiting for clients. So I spent a lot of time at a gym getting rid of my frustrations and working at staying fit. The gym owner noticed that I was in better shape than any of his personal trainers. He offered me a job, part-time at first, and guided specific clients in my direction. Malcolm Wudbine was one of those clients. It soon became clear to both of us that I had the right competencies to serve in a variety of roles in his personal and professional life. In addition to being a skilled personal trainer, I have commercial licenses in both fixed wing and rotary, and I can manage a security operation.

"I probably wouldn't have picked this kind of work. It's very intrusive on my personal life. However, Mr. Wudbine provided generous remuneration and benefits. I thought it was something I could do for a year or two."

"Tell me about the security part, especially up here."

"I did some one-on-one work for him as a bodyguard. I also worked as a liaison with the security firm that provided services to his offices, his apartment in the Loop, and their house in Kenilworth. When we came north, my job really was pilot and personal trainer. He didn't feel he needed protection here. I did keep my eyes and ears open for any possible dangers. I did a security assessment of the colony and environs, including the actors and other people connected with the theater. Most of these people have known one another for decades. There were no apparent threats."

"What were your other job responsibilities?"

"To be available at all times as a pilot, trainer, chauffeur, or companion. I usually accompanied him on trips to town and around the area. I think for him it had more to do with companionship than any security consideration. He liked being chauffeured, he liked having someone to talk to."

"This perceived need for security, was it caused by any specific threats or...?"

"There were no specific threats. But as you know, Sheriff, there are a lot of people out there with anger toward corporate types and Wall Street. You never know when some crazy is going to pop up. Mr. Wudbine was a public personality, his many charitable activities attracted media attention. I think he was just showing proper caution."

"So you told us that you dropped him off at the theater. What time was that?"

"He was running late. I think it was getting close to eight. We had flown to Traverse City to pick up Elliott. His plane was late, weather slowdown in Chicago. When we got back, I ran them up to the house from the heliport. As soon as we went in, the two of them disappeared into Mr. Wudbine's library. Eventually, I drove Elliott to his cottage and came back for Mr. Wudbine and drove him to the Assembly Hall."

"So what did you do then?" asked Sue.

"I parked the golf cart away from the building under a tree. I had a seat at the rear of the auditorium. I was planning to watch the play."

"Were you alone?"

"No, Elliott had a seat next to mine. He arrived just before the curtain went up."

"Continue."

"Sometime after the opening curtain, it really started to pour. I slipped out and moved the golf cart down to the picnic shelter. After I toweled off the cart, I stayed put waiting for the rain to let up. Elliott called as I was checking my e-mail. He said his father had been killed. I picked him up at the stage door, Jill and Pepper also, and brought them back to Gull House."

"What did you do then?"

"I stayed with the family. And soon after you appeared, I excused myself. Can I ask a question?"

"Please," said Ray.

"How was Malcolm killed? Elliott said something about him being stabbed."

"I'll know more when I get the autopsy results, but that's essentially correct. You seem to be extremely aware of what was going on in Mr. Wudbine's world. Was there anyone who had a motive to kill him, anyone in his professional life, his personal life, or his family?"

"Sheriff, I've thought about that a lot. I didn't sleep much last night, and I've been consumed by that question all day. The answer is no." She paused, brushing aside loose hairs again, and continued, "However, this clearly wasn't a random act. Sheriff, my primary job here was to look after Mr. Wudbine's personal security. Obviously, I failed. Yet, I don't think I could have done anything differently. He was the employer, he dictated the terms of the security envelope I provided for him. When he was in the colony, he often wanted to be solo. That was especially true with rehearsals. I wish I had more for you, but I don't."

"I'll probably need to talk to you again. What are your immediate plans?"

"Jill Wudbine has asked me to continue in their employment for at least the next month. I will be staying in the area as long as she is here."

"You were awfully quiet," said Ray to Sue as they watched Alyson Mickels march up the sand trail.

"Sometimes I just want to observe. It's hard for me to watch for nuances if I'm concentrating on forming questions."

"So what did you see?"

"Mickels checked you out. I won't say she undressed you—sorry, no such luck boss, but she did take in everything. Then she looked me over carefully. I was quickly surveyed. You were carefully examined. I was amazed by the way Mickels mapped the room, her so-called 'environmental scan.' I've never seen such discipline and focus. She was listening to your questions and always took a few seconds after each one to formulate her response. And before her words were out of her mouth, she was anticipating your next question. I suspect, and I'm using her parlance here, she was doing a 'threat analysis.'"

"So you think she's involved?" asked Ray.

"I didn't say that. But she certainly wants to know where she's going to end up in this whole affair. At a minimum, she hopes that she's not going to be pulled into anything that will tarnish her reputation or damage her employability."

"And at a maximum?"

"I'm not ready to speculate on that. She could have delivered the fatal thrust to Wudbine with a dull teaspoon. Mickels is a trained killer who knows we are going to be giving her a close look, so she's carefully weighing her options. She wants to come out of this unscathed." Sue looked at her watch. "I know you like to have a second set of ears, but I've got some things that need to be done."

"Fine, what are you up to?"

"I want to see if I can lift any fingerprints from the main shutoff switch. There are also backstage areas I want to look at again. We focused on the trash because it was going away. Now I want to attend to other areas I skipped over like the carpentry shop, lots of old tools tossed in boxes and drawers in no order. Then there's the kitchen area with a variety of sharp things. And using the playbill and the other names we've collected so far, I'll start checking for priors or outstanding warrants and also see if Wudbine was currently subject to any litigation. E-mail me the audio files of the next two interviews, and I'll listen to them sometime this evening. When we meet tomorrow at 7:00, we'll be on the same page."

"I didn't say anything about meeting at 7:00."

"You didn't need to."

23

The first thing Ray picked up on as Pepper Markley carefully settled in her chair was her perfume, subtle, not cloying, but distinct and impossible to miss.

"How are you doing?" he asked.

"Struggling. The initial shock, too little sleep, just trying to come to grips with the whole thing."

"How long have you been with the Wudbines?" Ray looked at her closely. He guessed that Pepper was about thirty. She appeared exhausted, but also very wary. Her dress was preppy, her hair skillfully cut and shaped.

"This is the start of my third and was probably going to be my last year."

"Last?"

"Working for Mr. Wudbine was a 24/7 arrangement. I am paid extremely well, multiples of what would be usual for this type of position, but I don't have much of a life. It was about time to move on."

"No vacations?"

"I was supposed to get a month each year, subject to Mr. Wudbine's schedule. It never seemed to work out. Like this June, I was going to take several weeks of vacation, but ended up serving as an administrative assistant to Elliott Wudbine when he visited clients in Asia and Europe. The person who usually accompanies Elliott was very pregnant, so I was pressed into service. That was unusual, I'd never worked for Elliott before. Elliott was a lot less demanding than his father. Mr. Wudbine worked day and night, didn't sleep much, and expected those who worked for him to be available at his beck and call."

"And your job title?"

"My contract reads concierge. Let me explain. I became an intern at Wudbine Investments right out of graduate school. After six months I was offered a full-time position to continue doing all the things I was assigned during my internship. When it came to giving me a contract, the HR director didn't know exactly what title my position should have. She had heard about some high-tech firms employing concierges and decided the term best described my work assignments."

"So what do you do?"

"Anything and everything. My major task is looking after his calendar and each item connected with that—travel and lodging arrangements, restaurant reservations, tickets for cultural and sporting events, and scheduling the corporate jet. Mr. Wudbine often made it available to his political friends. There were related secretarial duties, also. And Mr. Wudbine demanded that his coffee be prepared in a specific way. I was a barista in college. I probably got this job because of the coffee."

Ray did his best to suppress a smile.

"And then there were the flowers. Mr. Wudbine wanted fresh-cut flowers in every room. Gull House and the home in Kenilworth have greenhouses and gardeners, so we produce some of the flowers we use. I also acquire additional stock from commercial sources. You might say I run a small florist operation."

"Do you do things for other members of the household?"

"Mr. Wudbine worked very closely with his daughter-in-law, Jill. I primarily worked for the two of them, and also occasionally for Elliott."

"How about Mr. Wudbine's wife, Brenda?"

"During my tenure she hasn't been around much. I don't think I'm giving out any secrets to tell you that Brenda is a hopeless alcoholic, an embarrassment, really. I'm sure you noticed her condition last night. She's either at Betty Ford or a health spa in Arizona, that's were she spends most of the winter. Brenda also has a serious heart condition. The spa has special diets and exercise for heart patients.

"Brenda hates Chicago, she's almost never there. She does like it up here. Shows up in the spring and stays until early September. I think it's the only time the two of them are in residence together for an extended amount of time. When she's up here, she takes over the flower arranging, something she did earlier in their marriage. I still look after the inventory and ordering."

"Yesterday, please outline where you were from…let's say midday until after the murder?"

"Like I was telling you, Mr. Wudbine worked seven days a week starting early in the morning and sometimes running into the evening. Yesterday was just another workday. He had several major projects going for the foundation, new initiatives for the fall. He had a long planning meeting with Jill in the morning. So I spent my morning with them. We had a working lunch. I spent the afternoon organizing the material we had developed during the morning. Then I went to the beach for about an hour, came back, showered, grabbed a quick dinner, and headed for the theater. I did a walking meditation, trying to get in the head of my character."

"And how about Mr. Wudbine? Do you know what he did the rest of the afternoon."

After lunch he's usually in his gym working out under the guidance of Ms. Mickels. After the workout they usually go sailing for a while. I saw them coming in when I went to the beach. Then he planned to have Alyson fly him to Traverse City to meet Elliott's plane."

"Have you noticed anyone around in recent days with whom you were unfamiliar—at the house, the auditorium, or the colony?"

"No." She paused for a long moment. "I mean, there are lots of people around, many I don't recognize, but no one who seemed menacing or out of place."

"Were you aware of any threats against Mr. Wudbine? He did have a security person here and the fairly elaborate system as well," Ray observed.

"Everyone does that. There's a lot of paranoia out there, not that Malcolm was particularly paranoid. And it may be sort of a status symbol, too. Mr. Wudbine liked showing off Alyson Mickels, she is a lot classier than any of the personal protection specialists in his circle. He was vain in that way. Don't get me wrong, Sheriff, Mr. Wudbine was an absolutely wonderful man. And he was enormously generous with me and a real mentor. But we all have our things, don't we?"

"So when did you arrive at the theater?"

"The curtain was at 8:00. I was there around 7:15. I was probably the first member of the cast to arrive. There was a cocktail party at Verity's cottage. Most of the cast attended. They arrived at the theatre as a group.

Running a bit late, I might add. There was a real scramble to get into costume and makeup. I'm so glad I was ahead of them. I needed time to settle in, if you know what I mean. I haven't been in a play since high school, and that was only a bit part. This role is very challenging, and I was quite nervous."

"When did Mr. Wudbine arrive?"

"He got there about 10 minutes before the opening curtain. He wanted my help dressing, but I was getting ready to go onstage. I had a major part in the first scene."

"Walk me through what happened from the opening curtain until you knew something was very wrong."

"Well, I was onstage sitting at the dinner table. I was incredibly nervous. Then the curtain went up, and we were off. From that point it just seemed so natural. There wasn't one muffed line, not one. I was feeling exalted when I got back to the green room. By that time Mr. Wudbine was in his costume. He had those horrible, bloody wounds and was capering around. To be truthful, I was a bit irritated with him. I wanted to be left alone. Fortunately, one of the crew led him onstage."

"And then?"

"Things got very confused. I've thought back over it. There was that lightning and thunder. The building shook, the lights flickered. A little bit later they went out. I was sitting at a mirror checking my makeup when they went out. I just stayed put. Then the lights came back on. I was still at the mirror when I could tell something was wrong. I could hear it in the tone of people's voices. And you know the rest of the story. Eventually we were allowed to leave."

"Then what did you do?"

"I left with Jill. Elliott was waiting outside the stage door. And Alyson was just beyond the auditorium. We all went up to Gull House. Jill broke the news to Brenda and the others. We were all stunned, people talked quietly for a while."

"And then?"

"Eventually I went back to my apartment, sometime after midnight. And this morning I showed up about nine to see if there was any way I could be of assistance to Jill or Elliott. I'm sorry, Sheriff, I don't know more. I just can't imagine why anyone would want to kill him. Like I said, he wasn't perfect. But he did a lot more good than harm."

24

Ray held Elliott Wudbine in his gaze. "I'm sorry for your loss and this intrusion on your time. I'm sure you understand that the investigation has to go forward as quickly as possible."

"Sheriff, I can't imagine what I might know that will be of any use. My father was a good man. I don't know why anyone would want him dead."

"When was the last time you saw your father alive?" Ray took in Elliott's perfectly ironed, button-down shirt, the smell of tobacco, and the bulge in his shirt pocket. Elliott was lean, looked worn beyond his years, his brown hair thinning at the temples.

"He came with Ms. Mickels to pick me up from the airport in Traverse City. It was a magical flight back, the brilliant sunshine, the lakes and forests. However, we could see a mass of dark clouds coming across the lake from the west. After what's happened, they were an ominous warning—if you believe in that sort of thing."

"So you arrived back at...."

"I think it was after 6:00. The helipad is on the back of the property. Mickels drove us up to the house in a golf cart. Father and I went into his library for a few moments to talk. We have a couple of acquisitions that we're negotiating, and I wanted to fill him in on the details. We had a drink, and then I excused myself. I wanted to see Jill before she left for the theater. I got to our cottage just in time. She was heading out as I arrived.

Then I found something to eat and wandered down to the theater in time for the opening curtain."

"Where were you seated?"

"In the back row. The annual summer play is always a sellout. There was some kind of screw-up. I'm not used to sitting in the back."

"Were you alone?"

"No, Alyson Mickels was already there. She had the seat next to mine. The curtain went up. Jill made it through her first scene. I know she was quite nervous, but you couldn't tell watching her. The scene came to an end, and by then the rain had started. After the curtain was down, I was on my feet. My back was killing me. Alyson excused herself, she was worried about the cart."

"So what did you do at this point?"

"I did these back exercises I can do standing in one place. Then I settled back into my seat and started looking at my e-mail. The lights went out. I sat there in the dark and continued to read my e-mail. Eventually the lights came back on. Then Richard Grubbs came out, and I couldn't quite catch what he was saying, but everyone was leaving. I walked off to have a cigarette and eventually got a call from Jill. I went in and got her, and Alyson drove us and Pepper up to Gull House to absorb what had happened and to try to figure out how to tell my stepmother. And not too long after that you appeared with Grubbs."

"He's your father-in-law, isn't he?"

"After a fashion. Jill had a falling out with him years ago. They don't talk. I bear him no rancor, I just never see him."

"Ms. Mickels has told me that one of her jobs was working as a liaison to the firm that provides security to your corporation."

"That's correct," he responded, pulling out a cigarette pack, looking at it briefly, then returning it to his pocket.

"Had your father been subject to any threats?"

"Not that I'm aware of."

"Why the need for…?"

"It's part of the business of doing business. There are threats out there, especially against the financial industry. You know, the growing class warfare and all. You've got to be proactive. Everyone is doing it: key cards, fingerprint locks, cameras, photo IDs. With the right planning and equipment, you minimize possible risks."

"But there was a problem, wasn't there. Your father was murdered. Can you think of anyone who might have a motive to kill him? There might be some history connected, someone holding a grudge for an actual or perceived wrong ten, fifteen, twenty years ago."

"I don't think so. I certainly knew my father quite well, better than most sons. That said, who of us knows everything about anyone else. We all manage to irritate people along the way. I'm sure he did that a lot. He was demanding, wanted everything done yesterday, and he wanted everything done his way. He was very direct, didn't beat around the bush. But I don't think his aggressive manner would be a motivation for murder. He just wanted the people around him to perform at the same level he demanded of himself."

"How about on the business side?"

"My father was hardly involved anymore in the day-to-day operations. He was chairman of the board. I run the business."

"Any pending litigation against your firm?"

"No, nothing."

"Any disgruntled employees or former employees?"

"Not in recent years. No one that I can think of."

"How about investors?" asked Ray. "I understand some of the colony residents once had investment accounts with your firm."

"That is true. In the 90s we had a division that did portfolio management for small investors. Our opening threshold was a million dollars. A few colony residents had accounts with us. They raved about their investment returns, and a number of other people approached my father asking if they could open accounts with us. Not one of them met our threshold, not even close, but Father created a special category for these people with a minimum investment of a hundred thousand. Back then you couldn't miss in this business, the market was exploding. All of our clients did well, much better than the Dow. And then the dotcom bubble burst. Everyone took a beating, our clients included. People of means tend to take the long view. They know markets are variable and will come back with time. It was the small investors that came unglued, in our case the very people that my father reached out to help. At that point my father decided that these small accounts produced more aggravation than profit. We guided these customers to other firms, or returned their money if they so directed."

"And everyone was happy with this arrangement?"

"When people lose money, even if it's money they made in the run-up, not funds they actually invested in the first place, they're unhappy. For the born bitchers in the group, providing logical explanations is a waste of time. What you need to know, Sheriff, is my father was no Madoff. The only losses our customers ever experienced were due to normal market fluctuations."

"Is your company currently experiencing any financial problems?"

"Absolutely not. One thing about my father, Sheriff, was his remarkable sense of timing. While he may have been out of the day-to-day operations, he still provided strategic direction to our investment strategy. We were out of stocks before this last market collapse, and we came back in about the time things bottomed out. So we've done extremely well. I've been in the business for about twenty years, and we've never made this kind of money before. My father poured much of his profits into his foundation. He was committed to doing good works the last part of his life."

"Is there anyone who would profit by your father's death?"

"No, well, I would. And I guess my stepmother would." His face reddened, Ray interpreted this as a flash of anger, but Elliot's tone was unchanged. "We're hardly starving. Our lives will not be altered by the inheritance. In point of fact, I could retire now and live comfortably for the rest of my life."

"How about his personal life? Any romantic relationships that might have soured?"

"Sir, my father has had a long, and by all appearances, successful second marriage."

Ray noted a second flash of anger. He wondered what was motivating it.

Elliott pulled out his cigarette pack again and fumbled with it. "When will we have my father's body? We want to start organizing the memorial service."

"Later in the week. I'll be able to tell you tomorrow. What are your plans?"

"Jill and I are working on that. We'll probably do something in Chicago. It's just too difficult to get flights into Traverse City before Labor Day if you have to come commercial. However, Father would have probably liked something up here. He looked on Gull House as the major accomplishment of his life. His will stipulates that his ashes be spread on the shore." He paused, withdrawing a cigarette from the pack. "Now, Sheriff, if there is nothing else...."

"I will need to talk to you again in the course of the investigation. Oh, and there is one more thing. Could I get a list of the people who are or were once customers of your firm?"

Elliott's response was slow in coming. "I don't know what to tell you, Sheriff. I'll need to ask our legal people, see if we would be violating any securities or privacy laws. I'll have to get back to you on that."

Ray watched him go, Elliott stopping briefly and lighting a cigarette as soon as he dropped off the porch onto the sand trail that led away from the building.

25

Hanna Jeffers was waiting for Ray when he returned home in the late afternoon. His boat was already secured to the roof of her Subaru. "I've got all you stuff packed."

Twenty minutes later they were carrying their boats and gear from a parking lot to the Lake Michigan shore. Ray launched first, Hanna Jeffers following him. Once he got beyond the pilings, the remains of a dock left from the lumbering days, he stopped and waited. As she approached he capsized, hanging upside down in the cool water, looking at the sand bottom, the kayak rocking in the gentle chop. Then he moved to the right side of his boat, pushed the paddle out of the water, swept the blade from the bow toward the stern, and gracefully rolled up. After a few breaths, he capsized again, slowly performing the same maneuver.

Hanna glided next to him, rafting her boat against his, bow to stern, leaning on his deck. "Good hang time. I was wondering if I needed to give you the hand of God."

"Silence, I wanted complete silence."

"What's going on?"

"Too many voices. I'm trying to get through the static."

"If you want to talk about it, I'm happy to listen."

"Let's paddle. I need to burn off some energy. That seems to work better than anything."

"Where to?"

Ray looked out to the Manitous, and then glanced at his watch.

"I'm willing if you are," said Hanna, observing his actions.

"We have about three hours of light and maybe an hour of afterglow. We would have to haul ass the whole way."

"So let's do a gear check. Radios, navigation lights, tow packs, food, and water."

"All of the above," answered Ray. "Tell me about the food."

"You will approve, but we will have to gobble it down. You checked the weather?"

"It is what you see. A modest chop left over from yesterday. The wind will drop away around sunset. We should be coming back on glass. You lead, you set a faster pace than I do."

Hanna headed into open water and pointed her bow toward the south end of the island. Ray fell in behind, later moving just off her port side. There was little conversation, just the rhythm of body, blade, boat, and waves. Once they neared the shore of the island, they paddled north until they found a sand beach for landing.

Ray sat on the bluff above the beach and looked across the Manitou Passage in softening light. From Sleeping Bear Point the massive dunes stretched south toward Empire, rising again and slowly leveling as they neared Platte Point. The passage was almost devoid of boat traffic, and the wave height had dropped to less than a foot.

"How about some smoked salmon?"

"Sounds promising."

"On a dark rye with cream cheese and capers."

"Now you are talking," said Ray, dropping at her side and accepting the sandwich.

"I know we should be sipping vodka, or at least white wine, but how about some seltzer with a twist of lime."

"Perfect."

They ate in silence for many minutes. Finally, Hanna said, "We take this all too much for granted. This view, this amazing water, this tranquility. I have to keep reminding myself of my good fortune in being here rather than at the edge of some killing zone." She looked over at Ray. "How goes the investigation or are we banning all work-related conversations?"

Ray's answer was a long time in coming. ""It's so complicated. Twenty or more possible suspects just in our initial review. The victim has had decades-long relationships with most of these people. It's hard to know where to begin. I spent the day listening to different versions of the same story, most of them coming through a filter that would put the speaker in the best light. Most of the colony residents expressed a dislike for the victim. And yet they seemed to tolerate him because he had the money and competence to keep things going."

Ray looked out at the water and checked his watch. "We should be back on the water. I want to get across the shipping channel before dark. Let's have the navigation lights in place and switched on before we launch."

Ray pushed Hanna's kayak away from the beach, and then launched his own. As they paddled away from shore, Hanna asked, "Should we put out a radio call that we're crossing the passage?"

"I don't see any traffic, but it's probably a good thing to do." He stopped paddling and waited as she transmitted "Sécurité, sécurité, sécurité, kayaks crossing Manitou Passage west to east from South Manitou to Sleeping Bear Point." She repeated her message, her voice echoing through Ray's VFR radio.

"How was that," she asked.

"Perfect. We've made a cautionary call, the lights are in place, and there are no other boats in sight. Let's boogie while we've still got lots of light."

Ray turned his bow in the direction of the headland and settled into a fast cadence, Hanna in a parallel course at his side. As Ray focused on his destination, he slowly ran the memory of each of the interviews of the cast, crew, family, and employees from Verity Wudbine-Merone to her son Elliott. He tried to remember the details of each encounter. What had he missed? While it was too early to dismiss the possibility that the murderer was from outside this group, Ray was quite certain he had talked to the killer or killers in the course of the day. The careful, split-second timing necessary to successfully carry out the attack showed extremely careful planning. Was the perpetrator motivated by some recent events or by some smoldering resentment?

"Ray," Hanna's voice had a sense of urgency. "There's a boat closing fast. I can't tell if they have seen us."

"Do another sécurité call."

They paused briefly as Hanna made her call.

"I don't see any response. They're coming straight toward us."

"They are at least a mile out. Let's get out of their way."

As they picked up their pace, Ray watched the lights on the approaching craft. He could hear the rumble of the engines, and then the music, a techno beat. As hard as they paddled, the yacht continued to close, as if it was being steered in their direction. Suddenly it veered off to the west, missing their boats by less than forty or fifty yards, the kayaks surfing on its wake. Then it slowly disappeared into the dusk, the engine noise blending with a heavy bass beat.

"Did you get a name?" asked Ray.

"No," said Hanna, still breathing hard, her arms and legs burning from the extended sprint. "I don't think they ever saw us. Was anyone on the bridge?"

"Auto pilot," said Ray. "The guy at the controls was talking, or texting, or watching TV or in the head. They had their VHS turned off or down so as not to be disturbed by the routine chatter."

"What can we do?"

"Be angry at them, and thankful that they missed us. That was a good-sized yacht. They probably wouldn't have noticed running over us."

On the beach in the dull light of the afterglow, as they packed their gear, Hanna asked, "Did you figure out who the killer was?"

"No, I was distracted. For a little while it became quite unimportant."

"Near-death experiences seem to put everything else in perspective," she said sliding into his arms. "This was a lot more interesting than dinner and a movie."

26

"What time did you get here?" asked Sue, observing the elaborate diagram—a collection of circles and ovals with connecting lines that covered the large whiteboard.

"I slept for five or six hours, and then I was wide awake. I was just lying there trying to figure out how to get on top of all this information. Eventually I got up and came in. This," pointing to the whiteboard, "is what I had to do. I needed to draw it out. Too many balls in the air, I can't do that in my head."

Sue settled into her chair and studied the diagram.

"How was your night?" Ray asked.

"It was good. Harry's trying to prove himself as a cook. I guess I've blabbed on too much about your culinary skills. I think he feels competitive. That's a guy thing, isn't it?"

Ray looked over at her, but was not quick to answer.

"Anyway, he did a good job. Fresh salmon and some corn he bought at a farm stand. Couldn't be better. He made a salad, too. And bought some of those chocolates from the Grocer's Daughter. I think the man has promise as a hunter and gatherer and perhaps even as a cook. Or he's being excessively charming in the hope of getting me to move to Chicago. The old bait and switch routine. He keeps talking about different law schools, other kinds of jobs I could pursue, and the joys of living in a great restaurant city."

"Is he making any headway?" asked Ray, uncomfortable with the conversation.

"We've had this talk before, Ray. I do have this nagging feeling that I should be thinking about the future. And as you know, this is the first relationship I've had in awhile that shows much promise. But I don't know. How about you? What did you do last night?"

"Fast paddle on the big lake."

"With the doc?"

"Yes. We went out to the south island and back."

"Did you have enough light?"

"We were pushing it on the return. Almost got mowed down by a large yacht, a thrilling end to a long day. And that sudden rush of excitement took my mind off this," Ray pointed to the whiteboard, "for a while."

"Did you report the incident?" asked Sue.

"We didn't catch the name of the boat. At the time it seemed to be more trouble than it was worth. I was exhausted. I just wanted to go home and hit the bed."

"You and the doc, this has been going on for what, six months now? Since I've known you, this is close to a personal best."

"Don't get too excited, Sue. I imagine she will wander off to do another residency in some exotic area of medicine. Let's get back on task," he said looking up at the board. "You can see what I've done, every interview gets its own balloon, below each of those I've added additional balloons with information I garnered from the interviews. You will remember some of this from our conversation yesterday. For example, look at Richard Grubbs. In the balloons below I have identity of daughter and suggestion of wife's affair with Malcolm in their own graphic. And in each of those two balloons you see the V indicating Verity was a source of the information."

"I need 10 or 15 minutes to study this," said Sue.

"Take whatever time you need," said Ray. "I'll go make a fresh pot of coffee for us."

"Questions?" asked Ray, returning to the table with an insulated decanter.

"It looks like Verity gets the most balloons."

"Yes," said Ray. "Verity had all kinds of information, lots of things she wanted me to know. We have Grubbs' wife and Malcolm, and we have Grubbs' daughter not talking to her father."

"And then Verity lets you know that said daughter has Asperger's like behaviors. I guess I should say 'spectrum disorder,' and that the replacement wife, Brenda, is an alcoholic," said Sue. "And I have to admit I thought Jill was a bit strange. In our long conversation she only made eye contact once or twice. Most of the time she was looking between us at the far wall. She was absolutely without affect. And then I think about her on stage. I wish we could run the tape back. She seemed like the other actors, full of life and emotion. She wasn't flat or cardboard. Jill really seemed to be into her part."

"I noticed that too," said Ray. "Interesting that Malcolm encouraged her to read for the play. I wonder what his motives were. He also got Pepper Markley to take a role. She told me they were having trouble finding someone of the right age and gender, and he coaxed her to participate."

"So he lets his concierge participate in amateur theater while she's on the clock?"

"Some kind of weird work arrangement was going on there," noted Ray. "Pepper said Wudbine wanted his people available around-the-clock."

"Can we go back to Verity for a minute. She had means, motive, and opportunity. And she was certainly dropping information bombs that would move you in several directions."

"Yes, but can you see her delivering the fatal thrust?" asked Ray. "Their marriage was over decades ago. She appears to have gotten on with her life. I don't see her as the…."

"Maybe not as the killer," said Sue. "But if we're thinking about a couple of people. She certainly would be able to flip a switch."

"But why? I don't see it. By all reports they were quite civil."

"I don't know. Maybe old wounds that have been festering for years."

"Verity did suggest that Wudbine had been working their son too hard. Again, probably not enough to motivate a homicide. We need to know more about Elliott and his relationship with his father," added Ray.

"What's Elliott like?" asked Sue.

"Intense, ill at ease. Hard to tell if that's his normal demeanor or a reaction to the murder. He's a smoker. A bit unusual, given his age and who he is. Could hardly wait to get out the door to light up. I asked him about who would gain financially from his father's death. He said most of Wudbine's fortune would go to the foundation, and that a trust was in place to provide for his stepmother. Elliott also indicated that he was already a wealthy man.

"So, as you can see," continued Ray, "two family members, Verity and Jill, would have easy access to Wudbine, as would one of his employees, Pepper Markley. At the back of the theater you have Elliott and Alyson Mickels. They could have slipped in without being noticed. In addition, there's Grubbs and the other actors and crew. And then there are the colony members, and the list goes on and on. Did you come up with any prints?"

"I've got a partial off the master switch. It's probably David Johnson."

"We should talk to him again today. I'd like to get him back up in the booth, switch off the power and time how long it takes for him to get to the rear of the building and turn it back on. Maybe we can jar his memory a bit. I also want to look at places where an assailant could hide offstage. Let's do some timing there. How many seconds would it take to move onstage and out the door, or back into the green room."

"And Brenda Wudbine?"

"They're really protecting her. Lots of comments about her alcoholism. We need to find a way to isolate her. I want to talk to her without anyone protecting her, and I've got a sense that Jill Wudbine and the people she oversees will do their best to prevent us from doing that."

"Why? What's their motive?"

"I don't know," answered Ray. "Are they just trying to prevent her making an embarrassment of herself? Given the level of her alleged addiction, I can't imagine that she's enormously aware of what's going on around her. But we do need to find out if she has anything that might help us."

"How are you going to pull that one off?"

"Just keep our eyes open. Be ready when the opportunity presents itself." Ray paused for a moment, then added, "I've put all the audio files in their own folder in the case file. You can access them if there's anything you want listen to. I've asked Jan to convert them into text files."

"So where do we start today?"

"Let me do some paperwork so people get paid on Friday. See if you can have David Johnson meet us at the auditorium at 9:00. Bring a stopwatch. Then we will look for possible hiding places and escape routes for the assailant. Next, we need you to go to Gull House and interview the cook, handyman, and maid while I start talking to the remaining members of the cast and crew. Talk to Grubbs, see if he can get the play people lined up for me. And see if Pepper Markley can line up the Gull House staff.

That's certainly something a concierge should be able to do. Let's leave a little after 8:00."

"One or two cars?"

"One. You drive. We can talk on the way."

27

David Johnson answered their calls as Ray and Sue came into the backstage area. He was already up in the light booth.

"Can we join you up there?" Ray asked.

"Sure. It's a bit tight with three, but perfectly safe. We won't all come crashing to the ground. Be careful, I'm sure this doesn't meet OSHA standards."

Sue grabbed hold of the ladder that was permanently mounted six inches off the wall and climbed up to the booth. Ray followed.

"Like I said, there's not a lot of room up here," Johnson explained once Ray had joined them in the booth, a decked rectangle with the dimmers on the wall side. Three sets of steel pipes, secured at corner posts, ran horizontally on the other sides to provide a safe enclosure. "I think it was probably designed for two people, max," said Johnson.

"Walk us through what happened on Saturday evening," said Ray.

"Where do you want me to start? I went through this with you yesterday."

"But now I'm up here, and I can see what you were referring to. As I remember it, you told me you arrived early and got the set lit for the first scene. Once you established that everything was working, you went off to the green room to visit for…."

"About ten minutes."

"Then you came back here."

"That's correct."

"So let's start from the point when you climbed back up. Tell us exactly what you did from that point forward."

"The board is still set up the way it was on Saturday. Do you want me to power things up and walk you through it?"

"That would be perfect," answered Ray.

"Okay, starting on the right-hand side, this rheostat controls the house lights. I should say dimmer, it's a rheostat dimmer. Don't want to confuse things with our lingo. So this switch would be thrown, and this dimmer would be all the way up, just like it is now. Let me power up the rest of the dimmers. I had to make a change in the lighting between the first and second scene to reflect the time of day. Okay, lights are on and the work lights above the stage are off. Like I think I told you, these old rheostats are 60 or more years. They are inefficient, hot, and have been known to cause fires. The new boards are all electronic. And the new, high-end stage lights use LEDs, you can control the colors from the board. Not that I could, but it can be done."

"And why couldn't you?" asked Sue.

"I had a stroke a dozen or so years ago. I've recovered, but I've been color blind ever since."

"How did that affect you professionally?"

"I closed my practice and did some teaching at the medical school before I fully retired."

Ray and Sue looked down on the brightly lit stage.

"It's magical, isn't it?" said Johnson. "The lights make it somehow all real."

Ray carefully scanned the area enclosed by the set and the backstage area from the booth to the back wall.

"So you can see what's happening onstage and on this side of the backstage area. The set completely blocks your view of the other side."

"That's correct. But you don't need to know what's happening there."

"So the first act has ended, you've made the changes to the lights, then what?"

"Like I told you yesterday, I remember seeing the prop girl come through. Then Malcolm and Florence came out. Once she had him situated, she left. So then I was sitting right here on this stool, waiting for Tony to give me the word on the house lights. We blink them twice, first at three minutes, and a second time at one minute before curtain. I bring the houselights down just as he pulls the curtain. And I was reading a piece from the Free Press, the sports section. Someone had abandoned it in the green room."

"And then?"

"The lightning strike, it had to be close. Everything rattled up here. And then a few seconds later things went black."

"And now the emergency exit lights should have come on, but they didn't," said Ray.

"Correct. There had been some kind of problem with the system last week. One of the units shorted out and started smoking. Grubbs has ordered replacements for the whole system. I can't remember that they've ever been needed before. Isn't that always the way?"

"Then what happened?"

"I took my trusty headlamp and cut the power to all the dimmers. I was told years ago that you don't want a big dead load when the power is restored; it can blow the main fuses. And I switched on the work lights in anticipation of the electricity being restored. This is our standard procedure. It's right here for anyone operating the board to follow." Johnson pointed to a laminated sheet secured with thumbtacks above the dimmers. "And then I climbed down and went out to see if there was something I could reset outback, or if it was the power company's problem."

"Did you see any lights in the stage area, or any lights anywhere else, for that matter?"

"No, not that I can remember. But I was pretty focused on the board and getting out back. If I saw anything, it didn't register."

"Okay, let's stop right here. We're going to climb down. We want to time you so we can get an idea of how long the place was in complete darkness."

Ray and Sue stood below the light booth, Sue holding the stopwatch. "Go through the process of powering down the dimmers and making the changes just as you did Saturday night. Then come down the ladder," instructed Sue.

"Start timing now," responded Johnson.

They could hear the snapping of the old switches, and then they watched Johnson cautiously come down the stepladder. They followed him across the backstage area to the door, down the hall, through the east exit, and around to the utility cabinet mounted on the back of the building.

"So I looked at these breakers here first. This is where I usually find the problem, but nothing seemed to be tripped. I thought that was strange, not what I expected. I'm trying to do it in the same way I did Saturday night so the time will be close. Then I looked at the main disconnect switch. It had been pulled. I pushed it back on and headed in."

"Time?" asked Ray, looking at Sue.

"In the vicinity of two minutes."

"Just continue, and we will follow along," said Ray.

"Like I think I told you, I hurried back in. I wanted to get everything on so we could get the play started."

As they followed Johnson into the building, Ray asked, "Did you see anyone along the way?"

"No one in the hallway, no one backstage. To be perfectly frank, I was seeing red. Well, you get my meaning. What kind of a prank was that, turning off the power. So I climbed up there and got everything turned on so we were ready to open the curtain. Then you and the others were onstage, and I was quickly herded into the green room."

"Having to retire early," said Ray, "that must have been difficult. I'm talking about the financial end."

"It was a shock. The last kid was just out of college. The next few years I was really going to focus on saving for retirement. If I hadn't moved my account over to Malcolm…." Johnson stopped suddenly.

"You told me yesterday you had never had any financial dealings with Mr. Wudbine."

"Well, I meant I didn't after the dotcom collapse."

"What did you lose? Give me a percent."

"About 65%."

"And that was part of your retirement savings?"

"No. That was the whole thing. And then the SOB cancelled my account. He sent me a check with a list of names of other wealth management firms that worked with small investors. I wasn't a small investor until Wudbine ran my retirement into the ground."

"Why did you tell me something else yesterday?"

"I don't want to be pulled into this investigation. I just want it to go away. I had nothing to do with his death. That's the truth."

"Is there any part of our conversation about what happened Saturday night that you want to change?" Ray looked at Johnson carefully. He could feel the anger and hatred.

"I told you exactly what happened. Is there anything else, Sheriff? I've got things to do."

"That's it for now, thank you."

After Ray and Sue were outside, beyond hearing distance, she said, "Still an open wound there, the financial thing."

"Yes," agreed Ray. "I wonder if financial losses are at the bottom of this? How many others are still bitter and angry?"

28

Ray could see the tall figure of Ron Waltham waiting for him in the small clearing near the front of the library. Ron greeted him warmly, extending a hand, his smile exuding goodwill and bonhomie. After exchanging pleasantries, they settled into chairs on opposite sides of the table at which Ray had been conducting interviews.

"How did you end up with the role of vicar," Ray asked. "Did you read for that part or was it something that Sterling Shevlin assigned?"

"Sterling told me he had just the part for me the first time I ran into him this summer. In fact, he greeted me that first time as Vicar," answered Waltham, with an amiable smile, his blue eyes contrasting with his steel gray hair and rich tan. "You have to understand there's a bit of a joke going on. Usually he greets me as 'padre.' I'm an ordained minister and serve in that role here at the colony. I left the ministry years ago, so it's just sort of a summer thing I've been, well, I don't want to say stuck with. But it's something that's sort of expected of me, especially since no one else wants the job."

"So does Mr. Shevlin assign most of the parts in this manner?"

"You never know about old Sterling. Did I get the role because I was the right age and look like an English country vicar, or was he thinking about my role here at the colony? Sterling seems to operate on four or five levels at all times. I think he's making connections and finding meaning.

Not that he shares any of this with us, not often anyway. He's an incredibly interesting man. You should get to know him if you have the opportunity."

"You were saying that you were an ordained minister."

"Yes. I was a philosophy major in college with an interest in comparative religions. By the time I was graduating, I didn't know exactly what to do with that. So I did a master's degree in theology, thinking perhaps that the ministry was my calling. I ended up as the youth minister in a suburban Detroit church. I could tell that that wasn't a good fit, although I tried to make it work for about two years. Then I had an opportunity to become a chaplain in a large community hospital. That was a better fit. But it was also one of those experiences that change you a lot. Families in crisis, that's what I was dealing with on a daily basis. Grief, sickness, or end of life situations are extremely stressful. As I was learning how to help families, I was slowly beginning to understand the complexities of these relationships. I started taking graduate courses related to family therapy, eventually ended up with a PhD in the area and then transitioned over to my own private practice. And that's what I've been doing for almost 20 years. Except, of course, when I'm up here for two months, where I'm back doing a bit of what I did at the beginning of my career."

"So what are your pastoral duties here?"

"Pretty limited, and that's the way I've tried to keep it. At the beginning of the season we always have a memorial service, out on the beach, for the members of the colony who've died during the winter. We give family members and friends an opportunity to share memories and then we join hands, and I give a brief prayer. Sunday mornings we have a service with music and different kinds of performances and presentations. It's all done by colony members, people of all ages. It's not a religious service, it's more of a spiritual nature. My job is to get this organized and make sure everyone is lined up and ready. Then we have a wedding or two or three, an occasional death or baptism. I probably average half a day a week, and that's all I want."

"How are you connected with the colony?"

"I'm not a direct descendant. I got here via marriage. My wife's family goes right back to the beginning, right back to the strong Christian abolitionist roots of this organization. We've had our own cottage here for about 20 years. Jeanine's brother, he's older by five years, ended up with the family cottage. We're close enough to see one another on a daily basis, and far enough apart not to intrude on one another's lives."

"Given your expertise in family therapy, are you called upon to…?"

"All the time. Everyone with kids, especially teenagers, is trying to get through some problem. I do my best not to get too involved. This is my vacation. This is my respite from the demands of therapy. If there is a real crisis, I'm happy to help. But I do my best to keep a low profile, if you know what I mean."

"How about the colony as a family?" asked Ray.

"Funny you should mention that. I've always sort of thought about it in that way. It's a large extended family, composed of individual families, some of whom have histories going back generations. There are very complex relationships here. Fortunately, most of the time this is an enormously successful cooperative community."

"How did Malcolm Wudbine fit into this family?"

"There was an interesting dynamic. We have Malcolm and Verity and their history. Then there's Malcolm and his relationship with his son and daughter-in-law. And last the rather strange relationship with Malcolm and the colony. He's been very good to this place, but at times he's been a brute and a dictator. Along the way he created a dependency relationship. We all became conditioned to look to Malcolm for his money and his skill at fixing things. It was sort of father and child relationship."

"How did you get along with Malcolm?"

"I did my best to stay out of his way. That's how I deal with unpleasant people. I am one of the few people living here who never had an acrimonious encounter with him. I don't know why I was spared. Perhaps my pastoral role afforded me some special protection."

"Did you ever have any financial dealings with him?"

"No, fortunately, but a lot of people did. I might have, too. But at the time I had no money. There was quite a frenzy back when he invited people to open accounts. There were lots of people hopping on board, everyone hoping to make a fortune. They all wanted a piece of the action and were convinced that Malcolm could deliver for them the same kind of wealth he had acquired for himself. Folks moved their longstanding retirement accounts over to his firm. I also heard that some people took out second mortgages, although I don't know whether or not that's true. The market was going up, all the old guidelines and questions didn't seem to matter anymore. And for a couple of years they did well. That was a regular part of summer gossip. And then the dotcom collapse quickly shattered those dreams. There was a lot of anger directed at Malcolm, and

Elliott, too. It clearly wasn't their fault. I'm not sure they handled it well. I heard they abruptly closed out the smaller accounts, and many of those people had huge losses. Even though it was more than a decade ago, there is still some residual anger."

"So what about the Wudbine family?"

"I really can't tell you much. I'm just an outsider. I'm sure that it's just as functional/dysfunctional as any other family. On a bell-shaped curve, they're probably around the mean, maybe a standard deviation on the side of strangeness at the most. That's pure conjecture. Really unfair of me to say that. I just don't know."

Saturday night, did you see anything unusual, anything out of place, people around you hadn't seen before?"

"No, nothing like that. But, Sheriff, my focus was on the play. Sterling had worked us very hard. We had started in chaos about a month ago. By Saturday night it all seemed like a well-oiled machine. I was having a wonderful time. I think the rest of the cast was too. There was so much energy and excitement. Even the lights going out just seemed to add to the total effect of the suspense and mystery. Sheriff, I was in shock. I still am."

"Where were you when the place went dark?"

"I was sitting in the green room. I was texting with one of my kids out in the audience. We just went on with our conversation until the lights came back on, and I had to get ready to go back onstage."

"You have any theories about who might have wanted Malcolm Wudbine dead?"

"None at all. The man could be a pain in the ass. But murder, I don't see it, not here. So many things happen between people. If I've learned one thing over the years, especially in my professional life, it's impossible to imagine the things that happen between people. And to take it one step further, it's difficult to anticipate how a person might interpret events or see a relationship. So who knows what might have inspired this rage. I'm really interested in knowing more about the killer and what motivated them to do this crime. I hope we can have a conversation about the case after the dust settles."

"I'd be happy to do that," said Ray, standing and extending his hand, "after the case is closed and adjudicated."

"One more thing," said Waltham, "I assume my son's on the list. He played my nephew, he's sixteen."

"Yes, one of the many people we have to get to."

"My wife took him downstate this morning. Football practice starts tomorrow. I doubt if he knows anything. He's been totally in love for at least three weeks and oblivious to everything and everyone else. When you're sixteen, a summer romance is a big deal."

Ray walked outside with Waltham and chatted a few more minutes, then returned to the library and keyed some additional notes on his laptop. His concentration was interrupted by the his phone vibrating on the tabletop."

"You better get out here, Ray," said Sue. "The family chopper just took off with Elliott, Jill, and Alyson Mickels. Brenda Wudbine is in the greenhouse that adjoins the staff quarters, alone and unguarded."

"I'm on my way."

29

Brenda Wudbine sat on a stool near a counter at the center of the small greenhouse, a collection of cut flowers spread out before her. Holding a near-empty glass with the remains of a Bloody Mary in her left hand, she eyed Ray and Sue suspiciously.

"We came to offer our condolences," said Ray, making eye contact with Wudbine, then quickly scanning the area for security cameras. He looked back at her.

"Condolences," she repeated, her voice unsteady, her word suspended in the moist air, redolent with the smell of earth and blossoms. "Funny, no one has said that. I'm the wife, the supposed widow, and no one has said that. No one has offered condolences. And that's what people do, isn't it?" She focused on Ray, her gaze unsteady. "Even my friends back in Chicago who have been calling, they didn't say it. But then they loathed Malcolm."

Brenda focused on the flowers for a long moment, then looked up at Ray. "Does Jill know you're here?"

Before he could answer, she continued. "Of course she doesn't know. If she did, she'd be hovering right here, making sure I didn't say anything that would give you or anyone else the wrong impression of our happy little household."

"Ms. Wudbine, we are investigating your husband's death, and we'd like to ask you some questions."

"Call me Brenda," she said in a gravelly voice, reaching for a cigarette. "I never liked the name Wudbine. It always sounded like part of an animal name, the Wudbine mouse or the Wudbine rat, or the peckerwoods. On our first date he told me he was related to English nobility that could be traced to Wudbine Castle in Northumbria," she stopped and lit the cigarette. "That was before Google. I would have looked it up and called his sorry lying ass on that lie. When I did look up the name, I didn't find his spelling. The variant was woodbine. Do you know what I'm talking about? It's a kind of vine, related to poison ivy. It creeps and climbs and smothers the plants around it. Yes, smothers the plants around it." She inhaled deeply, exhaled, coughed, and then cleared her throat. "I should have known, but he was rich, charming, and handsome. He showed me a world that I didn't know existed."

"When was this?"

"Twenty-some years ago. Chicago. I was working in a flower shop near his office. Malcolm wanted fresh-cut flowers every morning. I took his order over one day when our delivery guy was sick. Malcolm called my boss, insisted that I do the delivery from then on. I was in art school, just getting by. He tipped me generously. Eventually, he started hitting on me, told me to stop by in the late afternoon sometime, and he'd take me out for a drink. He was just some guy. I wasn't interested. He kept pestering. Eventually I gave in. And then it was a slippery slope, a slippery slope. A drink, then a dinner, then a weekend in New York visiting the Guggenheim and the Met. A month later it was ten days in Paris visiting the Louvre and Musée d'Orsay. Eventually, I moved into his penthouse. I was perfectly happy with that arrangement, but he wanted us married. The early years were good. But you don't want to hear the story. I should tell it on Oprah." She looked away, then back at them. "So how exactly did he die? No one gives me the details."

Ray looked over at Sue.

"He was stabbed," she said.

"Where?"

"In the back."

Brenda repeated the phrase, "In the back. And I imagine that you're talking to me because you think I might be able to lead you to the killer?" She looked up at them and took another long drag on her cigarette before slowly crushing it out in a large crystal ashtray. "Well, you came to the right place. Stabbed in the back, ha. You're looking for a killer with a sense of irony, someone who sent him to the great beyond believing that he was meant to die as he had lived, a backstabber."

"Can you lead us to the killer?" asked Sue.

Wudbine was slow in responding. "Malcolm would have loved to get rid of me years ago. I was getting used up. My looks were starting to go. I was no longer the beautiful young woman he could show off. But Mr. Financial Genius screwed up early on. In our prenuptial he specified a percentage of his then net worth rather than a definite amount. He was only a millionaire back then. He could have unloaded me on the cheap in those days, especially during a bear market. Malcolm didn't foresee how his wealth would explode over the next couple of decades. In the end, he was too greedy to get rid of me. So he marginalized me. He hardly talked to me the last couple of years. I think he was hoping I'd drink myself to death."

"Why didn't you seek a divorce?" asked Sue.

Again, the answer was slow in coming. "I tried. Malcolm said no, said he would make sure any action was stalled in the courts forever. He told me to just hang in there. I'd have plenty of money and my freedom when he was gone. And now he is gone, and my stepson and his wife are probably doing their best to try to screw me out of my inheritance."

"Brenda," started Ray, "let me ask this question again. Do you know who would have a motive to kill your husband?"

"Me. I had a perfect motive. Battered wife syndrome. Not battered physically, but years of psychological warfare, anger, and verbal abuse. He brings in his new toys, runs them under my nose, calls them employees or interns. But he knows that I know what's going on."

"So did you kill your husband?"

"Of course not."

"Did you arrange to have your husband killed?"

"Wrong on that one, too, Sheriff. I do admire the way it was done, but I told you that already."

"Brenda, you are wasting our time. Do you have any idea who might have killed your husband?"

"No, no one in particular. But I'm sure along the way he screwed a lot of people. Malcolm was always looking out for number one, whether we're talking about his net worth or his bed. You can't do that for fifty years without pissing off a lot of folks. If you want specifics, Sheriff, I can't help you out. That's what you get paid for. My job now is to hang around until we put poor Malcolm in the cold, cold ground."

"Do you know what the funeral plans are?"

"They don't talk about those things to me. It's Elliott and Jill, probably more Jill. She seems to wear the pants. But I did ask Elliott. He said he'd let me know." Brenda glared at Ray. "It's like you don't get it, Sheriff. I'm a zero here, an empty shell. They will let me know. Maybe I'll get to sit with the family at the funeral. Of course, I'll have to be sober enough not to make a spectacle of myself. And I'll have to promise on a stack of WSJs that I won't be sarcastic or do anything unseemly. I'm sure they're planning a great show, and I'll have to promise to stay in character to the end, the bloody end.

"And what if I don't show," she continued, looking off into the distance, verbalizing an interior monologue, no longer quite aware of her audience. "How would that look? The happy family, minus the grieving widow. I'm sure they will come up with an almost credible excuse. 'Too distraught to attend a public event, a victim of uncontrollable grief. She's under her doctor's care and resting comfortably.' Well, I've got news for those bastards. I'm going to do my best to get there, but I'm not going to throw myself on my dear husband's funeral pyre. He can roast in hell on his own."

Brenda looked up, "I'm getting bored with our conversation, Sheriff. I will leave you to look at the flowers while I wander off to get a fresh drink."

Ray looked over at Sue. She could feel his frustration.

"Ms. Wudbine, Brenda, we're trying to find your husband's killer. And you are not giving us any help. Aren't you interested in seeing the murderer brought to justice?"

"You just don't get it, dearie, do you. I don't care. Bravo to the killer for a job well done. Now listen carefully. Glue your eyes on my mouth. Open your ears. I had nothing to do with it. I have no idea who the killer may be, and I don't give a damn." Brenda pulled herself to her feet and gently pushed Ray to the side as she passed, her right hand on his chest. Then she disappeared out the door.

"You really broke that suspect down," said Sue.

"And your interrogation skills are equal to mine," said Ray, shaking his head and smirking.

"We may not be able to isolate her again."

"I know. I'm not sure it matters," said Ray. "How did it go with the cook and maid?"

"The cook, Grace Rodrigues, I think she was trying to be helpful, but her English is quite limited."

"I thought you were bilingual," Ray chided.

"Yeah, sure. Four years of high school Spanish, two more in college, proficient enough to order a meal in a Taco Bell."

"Citizenship?"

"She has an Illinois operator's permit. I didn't push it. She's a recent hire, and I don't think she has anything to tell us."

"How about the housekeeper, what's her name?"

"Jane Propst, she's local, lives in town. This is her second season at Gull House. What's your term, omerta? All she knows is that the Wudbines are a wonder couple. They are the best, most generous people she's ever worked for. And she just doesn't know how anyone could hurt Mr. Wudbine. She said, and I'm quoting here, 'The earth must be spinning off its axles.'"

"Well, if not its axles, at least its rails. So what are you telling me?"

"I don't think she knows anything. I pushed her hard. Nada, nada, nada. She works 8:00 to 4:00 seven days a week for the twelve-week season. And she comes in during May to open the place and works through September to close things up. During those months she's on a five-day schedule. The rest of the year she's on a retainer to be available when they occasionally use the place. And, of course, she's worried that this arrangement will disappear."

"How about the handyman?"

"He's off on weekends, and had today off to see his cardiologist in Traverse City. We'll have to catch him tomorrow or the next day. What now?"

"We still have the rest of the cast and crew. Grubbs is helping line them up. Maybe after lunch we can split the list and talk to all of them."

30

In the course of the afternoon Ray interviewed most of the remaining cast members while Sue, working in the auditorium's green room, met individually with the crew members. The one exception to the one-on-one rule was her planned meeting with the five teenage girls who served as ushers. That interview was scheduled for the end of the day.

Most of the remaining actors were younger than the ones Ray had first interviewed, people in their 20s and 30s, none of whom seemed to have a history with Malcolm Wudbine or his family. The interviews went quickly and provided no new information. The one exception was eighty-seven year old Lenore Beeson—tart tongued and venomous, especially toward Malcolm Wudbine. She played the gossipy Mrs. Price Ridley. Frail and unsteady, she was clearly not a possible suspect. She did explain in great detail how Wudbine had robbed her of much of her retirement while making millions for himself. But beyond her vituperations directed at Wudbine, she had little to add.

Soon after Lenore Beeson departed, Sue called Ray, asking him to come to the green room. He found her sitting at the head of a table with five young women, teenagers. One by one, Sue introduced the ushers: Samantha, Brittany, Megan, Kayla, and Anna.

"I would like to cover the same ground again," said Sue, "this time with the Sheriff listening. She looked over at Ray, "Samantha and Brittany were at the west entrance, Megan and Kayla were at the east entrance, and Anna was at the doors in the rear of the building. Okay guys, let's talk about the flashlights first."

"Who should start?" asked Kayla.

"Doesn't matter."

"There's been some kind of trouble with the lights over the doors, the ones that should turn on if the power goes out," said Kayla. "Mr. Grubbs told us about it the day of the dress rehearsal. We were there with the cast and crew, just like this was the actual event. He gave us flashlights, new out of the box, and told us in case the power went out we were to open the doors, block them open, and use our lights to help people exit the building. But he said having to do that was unlikely. In the thirty or forty years since the emergency lights had been installed, they had never been needed, but he said it was better to be safe than sorry."

"So how did that work out?"

"Not exactly as planned," answered Megan. "The first scene came to an end. We had been told that it would be a ten-minute scene change and lots of people would be going out to stretch. As soon as the curtain closed, we propped the exit doors open."

"We did the same on our side," said one of the other girls.

"And then what did you do?"

"Well, since I had ten minutes I went to talk to people," said Samantha. "We wouldn't be needed again till the lights blinked, indicating that the play was starting again."

Ray looked at the other girls, they all looked slightly abashed. "We all did the same thing," said Brittany. "How were we supposed to know the lights would go out in the middle of an intermission?"

"And then," said Ray.

"I used my light to get back to the door, not that I really needed it," said Brittany. "And shortly after that the lights were back on. It was no big deal."

"Did anyone leave early, before the end of the scene?" asked Ray.

"Not on our side," said Brittany.

"Or ours," said Megan.

Ray looked over at Anna, the girl responsible for the back entrance. She looked down toward the table.

"Same thing for you?" said Ray looking in her direction.

Anna's answer was slow in coming. She lifted her head and looked at Sue. "I wasn't there. I slipped away for a few minutes after everyone was seated. I was planning to get back. I just lost track of the time. And then it started raining so hard. I didn't think it would matter."

"Where were you?" asked Ray.

"I was over in the library."

"Catching up on your reading?" giggled Megan.

"One of my friends was leaving this week," she said, directing her answer to Sue and Ray. "I just wanted to spend some extra time with them."

"So let me summarize here," said Ray. "During the first act, no one left the theater from either the east or west exits. And we don't know about the back entrance."

One of the girls answered, "correct," and the rest nodded their agreement.

"So you were here for the dress rehearsal and the performance. And you are all residents of the summer colony, correct."

Ray had everyone's eyes. They nodded their assent.

"Have you seen anyone around who wasn't part of the colony in recent days?"

After a long silence Megan said, "Well, there's crazy Tom."

"Who is that?"

"I don't know what his last name is. He's been hanging around. I know Grubbs talks to him all the time and sometimes asks him to leave. A day or two later he's back."

Ray looked over at Sue. Her nod told him that Tom wasn't on their radar.

"The guy creeps me out," said Megan. "He likes hanging around the beach. I don't like the way he looks at me."

"He's been around the theatre a lot," said Brittany. "I think he wanted Mr. Shevlin to give him a part in the play. And someone told him to go away last week, maybe that old guy that works the lights. Tom got nasty. I heard him drop a few f-bombs as he was leaving."

"What does this Tom look like?" asked Ray.

"Like a street person. He's got long hair and a beard. It's a narrow one that just covers his chin, but it's sorta long. He's tall, real tall, and his jeans just hang on him," added Anna. "And he reeks of cigarettes. You can smell him coming."

"But the real creepy thing is that he's always jabbering away on his phone, loud conversations, lots of laughing and hand waving," added Megan.

Ray held her in his glance.

"Well, you have to understand. It's not a phone. I saw it up close. It's just a piece of wood about the size of an iPhone. It's colored up with pencils or markers to make it look like a phone."

Ray looked over at Anna. "This Tom has been hanging around the theatre a lot?"

"She'd know," chimed in Samantha. "She's hardly left the place since rehearsals started."

"He's been hanging around. He would often sit way back in the rear of the auditorium. In the beginning he didn't bother anyone, and no one said anything. Lots of people drop in and watch the play practice. About a week ago he had one of his famous phone conversations, and Mr. Shevlin asked him to leave. He started out being very nice, but Tom said something, and Mr. Shevlin lost his temper. And then there were a lot of obscenities from both sides. And Mr. Grubbs showed up. He got Tom in his car and drove off somewhere.

"I didn't see him for a few days, but he was around the other day, not in the theater, but around back. One of the older women said she thought he was looking in the windows. Anyway, that other man I told you about asked him to go away, and there was some more shouting. Not as bad as the day with Mr. Shevlin."

"Did you see this Tom on the day of the play? Any of you?"

Brittany answered. "Yes, He tried to get in my door. He gave me a piece of paper and said it was a ticket. It was just a piece of paper with 'ticket' written on it with pencil. I told him he couldn't come in, and that I was going to get Mr. Grubbs if he didn't go away."

"He tried our door, too," said Kayla. "I was sweet about it, but I told him he couldn't come in. He didn't argue, he just disappeared."

Ray turned toward Anna.

"I didn't see him."

"Did you stay at that door until the opening curtain?"

"Yes. My friend has a few lines near the beginning of the scene."

Ray looked over at Sue, "Anything else?"

"Girls, here are my cards. Please feel free to contact me if anything comes to mind that you think I should know."

After they trooped out, Ray asked, "What did we learn?"

Sue smiled, "Libraries are romantic places. Summer romances are special, especially when you are sixteen. And we need to talk to Weird Tom."

"Let's start with Grubbs. I imagine he can point us in the right direction."

31

Richard Grubbs was working at a keyboard when Ray and Sue came through the screen door of his office. Grubbs looked at them over the top of his glasses, nodded his head in recognition, and turned back to the screen for a few seconds.

Looking back at them, he said, "I didn't mean to be discourteous. I just needed to finish the sentence before I lost the thought. Even though I've been using these things for decades," he gestured toward the Mac computer on his desk, "I still work the way I did when I used a typewriter, forming the whole sentence in my head before the first keystroke, typing to the period, and then starting all over again on the next sentence. I've watched the kids here, the girls who help me do the weekly newsletter. They just rattle away, move things around, deleting words or some times whole sentences. In the end it seems to work. But when they start, I don't think they have any idea where they are going. Their brains are different. It's the computers. The kids don't really learn to think things through. I could see that in student papers my last few years of teaching. Random thoughts cobbled together with rock and roll bouncing off the sides of their brains from the omnipresent ear buds. But I don't think you dropped by for a Luddite rant, Sheriff."

"Tell me about someone called Tom, or weird Tom?"

"How did that poor fellow get dragged into this? That's the last thing he and his mother need."

"The ushers, they talked about him."

"Sheriff, throughout the history of this colony we have always practiced and taught toleration. I think what you're telling me is most unfortunate. The chatter of a group of slightly hysterical teenage girls should not become a police matter. This isn't 1692, we're not in Salem."

Ray could see that Grubbs was extremely angry. "I don't think it was any hysteria. I asked the young women if there had been anyone around the night of the play who wasn't part of the colony. They indicated this Tom character fit that description. The 'weird' tag seems to me to be normal teenage jargon. I would like you to identify this person, provide whatever background you can give me, and tell me where I can find him."

"He is very fragile," said Grubbs, continuing his protest. "The last thing he needs is to be questioned about something that he couldn't have been involved with. Tom won't know what you're talking about. You'll just add to his already paranoid state. Trust me, you're wasting your time."

"Sir," said Ray, "I'll judge whether or not it's a waste of my time. Tell me about Tom."

Grubbs rocked back in his chair and looked at Ray and Sue. "You better have a seat, this will take a few minutes." After they were seated he continued, "His name is Thomas Lea. Historically, his family has owned cottages in the colony for decades. They don't any longer. They sold the last property 10 or 15 years ago and bought an all-season house just south of our beach area. At that time I don't think Tom was a teenager yet, well maybe a young teen. After they moved from the colony, he continued to spend a lot of time here. We have an arts and crafts building with a couple of college kids who oversee a whole range of activities. I know he liked doing crafts, and he also continued to show up for the youth choir. Now, technically, he wasn't part of the colony anymore, but like I was saying, we are a tolerant community. His participation wasn't costing us anything, and he wasn't disruptive or offensive in any way. Tom seemed lonely. He needed a place to be. Then he disappeared for a lot of years. I'd almost forgotten about him, and then he reappeared. The kid I remembered was exactly that, a kid, not five feet tall. I hardly recognized Tom in his new iteration, more than six feet tall, rail thin, almost wasted looking, and old beyond his years. But once someone identified him, I could see the boy in the man."

"When was that?" asked Ray.

"It was last summer. Not the beginning of the summer, probably more like the middle of July. He was hanging around, like he was a kid again, the same activities. One of the arts and crafts instructors came to get me. She was quite unhinged by Tom, thought perhaps he was a child predator of some sort. I didn't banish him from the colony. I did explain that he couldn't participate in the children's programs any longer. He was just too old.

"Tom seemed to comprehend what I was telling him. Then I took him home. His mother was there, and I had a long talk with her. He wasn't around to hear the conversation. She told me that he had had a major breakdown his senior year in college, and was diagnosed with paranoid schizophrenia. At the time she thought the problem might have been stress related and wondered about the possibility of the condition being drug induced. They took him over to Rochester for a workup. That's where they got the diagnosis. So now he's on drugs, you know the prescription kind, and getting therapy.

"And this summer he started coming around again. He doesn't do any harm, he's just rather bizarre, especially when he's talking on his imaginary phone. His conversations are very animated and loud."

"One of the ushers, Anna, I believe, mentioned that he had a confrontation with Sterling Shevlin. Do you know about that?" asked Ray.

"Sheriff, I know about everything that happens here. And, yes, I'm well aware of their face-off. If Sterling had just come and gotten me, I would have guided Tom out of there. The worst thing you can do is to confront Tom directly. He totally loses it at that point. Like I said, he is paranoid. He believes that people are out to get him. Tom doesn't understand that having a loud phone conversation in the back row of the auditorium during a play rehearsal isn't appropriate behavior."

"They also said he was around Saturday night for the play, that he tried to get in with a ticked he had created."

"A ticket he had created. That's part of his charm. Tom knows he needs a ticket, so he makes one. As you can see, there's a bit of disconnect there. Not too dissimilar from his creating an imaginary phone conversation. And I have to tell you they are wonderful, the side that I can hear, anyway, always upbeat and full of humor. I wish I knew more about psychiatry. Tom has this way of connecting things together, not that it's completely comprehensible to the rest of us."

"We need to talk to him."

"Why, Sheriff? Tom knows nothing. He's a total innocent. You will just frighten him. Like I was saying, he's paranoid, terrified by police. That's why…." Grubbs stopped midsentence, biting his lip, letting his gaze drop to his hands that rested on the tabletop.

"That's why what?" prodded Ray.

"A little while after Shevlin's confrontation with Tom, Malcolm came storming in, demanding that I get a court order prohibiting Tom from stepping on colony property."

"And did you?"

"I started the process, called our attorney, and asked what steps needed to be taken."

"Did you authorize them to go forward?"

"Actually, no. The summer is almost over. I talked to Tom's mother and tried to impress on her that it was important for Tom to stay away, at least for the rest of the season. You have to understand, Sheriff. Malcolm made a big brouhaha, but most times by the next day he was onto something else. Over the winter lots of things could change. Perhaps Tom won't be around next summer. My hope was that the problem would go away."

Ray looked over at Sue and then back at Grubbs. "We need to question this Tom. If he was in the area of the theatre, he might have seen the person who turned off the power."

"Oh, Sheriff, I assure you that anything he might tell you would be absolutely untrustworthy. He lives in his own fantasy world. He would be sending you in the wrong direction and wasting your time. Besides, he's very wary of males, especially police officers. In the past they are the people who have taken him to the hospital when he's had his meltdowns. If he sees you coming, he'll probably will do a runner and disappear into the woods and only God knows what will happen then."

"Mr. Grubbs, we have to talk with this individual. As you know, someone pulled the main disconnect, giving the perpetrator several minutes of complete darkness. If this Tom person was circulating around the exterior of the building, maybe he saw the person who caused things to go dark."

"He's not going to tell you anything, but if you insist, maybe your colleague here can talk to Tom. Like I said, he responds better to women then men."

Ray looked over at Sue, then answered, "I'm good with that. Will you go with her and do the introductions. Then she needs to talk to Tom in private. Will that work?"

"Yes, and I'll drive her in my car. Don't want to spook him with a police car."

32

Richard Grubbs opened the passenger-side door of his sagging Volvo for Sue Lawrence. She settled on the seat cushion—torn vinyl exposing crumbling foam rubber—and peered out through the windshield at the dull, oxidized finish on the hood. The interior smelled of gasoline, mildew, and petroleum-based grime.

"Just got a 400 thousand mile badge from the company," bragged Grubbs after he dropped into the driver's seat. "Sure hoping this baby will make a half a million."

Sue sent a weak smile his way. "How far are we going?"

"Just a few blocks. We probably should have walked. I'll go in and introduce you to Tom and his mother. Then I'll disappear. If you need me, I'll be here reading a book. If Tom has a meltdown, come and get me. I'm good at talking him down."

Grubbs parked near the back of the cottage next to a late model Chrysler van, and they walked to the rear entrance. His gentle rap brought an almost instantaneous response.

Pushing the screen door open, a sixtyish woman stepped out, gave Grubbs a quick hug, and then held Sue in a long, suspicious gaze.

"What's going on, Grubby. Some sort of problem involving Thomas?"

"Nothing of the sort. Sergeant Sue Lawrence, here, is with the Cedar County Sheriffs Department. She's investigating the death of Malcolm

Wudbine. Several witnesses saw Tom near the auditorium Saturday evening."

"He's not suspected of...."

"No," said Grubbs, reassuringly. "But if Tom was in the area at the time of the crime, they are wondering what he might have witnessed outside the Assembly Hall. Sergeant Lawrence would like to have a conversation with Tom."

"He's out on the beach smoking. He's not allowed to smoke in the house. We have this agreement about where he can smoke. I'll walk you out there, but," she looked toward Grubbs, "have you explained Tom's fear of the police?"

"Alice, yes. And I've made it clear to both the sheriff and Sue that this questioning might have unexpected consequences. They were most insistent."

Sue followed, letting them lead the way across a chamomile lawn, and onto a path through the dune grass to the shore. She held back, giving Grubbs time to explain to Tom the situation before she entered the circle.

"I don't want to talk to her. Why is she here?"

"Tom, I just told you. She only needs a few minutes of your time. Will you please cooperate?"

"Do what Grubby says," counseled his mother. "You know he's always been your friend."

Tom looked over at Sue, then back at Grubbs and his mother. "Okay, but I've got important things to do. She can have five minutes."

"Can we sit over there?" asked Sue, pointing to weathered picnic table.

Tom stood up, brushed the sand off the back of his jeans, and ensconced himself on one side of the table.

"We'll leave you now," said Grubbs. "I'll wait in the car."

"What do you want?" asked Tom, lighting a cigarette.

"Saturday night, the night of the play, were you near the auditorium?"

"That was awhile ago, I don't know."

"People saw you there, you had a ticket to the play."

Tom looked thoughtful, "Ticket?" Then he smiled with delight. "It was a wonderful ticket, a piece of art. But those crazy little bitches, they wouldn't let me in. I went to one door and then the other. They laughed at me. I don't like that. I hate it when people laugh at me."

"When you couldn't get into the theater, what then?"

"I think I watched through a window, they were open. I could hear what was happening until it started to rain and thunder."

"Then what did you do?"

"Well, I don't know. I think I went down to the picnic area. It's covered. Yes, that's what I did. The picnic area."

"Could you see the Assembly Hall from there?"

"Lady, it was raining so hard I couldn't see anything. And then I almost got electrocuted. Boom, crash. I could smell sulfur. I knew the devil was lurking."

"Were there any lights on in the back of the auditorium?" asked Sue.

"There's one, you know, the kind that turns on when it gets dark. It's on the wall above some equipment stuff. It's always on, summer and winter."

"Was it on Saturday night?"

"Probably, till everything went out."

Tom tossed away the cigarette with his left hand.

"Do you remember seeing anyone on Saturday?"

He pulled another cigarette from a crumpled pack, removing the filter and flicking it with the index finger and thumb of his left hand toward the beach. He fumbled with the lighter, his hand unsteady, finally igniting the loose strands of tobacco that extended beyond the paper.

"Like I was telling you. There was someone out there. I remember wondering why they were in the rain. I thought maybe the devil. Maybe a witch." He looked at Sue, his eyes wide, his grin displaying tobacco-stained teeth.

"Man, woman?"

"It was…it was…a woman."

"Are you sure?"

"I know the difference…I gotta take this call." He fished a phone-like object from his pocket, gave Sue a quick glance, and said, "I had it on vibrate so we wouldn't be disturbed." Tom brought the object to his ear. "Hello. Garr. Hey dude, what's happening? How's the weather?"

He waited for the answer, then responded, "Hot. Hey, I'm not surprised, man. You were into some pretty deep shit…What am I doing? I'm talking to some police lady."

Tom listened for awhile, nodding his head, his eyes focused on Sue.

"Fuckers! Shot up the place! RPGs and firebombs! I know, get a lawyer and tell them to stay the fuck away! I'm on the case, dude. I won't tell them shit."

Tom stood, as he dropped the phone back into his pocket, he leaned over the table, his face only a few inches from Sue's. "Garr said you were the one. You were shooting at him. You blew his place up. You sent him across the river Styx. Bitch!" His final word was accompanied by a spray of spittle.

Sue remained still, fighting the impulse to push him out of her face.

"I'm not talking to you anymore. I know my constitution, my God given rights. Don't think you'll get me like you did Garr. Now I'm getting the fuck out of here. I just hope you don't shoot me in the back like you did to Garr."

Tom pushed himself up and then scampered down the beach in long strides, turning and looking back once just before he disappeared into the dunes.

Sue sat for a long moment, stood, and walked to the lake's edge. She looked at the point where Tom had entered into the woods, then quickly scanned the beach before reaching for her phone.

"I think we have a problem," she said when Ray answered. After the conversation, she walked back to the cottage to tell Grubbs and Alice Lea how her conversation with Tom had ended.

33

Ray stood near the empty boat slip with Terry McDaniel. As he listened, he looked down river past the seawall on the left to the open water of Lake Michigan. The wind was calm and the lake flat, with only a gentle swell breaking the mirror-like surface.

"I had just brought the grandkids in, my wife was running them back to the cottage. I was going to get more gas and do a few small maintenance jobs I had been putting off." McDaniel looked at Ray, "To be honest, Sheriff, I was looking forward to some quiet time. We've had the grandkids, four boys from five to ten, for almost two weeks. Don't get me wrong, they're great kids and all that, but two weeks. My wife does better at this than I do. But then, she used to be a third grade teacher."

"So tell me exactly what happened," pressed Ray.

"Well, Tom comes springing in here all breathless like. I've known him since he was a boy. So much promise, smart as a whip. You just never know what's going to happen. I guess we were lucky with our own kids. You know what I mean.

"So Tom arrives, says someone's after him. He wants to know if I would take him out on the lake for a while. I explain that I'm almost out of fuel, that we would have to stop at the marina. And I try to stall for a little while, saying there are a couple of things I need to do onshore first. As I climb on the dock, he jumps into the boat. Initially, I didn't think anything about it. I've been taking Tom out for years. It's very therapeutic for him. Being on the water is enormously healing, and I think it gives his mother a break. Alice, that's his mom, we go back a lot of years. Knew her when we were at Albion. That poor woman has…."

"Then what happened?"

"Well, I walked back to my car. Like I already told you, my wife had our other car with the grandkids. When I got back here, the slip was empty and my boat was heading down the river with Tom at the wheel. I've let him drive a lot. He's perfectly competent. I yelled at him, but I'm sure he couldn't hear me over the sound of the engine. This is a no-wake zone, but he wasn't paying attention to that. Tom was hell bent for open water. I don't know where he's going, but he doesn't have too much fuel."

"How far can he get?" asked Sue, who had been silent up to this point.

"I don't know for sure. There was a quarter of a tank, maybe less. If he holds it at full throttle, he'll burn it real fast."

"Any idea where he might be headed?"

"He likes the islands up north, but there's not enough fuel." He paused and looked out toward the lake. "Good thing its calm out there. He's not going to get bounced around waiting for a tow after the tank runs dry."

"When did this happen?" asked Sue.

McDaniel pulled a phone from his pants pocket and looked at the screen. "Musta been about an hour ago."

"Why did you wait so long to call us?" she asked.

"Tom can be a real joker on his good days. I thought he might turn the boat around, come back, and we'd have a good laugh. But that doesn't seem to be the case. He's probably off his meds and in full meltdown. He does that from time to time. If that's the situation now, who knows what might be going on in that screwed-up noodle of his."

"Was Tom carrying anything?"

"Like what?"

"A backpack where a gun or other weapon might be hidden."

"No, it was Tom in his summer uniform, old jeans and a T-shirt, the kind with the pocket for his phone and cigarettes. I never let him smoke on the boat."

"Have you called his mother? Does she know what's going on?"

"No, I thought I'd call you first. I didn't want to worry her. She will be frantic as soon as she hears. The poor woman has dedicated her life to that kid. Where will this all end?" McDaniel looked at Ray. "What are you going to do about this, Sheriff?"

"I'm thinking. What's the make, model, and color of your boat?"

"It's a Four Winns Sundowner, mostly white with some blue and tan trim."

"Do you have the registration number?" asked Ray.

"It's on the boat in my wallet. Like I said, I was going to get some gas. Is that going to be a problem?"

"No, we can pull it off a database if we need to. Are there any weapons on the boat: firearms, knives, flare gun?"

"No, nothing of that type. Sheriff, I don't want Tom arrested. I'm not going to press charges or anything. I just want him safely back on shore, and I'd like my boat back. This is all my fault, well at least partially."

Ray looked over at Sue. "Why don't you talk to Tom's mother, explain what happened, and that we are starting a search for the boat. And see if you can get a sense of the best way to talk him down."

"She may not be there," said Sue. "She and Grubbs were going to look for him. She tried to reassure me that it was probably nothing I did that set her son off. She said he has these episodes. He usually wanders home on his own, or she goes out and finds him."

Ray walked Sue to her Jeep. "Did you learn anything from Tom?"

"We just got to a point that sounded interesting. Tom said when it started raining he went down to the picnic shelter. He saw someone near the back of the auditorium."

"And?"

"Then he took a phone call, a call from Garr. And then he flipped out, accusing me of killing Garr. I really thought he was about to attack me, but he took off down the beach instead."

Ray just shook his head, "We better get going. There are only a few hours of light left. I'll establish a rendezvous point when we get a fix on the boat."

34

"This is Tom's usual pattern after he's had a meltdown," Alice Lea explained to Sue. "He goes into full panic mode. He believes that anyone who comes close to him is trying to kill him. And that's how he's gotten in trouble with the law. There have been a number of incidents where people have called the police for assistance in handling him when he's gone out of control. Tom just thinks he's going to die, but he's going to put up a good fight on the way. He sometimes ends up assaulting the police officers…it's just not pretty.

"I thought you would be okay, that you could question him without incident. He likes the attention of attractive women. Usually he's quite charming." She gave Sue a weak smile. "There are parts of his brain that are normal. In terms of threats, he differentiates by gender. Males are bad, women not. The really bad confrontations have always been with men. And most of these have led to his hospitalization."

"Can you walk me through one of the episodes?" asked Sue. "We need to know what to anticipate when we locate him."

Alice Lea looked thoughtful. "Simple question, complicated answer. The safest response is that there is no pattern you can depend on. That said, most of the time he crashes after one of these episodes. He falls into a deep sleep, sort of a stupor. When he wakes, he's usually lethargic the rest of the day. But that's not always the case. Sometimes he goes through this whole cycle a second time." She looked at her watch. "He gets his meds twice a day, so he's long past his afternoon doses. I don't know if that will make a difference."

"Does Tom have any weapons—guns, knives—or does he have access to anything like that in your house?"

"Absolutely not. There was a shotgun from my grandfather's time. I gave that away years ago. Tom has suicidal tendencies. He's tried it more than once. I've made sure there's nothing around that would give him an easy exit."

"He told me his friend Garr gave him a gun."

"Garr is a fantasy friend. I don't think he ever knew the man. But that's all Tom has talked about since that horrible day. Tom has some kind of romantic fantasy about that whole incident." She paused and looked at Sue, "What's going to happen now?"

"We will try to locate the boat. Mr. McDaniel told us there was very little fuel onboard. So if Tom took it way out into the lake, he's probably just sitting there. Or he might have landed somewhere and is off on foot."

"I need to be close by when you find Tom. His big fear is going back to the hospital. If he sees me, he knows he's alright."

"We will do our best to make sure that happens. Give me your cell number, and we'll stay in contact."

"I'll be back in a second, let me go write it down." Lea disappeared into the kitchen, reappearing a few minutes later.

She handed Sue a slip of paper, "I went to an early morning yoga class today. I had Tom's pillbox laid out with his breakfast," she held up the blue, plastic container. "He didn't take his meds this morning. This is not good."

"I will call you when we find him. Please bring those with you."

Ray handed Sue the binoculars. "You can see the boat just left of the island. That was probably his destination. He ran out of gas a few miles short and right smack in the shipping lane."

"Any signs of life?"

"Not that I've seen. The pilot of the coast guard chopper says someone is sprawled on the floor."

"That's consistent with what his mother told me." Sue quickly summarized her conversation with Alice Lea.

"So what's our plan?" Sue asked.

"Brett's on his way with the Zodiac. I thought we'd run out and tow him in. But given what you've just told me, that's not a good idea."

"There's not a lot of daylight."

"Two hours at best," said Ray.

Hanna Jeffers joined them. "Are we paddling?"

"No, change of plans. I'm sorry I didn't get back to you." Ray explained the situation.

"How about the doc?" asked Sue, looking at Hanna.

"We can't put her in that situation."

"So what are you suggesting?" asked Hanna. "I paddle out there, check out the situation, and see if I can get him comfortable enough that you can tow him in without him jumping into deep water?"

"That's the idea?" said Sue.

"We can't put a civilian…."

"I've dealt with this kind of situation lots of time, especially in Iraq. Help me get my boat off the car."

Hanna Jeffers dipped one paddle blade into the water, then the other, side to side, catch, pull, rotate. Connected acts, each contributing to the rhythm that propelled her long, slender kayak through the mirror-like surface. From the launch point, her destination was less than two miles out. The marine radio on her chest was switched off, as was the phone in the waterproof bag secured under the bungees on the deck in front of her.

Her target had been in view from the moment Ray pushed her kayak away from the shore. As she approached nearer, she could make out the lines of a speedboat sitting dead in the water. When she was twenty yards away, she stopped paddling and listened. A steady, pulsating sound came from the direction of the boat, deep breathing or perhaps snoring.

She closed the distance by half and shouted in the direction of the craft. "Hello, anyone on board?"

No response, just the sound again, louder. She paddled to the stern of the powerboat and secured her boat to the teak swim deck. She released her spray skirt and carefully climbed onto the deck. Then she peered into the boat. Tom was sprawled on the floor, eyes closed, chest gently rising and falling.

"Hello," Hanna said. She repeated herself three more times, raising the volume of her voice each time. There was still no response. She moved closer, grabbing a shoeless foot and shaking it, first gently, and then more vigorously, her gaze fixed on Tom's face.

One eye opened, closed, and opened again, this time wider, slowly moving in her direction.

Hanna tensed, surveying the boat for possible weapons and routes of escape. She had been in this situation before in the military, dealing with patients emerging from psychotic episodes, some quiet and spent, others physically and emotionally out of control.

"Are you okay?" she asked softly. She held her position beyond his grasp.

The other eye opened. "Bitch, you killed…."

" I didn't kill anyone. I'm here to help you."

Tom crawled forward to the front of the boat, sprawled on the cushions and looked back at Hanna.

"Where did you come from?"

"My kayak, it's tied up back there. I saw the boat dead in the water. I thought maybe the driver had a heart attack or something. I'm a doctor. I came onboard to see if someone needed help. What's your name?"

"I don't need any help."

"It's going to be dark soon. It's already starting to cool off. Don't you want to be on shore? Get a warm meal."

"I'm good to go. I like sleeping under the stars."

"Storm coming in later tonight. You're going to get tossed around when it hits."

"I'm thirsty. Got anything to drink?"

"Water. Want me to get you a bottle?"

"I need caffeine. How about Rock Star or Red Bull?"

"All I have is water. You want a bottle? I have to go back to my kayak."

"Okay, water."

Hanna moved toward the stern, her eyes fixed on Tom. She crawled onto the transom and pulled a plastic water bottle from under the bungees. Then she moved forward in the boat and rolled the bottle toward Tom.

"How do I know you didn't put anything in this?"

"Check it out. It's sealed. Just twist the top."

"Are you a cop?"

"I told you, I'm a doctor."

"Why are you wearing a knife on your life vest?"

Hanna looked down at knife. How could have I been so stupid? she thought.

"It's a piece of safety equipment. It's for emergencies."

"Let me see it."

"You want a power bar. You must be hungry."

"I want to see your knife."

Hanna pulled a bar from her vest and tossed it in his direction. "Double chocolate. Red Bull in a bar," She moved back in the boat, getting into a defensive position. In a soft voice she instructed, "Eat the bar. It will make you feel better." She switched on her radio.

"That water was poisoned, and now you're trying to give something else. You cops are all alike. You killed Garr and now you're after me." He tossed the bar at her, then the water bottle. Pulling himself to his feet, he started toward her, finally lunging in her direction. Hanna moved to the side, tripping him with her hand as he went past her. He fell hard on the carpeted deck, his head striking the back of the boat.

Hanna scrambled toward the bow and waited for Tom's next move. After a minute or two she cautiously crept closer. He appeared to be unconscious.

"I need help now," she said, squeezing the transmit button on her radio. The Zodiac that had been lurking a half mile off the stern, roared to life. Soon Ray and Sue were at Hanna's side as she checked Tom's vitals.

Hanna was in scrubs, waiting as Ray came through the emergency entrance. "I just talked to the radiologist. The CT scan is unremarkable. They sedated Tom for the scan. He's awake now, but remains quite subdued. His mother is with him. He's been admitted for observation and most likely will be released in the morning." She chuckled.

"What?" asked Ray.

"I was in the room when Tom started to become aware of his surroundings. He kept looking at me with this confused expression. Finally he said, "You really are a doctor.""

35

$\sim$

S hortly before 9:00 A.M. Ray slowly rolled through the three-block long business district of the Harbor Village. Most of the brick buildings lining both sides of the street were constructed after the great fire of 1906. Once a thriving mercantile hub for farmers, lumbermen, and sailors, the stores now catered to the tourist trade with windows filled with t-shirts, sandals, summer frocks, and regional art—seascapes in oil and watercolors. The summer people and tourists were already filling the streets, heading to the coffee shops, the bakery, and restaurants in search of breakfast.

A few blocks away from the lake, a series of widely spaced, single-story structures—most constructed of cement block—housed auto and marine repair facilities and the shops and businesses of the local tradesmen. Ray pulled onto the blacktop lot in front of North Lakes Electrical and Fire Equipment. He sat in the car for a few minutes, not wanting to interrupt the final movement of Schubert's Trout Quintet. As the last note faded, he switched off the engine and emerged into the hot, humid air of the August morning. He crossed the threshold, the front door propped open by an old electric motor.

The counterman, short and round, looked up from the sports page of the Record Eagle as Ray approached. "Can I help you, Sheriff?"

"Is Dale in?"

"He's back in his office." He pointed to a hallway that ran along the left side of the building. "It's the one at the end."

Dale Van Beers was on the phone, his head bent to the right holding the phone, his eyes on a computer display, his fingers moving on the keyboard as he talked. He noted Ray's presence with his eyes and a nod. Ray could tell from the conversation that he was doing his best to bring it to an end. Finally, Dale rang off.

"Hey, Ray. It's been awhile," he said extending his hand.

"How's business?" asked Ray, settling onto a gray steel chair.

"We're keeping the lights on. That's an achievement in this economy. What can I do for you?"

"You service the fire extinguishers and other safety equipment over at the Old Mission Summer Colony?"

"Yes, have for decades. That was one of my father's accounts, maybe my grandfather's, too."

"That includes the emergency egress lights, the ones in the Assembly Hall?"

"Yes? What's happened?"

"They lost power Saturday. And…."

"Half the county was out, on and off. And I was worried about those lights in the Assembly Hall. I was hoping that situation wasn't going to come back and bite me in the ass. Am I in trouble?"

"Dale, this is part of a murder investigation."

"Yeah, the murder. I read about that. Guy was a big shooter, huh. Big bucks from Chicago with that concrete and glass house. I bid on that house. The job would have covered my retirement."

Ray nodded. "Yes, all of the above. And the egress lights not working just seemed way too convenient. I was wondering if…."

"If you're thinking about sabotage or something, there's a possibility. I can even name a suspect, not an actual suspect by name, but I can provide a pretty good description."

Ray noted that Dale's expression had gone from one of concern to one of mirth.

"That whole egress lighting system is older than the hills, first generation stuff that was installed right after the fire code made those things mandatory. It's needed replacing for years. We do the whole nine yards out there, routine inspection and recharging of the extinguishers, no problem there. The cost is built into the colony's maintenance budget.

Same is true for the service on the egress lights. They need to be inspected and the batteries and charging units need to be swapped out from time to time. But replacing the whole system, that's a problem. It's a capital expense item, and Grubbs never seems to have the funds for it. So we've been cobbling the system together the past several years. The original manufacturer has moved all its production to China and is no longer providing parts for these old units. The last few years I've been getting parts by cannibalizing units we've pulled from churches and schools as they've upgraded. The colony is the last of our customers that still has this old stuff. But we had an incident last week that…well…brought everything to a head.

"What was it, Thursday, Grubbs calls all concerned about an electrical kind of burning smell in the back of the Assembly Hall. I rushed over there personally. As soon as I got into that back hallway, I knew where the problem was. The egress lighting unit over west door was smoldering."

"And the cause?"

"Mice. It was crammed full with acorns. They must have been chewing on some of the wires, too. This has always been a problem with those units, especially in a building like that. It's easy for the mice to run along the walls and follow the Romex into the unit. Probably a great place to spend the winter, a heat source and a good supply of food.

"The unit was toast, Ray. Grubbs wanted me to repair or replace it, but I didn't have anything. So I made a pitch that this was the time to replace the whole shebang. First, pointing out that they had become a fire hazard. Then I gave him my usual sales pitch, and it's all true. The new units are more reliable, energy efficient, and have come way down in price. They are also rodent proof, according to their manufacturer. He said he'd find the money, and I put in the order as soon as I got back to the office. The replacement lights came FedEx late yesterday. I'll have everything back together by quitting time."

"Sure it was mice, no chance of sabotage?"

"Yup. It isn't the first time it's happened. There was no sign that anyone not having four paws had tampered with the interior." He looked at Ray, his tone becoming more serious. "So here's what I was dealing with. I had to take this unit out of service. I could have wired around it, but I started to wonder about the other units. Grubbs was telling me that he didn't think the system had ever been activated, not once in his memory. So the easiest thing to do was pull the breaker. I didn't want anyone noticing it was tripped and flipping it back on. So I deactivated the whole system, all the egress lights. I'm the responsible party. Grubbs told me about the play, and I advised him to make sure that every usher had a flashlight, a new one that worked for sure on the off chance that there was a need for emergency lighting. So am I in trouble with the law?"

"I think you were being prudent, and you gave Grubbs good counsel. I imagine the fire marshal will be pleased to see the improvements on his next inspection."

36

~

"Just the lunch you ordered," said Sue, unpacking a brown paper bag. "One tofu burger with a side of chipotle, brown rice, and a kefir ginger shake. Bon appétit." She gave him a mocking glance and under her breath said, "I couldn't live like that."

"And what are you having?" asked Ray, noticing a grease spot on the side of the bag.

"A half-pound burger from free-range buffalo, topped with farmhouse, aged-goat cheese from the new creamery up in Northport, and organic sweet potatoes fries. I just go for the healthy stuff now. It's your influence, Ray." She gave him a mocking smile. "I see you revamped our suspect chart."

"I'm trying to get some focus. I would like to see if we could start dropping some people, at least tentatively. I would like to get them in rank order and start a second round of interviews." He studied the chart and looked over at Sue. "I had trouble sleeping last night. With all the summer people leaving in the next two weeks, I can just see this case slipping away. By Labor Day we'll be talking to ourselves."

Sue, eyeing the chart, said, "You've got another column on the right."

"Yes, we've discussed this. It would have been difficult for one person to pull off this murder. With some careful planning and execution... unintended pun...."

"But the perfect word," agreed Sue.

"What I'm getting at is another way of looking at suspects. Who is the killer, and who assisted them? It might be easier to identify the person who turned off the power, and then go after the killer."

"Agreed, but everyone on your list could have flipped the switch. That's the painless part of this crime."

"I was thinking that the switch puller might be easier to break down than the killer. My theory is that we're dealing with two personalities."

"What did you learn from the fire-safety guy?"

"Dale Van Beers."

"Exactly."

"I learned that neither Grubbs nor anyone else could have tampered with the egress lights. Mice and acorns, not humans. Grubbs called him late last week when one of the units was smoldering. Van Beers diagnosed the problem then removed the circuit breaker as a safety precaution. He's got replacement units going in today."

"Good for the mice. Damn convenient of them to lend a helping paw."

"This crime had to be weeks in the planning. But with the egress lights being deactivated, the perp must have thought everything was falling their way. Back to the chart, look at Grubbs. If we were doing this just based on ticks on the chart, he'd be the big winner, or loser. Multiple motives perhaps involving his late wife, his estranged daughter, and years of taking abuse from Wudbine. So how does he set up the murder? He invites us to the performance, slips away at the break, and has an accomplice who pulls the switch. Then he calls us to the site of the crime."

"That would be quite brilliant," agreed Sue. "And he is clearly not lacking in intelligence. I'm sure he could envision this crime on all sorts of levels, like one of the multi-tiered chessboards. He knows the place, the people, and all the complex histories. And he'd know where to dump the murder weapon. He could have even done that in stages, maybe get it out of the building on his way to fetching us, and then move it a second time while we were attending to other things."

"And who would handle the power?" asked Ray. "Verity?"

"Possible. They have a long history here. Or how about his daughter?"

"That would be clever. The kid he's been estranged from for years helping him pull off a murder. What would be her motive?"

"Maybe she's tired of her father-in-law treating her husband poorly. With Malcolm out of the way they could sell off the business, move to Provence, buy a small farm and some goats, and start producing artisanal chévre. That would have to be much more rewarding then peddling stock and bonds or looking after the legal affairs of a cantankerous old fart."

"I think the chévre in your sandwich has gone to your head. Or are you telling me about a new pastoral fantasy? Are you and Harry getting ready for a year in Provence?"

"I don't think so. I was going to be the consummate tour director this week. Remember, I was going to take the week off. Instead, Harry is spending days looking after Simone and evenings with a slightly grumpy me."

"You're never grumpy."

"Yes, but something weird is going on. Maybe I don't like my space being invaded. He's been working hard to make really nice meals. I appreciate that. But he leaves the kitchen a mess. In Chicago, someone cleans his apartment every morning. I don't know if he's inherently messy, or it's something he's learned he can get away with. I mean, he tries to clean up, but it's just not good enough. I'd be happy with Healthy Choice and no cleanup. And I'm not sure that…. enough of this. Let's go back to your chart."

"Hold that for a minute. Let's think about the perp. To pull this off they have to be able to isolate Malcolm. That's not easy to do. Having him alone and in a vulnerable position is most unusual. Whoever did the crime was very familiar with Malcolm's movements."

"Members of the cast would be aware of that."

"Yes, and they would know the history of the electrical problems, how to turn the power off, and the possible impediments to achieving success."

"Like David Johnson, the lighting guy."

"You got it," said Ray.

"David seems to have motive, and he was less than honest with us," said Sue.

"No one likes being a chump, especially smart people who think they know about money and then lose a pile in a bad investment. You can understand his anger. Much of his retirement went away, and Malcolm seemed unscathed."

"But that was just a normal market fluctuation," countered Sue. "We've talked about this before. There's never been a suggestion that Malcolm was running any kind of scam. The SEC isn't after him. There are no criminal cases pending. Johnson is a smart man. In spite of his rage, he knows Malcolm wasn't really responsible."

"Shortly before you were hired, we had a case where a man shot his doctor because he was chronically ill and not getting better. The shooter wasn't dotty, mad, drunk, or on drugs. He seemed to be absolutely all there when I questioned him. He needed someone to blame. He needed a focus for his rage. His anger was really at his body because it was failing him, but he externalized it and went after his physician."

Ray paused, "But Johnson is of interest for another reason. He was the one person who had a clear view of most of the backstage area, the exception being the far side of the set. To pull this crime off, the perp had to get him out of his loft. They also had to know that when the lights went out, Johnson would be the one who would go into action. And they timed it, just like we did."

"But Johnson could be the perfect accomplice," said Sue.

"But he would have to know that we would be looking at him closely. I think he's too smart for that. As you know, I never claim infallibility, but I don't think he's involved."

"And then we have Tom Lea's claim that it was a woman who pulled the switch."

"Did he give you anything more?"

"No, that's when we were interrupted by the phone call from Garr. How would you like to see Lea on the stand as a witness for the prosecution?"

"Well, he could never do that, but what if his observation was correct? Not that we can go with it 100%, but the possibility is important. I wonder if you could talk to him again and see if you could get anything more?"

"Based on my track record from my last interview?"

"Phone his mother, explain the situation. Ask for her guidance. Let's see what happens. Essentially, you have one or two questions. Five minutes."

"The changes in the chart?" Sue was looking at the whiteboard. "Friends and family, or more correctly, employees and family."

"When we're not moving at warp speed, in a case like this we'd start with the family and close associates. In the beginning we focused on the scene, searching for the weapon, and looking for other physical evidence. It also seemed that someone—cast, crew, ushers, Grubbs—would have seen something that might have led us to the perp. Nada. So let's really look at the family."

"But we haven't interviewed everyone who was backstage yet."

"I know, but we talked to them en masse, gave out cards, and asked for their assistance. And I talked to Grubbs about the folks we haven't interviewed this morning on my way back. We went one by one through the list. They are mostly in their 20s and 30s, with a few teens thrown in. Grubbs doesn't believe that any of them have a history with Malcolm. So I think we should put them aside for the moment."

"Makes sense." Sue was silent for a long moment, looking at Ray. "You look tired."

"I needed to sleep last night, and it didn't happen. All of these people were floating through my brain. I need to go for a long paddle, a couple of days, where I don't think about this. But we don't have that luxury, do we?"

"So what's the plan?"

"I wish we had a solid reason to request a search warrant for Gull House and the out buildings."

"What are you looking for?"

Ray chuckled, "That's why we don't have a good reason. It would be fishing trip, a chance to snag something that might move the investigation forward."

"In the meantime?"

"I want to talk to Verity again. I want Grubbs to tell me how he found the body. Why was he onstage? Then I would like to chat with Pepper and Alyson, separately. Malcolm surrounded himself with beautiful young women. What was going on there? Did he give these women a motive to off him? Then there's Elliott, and his wife, the devoted daughter-in-law. I think we're just starting to understand the complexity of all these relationships."

37

Ray knocked, paused, and then knocked a second time. Just as he was about to leave, the curtain moved. A blurry-eyed Verity peered out at him. "What do you want?"

"I have a few more questions for you." He stood and waited, finally the door swung open.

Verity blocked his entrance. "I have nothing more to tell you. You're wasting my time and taxpayers' money," she argued, her breath reeking of alcohol.

"I need to clarify a few things."

"Alright, alright, come in. Sit there at the table. I've just made some coffee. Do you want a mug?

"Please. Black."

Verity placed a mug in front of him and filled it with coffee from a thick glass carafe, spilling some on the table and muttering an obscenity. She came back with a dish towel and clumsily wiped the surface. She dropped into the chair across from him, adding brandy, sugar and cream to her mug, and stirring slowly.

"I don't know why you bother with me. Can't you leave an old woman to her own grieving and sadness?"

"From our last conversation, I didn't get the impression that you were going to do much grieving."

193

"I'm not grieving for that bastard, Malcolm. The devil can take him. I'm grieving for all of us. This is our little paradise, and it's been ruined, at least for this year. And for me, at my stage of life, every summer is magical, a special gift. And it's been stolen away.

"And like I said, I don't know why you are talking to me. You just don't seem to get it, Sheriff. Malcolm was part of the billionaires' club. Somewhere across the face of this planet people are celebrating. Maybe they are in Dubai or Abu Dhabi, perhaps Hong Kong or Beijing, or close like New York or Chicago, or somewhere in Europe, Paris, London.

"What you have to understand is Malcolm was a giant in a very exclusive club. He was smart and very shrewd. But perhaps most importantly, he was a worker. When he was on a project, Malcolm's focus was there for 12, 14, 16 hours a day. People thought he was a gambler. He never gambled. He carefully calculated every investment and didn't buy in until he knew that he was going to be successful. If that had been the end of it, it wouldn't have been so bad. But Malcolm needed more. After he crushed someone in a business deal, he'd go out of his way to humiliate them further if he could.

"I don't mean to be disparaging, Sheriff, but you are out of your league. In your wildest imagination you can't envisage the world I'm talking about. You're giving those men in far away places a good chuckle. There's no way in hell that a backwoods sheriff in a one-horse town is ever going to figure this one out. You'd need the FBI and Interpol and scores of lawyers and accountants to discover what Malcolm's been up to and who he's screwed. What I'm telling you is that he had a heart of coal, as black as they come. He was a greatly flawed person. He obviously pushed the wrong people too far.

"And you can't even begin to fathom the resources that were brought to bear in this assassination. I wonder how many people were on the ground, blending in, casing the place. Look how perfectly everything was done. And then they were gone. And ever since, you've been muddling around, looking through people's trash, making a nuisance of yourself. You can go around and annoy people till hell freezes over, and you're not going to find anything. There's nothing here. Nothing." She took several gulps of coffee and added more brandy. "So why don't you just leave us alone?"

"If you're finished with your rant, I've got a few questions for you," said Ray.

Verity didn't respond verbally, she just looked across the table scornfully.

"You're telling me that this murder was done by outsiders, hired killers, right?"

"Absolutely."

"But when we last talked, you told me you didn't remember seeing anyone who looked out of place. Now you're telling me that a team of assassins, hired by Mr. Wudbine's enemies, is responsible for the crime."

They sat in silence for several minutes. Then Verity responded, "Well, I think I told you that no one in the colony was responsible. Given the way you and your people have been running around here like chickens with their heads cut off, you obviously didn't get the message. I compliment you on your diligence, and forgive you for your complete naiveté."

"My lady doth protest too much, methinks."

Verity gave Ray a startled look and chuckled, "So what are you thinking. I'm like one of those plovers on the beach trying to lead you away from my eggs?"

"I'm just reflecting on what you've told me. You've been a summer resident all your life. You know everyone connected with this place and their histories. You've told me you don't recall seeing anyone around in recent weeks who shouldn't have been here. And then you very aggressively contend that the murder was the work of professional killers hired by billionaires from far-off places. It doesn't add up. And even if you don't have any knowledge of the crime, you do have people you would probably like to protect: your son, perhaps your daughter-in-law, and Richard Grubbs, among others. And then there are people like Brenda Wudbine. If you thought she helped off your ex, perhaps you would feel you owed her some loyalty." Ray paused and looked at her. "It would be ever so convenient if we went away. That's not going to happen."

Verity looked across the table, stood, picked up the carafe, and reached over and filled his mug. "It may be a bit tepid. Do you want me to put it in the microwave?"

"No. Let's go over the same territory again. The night of the performance and during the weeks leading up to that time, did you see anyone around who didn't seem to fit here?"

Verity was not quick to answer. "Like I said, lots of people come through here, visitors and whatnot, but I can't say I saw anyone suspicious lurking about."

"Elliott, your son, how did he and his father get on?"

"Do I have to answer questions about family members?"

"No. And if you know anything incriminating, I'm sure you wouldn't tell me."

"I won't say Elliott adored his father, but they seemed to have a good working relationship. I was almost a bit jealous of how close they were."

"And the daughter-in-law, Jill?"

"She was Malcolm's right-hand person. He's been obsessed with his legacy, as if good acts now would compensate for all the crap he's pulled over the years. Jill has been the key player in his foundation. She's the person that's made it all work."

"How do you get on with her?"

"Like I think I told you in one way or another, we don't really have a relationship. I don't understand why. I've tried. We've never clicked."

"You told me you were reviewing your lines before the second scene. Do you remember seeing her about that time?"

"Yes and no. There was a swirl of activity in the green room. I probably saw everyone unconsciously or…well, you know what I mean. I don't remember having a conversation with anyone during that time. I can't say that I saw her or didn't see her."

"How about Pepper Markley?"

"The same."

"How about Alyson Mickels?"

"You should ask some of the male cast members, she's a real head turner. Alyson was around a lot. She was just part of the usual scenery. I wouldn't have especially noticed her.

"You know…and this just occurred to me, if someone wanted to get close to Malcolm, that would be the way to do it. For decades he's been surrounding himself with his 'special' assistants. And they all come out of the same mold: young, beautiful, and ambitious. And they are smart, I've got to give them credit for that."

"The tone of your voice, what are you suggesting?"

"Come on, Sheriff, you weren't born yesterday. His special assistants… how should I put it? Of course, he was sleeping with them. I have been told that Malcolm bragged about a casting couch. It has also been rumored that he joked about a farm system where he developed new talent. You see, Sheriff, it's about sex, but also a lot more than sex. It's about dominance and control. He loved travelling around with a beautiful young woman attending to his every need. He liked to show off for his competitors. I don't know if they were impressed or just thought he was an old fool."

She paused and refilled their cups again. "This is what I'm thinking, Sheriff. If you wanted to get close to Malcolm, buy one of his assistants. Take Pepper, for instance. She handled his daily schedule, made all his travel and hotel reservations. And, of course, she was in the Murder at the Vicarage. Pepper could provide key information for anyone planning an assassination. And I imagine much the same could be said about Alyson. Two beautiful young women, who already have a track record for making their services available to the highest bidder. For a million dollars, maybe less, I'm sure you could buy their services."

"Do you have anything to support this scenario?" asked Ray.

"No. But, Sheriff, you are such a provincial. I'm just trying to open your eyes to the possibilities. You're not going to find the killer in the colony. You're wasting your time."

"How about Brenda, Mrs. Wudbine," asked Ray, "why would she tolerate the behavior you are suggesting?"

"Brenda was one of those special assistants back in the day. Now she's an incurable alcoholic with a very bad heart. The alcohol, that's how she dealt with it. In recent years she's been smashed most of the time. They lived separate lives. I imagine Malcolm was just waiting for her to go away. In fact, that thought had crossed my mind. I was wondering who Malcolm would end up with if dear, dear Brenda suddenly exited her worldly existence."

She looked at Ray. "You see what this conversation has done. It's brought back all the anger. For years I've done my best just to think about the positive parts of Malcolm's personality. And now you have me blathering on about his heart of coal."

"So tell me about the positive parts."

"He has an extraordinary eye for beauty, and not just in women. Look at that house of his. Yes, he hired a gifted architect, but he was a major player in the design. And when you walk through the place, it's a museum of the best modern furniture of the last 100 years. Every piece is iconic."

"And the piano?"

"Yes, one of many he's acquired along the way. If I'm not mistaken, that's a Bosendorfer. Very contemporary, isn't it. I imagine it was a custom design." She paused, then continued, "Like I was saying, positive things. Malcolm was a terrific jazz pianist. He liked to spend time in New Orleans, hanging out in the jazz clubs, getting invited to sit in. His foundation has supported starting jazz programs at traditional Black colleges. See, he did many good things."

"How about the bass standing next to the piano. Did he play that, also?"

"No, that's my daughter-in-law's, the ice princess. You wouldn't know that watching her play. She dances with that instrument. And she smiles, most uncharacteristic of her. When she and Elliott decided to marry, there was a rumor going around that Malcolm had arranged the whole thing so he would have a bass player available at his beck and call. And she certainly has been more of a devoted assistant to Malcolm than much of a wife to Elliott, not that he probably noticed."

"I'm not quite following,"

"It's hard to follow, Sheriff. You are listening to an angry, rambling old woman. Elliott, my dear son. He's smart, but he's very weak. There came a time when I could no longer protect him from his father. He, too, was a faithful servant. And I've never understood that marriage. Elliott seems to be asexual, an absolute contrast to his father. When he was younger I wondered if he was gay. And his wife…well. Sheriff, I'm tired of talking. Is there anything else?"

"Not for now, thank you."

"Remember, the killer is not among us. I'd call the FBI. You need some serious help."

38

S ue parked her Jeep off the side of the road at the bottom of the drive and walked up the sandy two-track toward the cottage.

Alice Lea greeted her halfway up the drive. "I see you're dressed in mufti today," she commented, eyeing Sue's jeans and light-blue polo shirt.

"Your son gave me an excuse to escape from my uniform for a day. This is a lot more comfortable."

"Well, you look good in jeans." Before they reached the cottage, Alice Lea paused and turned toward Sue. "I wanted to chat with you a few minutes before you meet with Thomas. First, I want to thank you and Sheriff Elkins for the way you handled that situation. I know that it could've ended quite badly for him.

"I have to take some responsibility for his meltdown. You see, Thomas was off his meds that day. I won't always be around, so I've been working to have him take responsibility for his medication. That morning I didn't check. This morning I did. There should be no problem. He's looking forward to talking to you. I've got some coffee set up in the kitchen, and I've given him permission to smoke. If you don't mind, I'd like to be in the area. If it looks like Thomas is going to have another meltdown, I can usually intercede and prevent it from happening."

"That's fine. I only have a few questions for him. I'm not sure he can answer them. But there is a chance he might have seen something on Saturday night that could help us find Malcolm Wudbine's murderer."

Unlike the last time, Tom Lea greeted Sue enthusiastically, shaking her hand and almost reluctantly letting go of it. They settled across the table, Alice pouring coffee and pushing a plate of cookies in Sue's direction.

Sue pulled her phone from her jeans pocket and pushed against the power button. "I'm turning my phone off, Tom. I don't want our conversation to be interrupted. I wonder if you could do the same?"

"I don't have to do that. It's got this built-in, artificial intelligence algorithm. It knows that when I'm having an important conversation I shouldn't be interrupted. Fantastic technology. Absolutely cutting-edge."

"We were interrupted in our last conversation," Sue chided. Instantly, she thought that was probably not a useful thing to bring up, but it was too late to pull it back.

"Yeah, I remember that. An unfortunate interruption. It won't happen. I downloaded the newest iteration of the software, 20.6.8. Now it knows when I'm having a significant conversation. No more interruptions."

"Remember what I was asking you about? You were telling me that you were under the picnic enclosure. From your vantage point you could see the back of the Assembly Hall. You said that you could see someone near the electrical panels."

"Yes, I remember."

"Tell me about the person you saw. Do you know who they were?"

"No, I didn't know them."

"What do you remember? Old or young? Male or female?"

"It was a woman."

"How could you tell?"

"She was wearing a raincoat. It was long, probably black or dark blue, maybe tan but darker because it was wet. And it had a belt at the waist. It was the shape of a woman. No man has a waist like that. Look at yours. It's clear that you're a woman. That's what I saw."

"And what did you see this person do?"

"They came up through the woods, not where I was but from the other side. The light on the back of the building was on, but she was staying in the shadows. Then there was a big crash of lightning and the lights flickered on and off and back on. By then, she was up near the side of the building. There must've been a hasp or something holding the doors covering the electrical panels closed, because she struggled with it for a moment. Then I saw her reach in and all the lights went out, and she came in my direction. She didn't see me. I got down, trying to stay out of sight.

I knew what she had done, and I sure as hell didn't want to get blamed for it. She came under the roof where I was hiding. I'm surprised she didn't see me. She stopped, lit a cigarette, and then got out of there fast. That's all I know."

"Did you notice anything else? Hair color? Tall or short?"

"Tall, maybe. But there was one more thing. The smell. It was the scent of a woman, but not perfume."

"Shampoo, soap, something like that?"

"No. It was one of those herbal things. Aromatherapy, you know what I'm talking about?"

"Thomas is an authority on this," offered Alice Lea. "Aren't you? It sometimes really helps him with some of his moods."

"Can you tell me anything more? Do you have a name for it?"

"Let me think. It helps with meditation. And it's very strong. People usually blend it with lots of other oils."

"Tom, does it have a name?"

"It's not sandalwood, or Juniper, or bergamot. It's just on the tip of my tongue. You know how it is when an idea is just floating around in your brain, and you just can't quite catch it. Maybe if you come back tomorrow, I'll remember. I'll keep a pad by me, so if it suddenly comes to me I can write it down."

Sue sat and looked across the table. She took several slow breaths, holding Tom in her gaze. "This is really important, friend. If you could remember the name, you would really be helping me out."

He pulled a cigarette from a package and carefully removed the filter, dropping it in the ashtray. He lit a kitchen match with the nail of his thumb, brought it to the cigarette, inhaled slowly, then exhaled, looking toward the ceiling. "Patchouli oil, I think that's it." He slowly spelled out the name, "p-a-t-c-h-o-u-l-i."

"You're sure of that?"

"Absolutely. Scents leave one of the strongest impressions on the brain. That woman was wearing patchouli oil."

Sue looked at her notepad. Finally, she thought. Finally.

"Aren't you going to asked me who else was there, under the picnic shelter? There were bundles of new shingles in stacks, and I was hiding between the stacks. I could see them, but they didn't have a clue that I was there."

"You took the question right out of my mouth," said Sue. "Tell me, who else was there?"

39

"It's good you got hold of me today. I'll be going back to Chicago tomorrow," said Pepper Markley as she plopped into a chair across from Ray. He perceived by the tone of her voice and her body language that something clearly was not right.

"You sound as if you're not planning to come back."

"That seems to be it. I got a call from the head HR person at Wudbine Investments early this morning, I mean it wouldn't have been 8:00 in Chicago yet. I've been terminated. Ms. Ridley said my last day is officially Friday, but that the family would prefer that I leave the premises at my earliest convenience. "

"How do you feel about that?"

"Stunned, just stunned. And get this," Pepper was shaking with rage, "the severance package, two weeks. Can you imagine? It's like getting knocked down and then stomped on. I was planning on leaving this position soon, but not like this. Malcolm had promised me that I would be well taken care of as I transitioned to my next job, either within the company or somewhere else in the industry. I was interested in becoming a stock analyst. Malcolm had taught me a lot in our day-to-day conversations."

Ray peered across the narrow desk that separated them. Before this interview he had been thinking about how he might get beyond the corporate loyalty she had displayed during their first interview. The Wudbines had provided some unexpected help.

"Did they give you a reason for your termination?"

"Not at all. Ms. Ridley, that's the HR person, young and officious, just said the family no longer needed my services, and that there was nowhere else in the company where my skill set met current job openings. Skill set, what BS. I've got an MBA from Chicago and almost three years of tutoring from one of the best minds in the industry. I can do almost any job in the organization.

"It's not just getting sacked, Sheriff. There's a whole question of housing. In the summer I live in an apartment on the grounds near Gull House. When we're in Chicago, I live in an apartment near Malcolm's penthouse. The housing was part of my compensation package. That was the arrangement. Mr. Wudbine wanted me close, so I was always available. Like I said, it's not just getting sacked. Now I have to find someplace to live, move, and then start a job search. This isn't how Wudbine Investments treats its employees. They always provide generous termination packages." She slowed, catching her breath. "The firm has been downsizing in recent years. Everyone who was downsized out received their salary and insurance for six months. And there was usually a fairly lavish handshake, too, depending on years of service. When I pressed Ridley about this, she just blew me off with some sarcastic comment about my lack of gratitude."

"You have no kind of contract?"

"Nothing like that, we are all at-will employees. But my getting sacked, this doesn't happen at Wudbine, not normally. On Monday, Elliott assured me that they would continue to need my services, now perhaps more than ever, those were his words. And today, this. Go figure. I don't think I'm even being credited for unused vacation. I'll probably have to sue for that."

Markley look at Ray, her anger now seemed to be directed at him. "Why am I here? I've already told you everything I know." She stared at him for a long moment. "They aren't trying to implicate me in this whole mess, are they? That would be the final…."

"Nothing of the sort. We're just beginning to conduct a second set of interviews with people who were close to the crime scene or had special knowledge of the victim. And you, obviously, fit both of those criteria."

"Well, I don't know anything more than I did a few days ago."

"We often find that witnesses, after overcoming the initial shock and horror of a traumatic event, remember details that help with an investigation. So I'm going to cover much of the same ground we covered before. First, how did it happen that you were in the play? Wasn't this a big time commitment, given all work responsibilities you've told me about?"

"I think I told you that Malcolm encouraged me to take the part. But it was more than that. No one showed up at tryouts who was right for the role. I'm talking about age and appearance. So, I was pressed into service by Mr. Wudbine. I sort of objected, but I learned long ago that was a waste of time. He always got what he wanted. I don't know what's the best way to describe him, persistent or insistent. And, in truth, it turned out that I really enjoyed being in the play. It got me away from Gull House. I met many interesting people that I'd only seen in passing during previous summers. I was having a wonderful time. It really strengthened my resolve to find a new job. And then everything fell apart."

"Ms. Markley, the night of the murder, the perpetrator was probably in the theater early on. The killer might have been someone who slipped into the stage area and secreted himself or herself very successfully, and after the crime effected a successful getaway. Or the murderer might have been one of your fellow actors, or a member of the crew. Someone had to notice something."

"You left me out of your list of possible suspects, Sheriff. And I should be near the top. I knew all the minute details of Mr. Wudbine's schedule, the inner workings of his home and office, and I was close to the murder scene at the time of his death."

"That's all true. Is there some reason I should move you up on the list? Can you suggest a motive?"

Pepper gave him a sardonic smile. "Saturday, I had no motive. Today there are several people I'd like to off. But Malcolm isn't on the list. I'm sure he had nothing to do with my current situation."

"Your relationship with Mr. Wudbine, had it changed in recent months?"

"By changed, do you mean was it strained?"

"That's one possibility," answered Ray.

"I don't think so. We both knew it was time for me to move my career forward. My leaving would have been a greater inconvenience to Jill. I really have been the concierge, taking care of the details in everyone's life. From dentist appointments and restaurant reservations to international travel itineraries, I've made it all happen. I've also handled all the staffing issues at their three homes. I suggested to Jill months ago that I should start training my replacement. Instead, she sends me on a long business trip with Elliott. And that turned out to be a disaster."

"How so?"

"Actually, the trip went fine. But before I left there's this big panic about Mr. Wudbine's cappuccino. Jill almost cancelled me out at the last minute. She was on one of her campaigns to rehabilitate Brenda. I was supposed to teach Brenda how to make coffee to her husband's specifications. It was a total disaster. Brenda is a poster child for learned helplessness. At the last minute we had to have a totally automatic machine FedExed overnight. I did manage to teach Brenda how to turn it on and push the right buttons. And to make sure there was backup, I trained the cook and Jill.

"And then while I was gone Malcolm got some mysterious illness. He was sick for several days with an acute gastritis. They rushed him to the local walk-in clinic. The initial diagnosis was food poisoning. I guess he recovered a bit, and then a few days later he had another episode. They brought his internist in from Chicago."

"What was the diagnosis?"

"I don't think that changed. Again, suspected food poisoning. When Malcolm was dieting, which was most of the time, he lived on these king prawns. He had a standing order with a supplier in Louisiana for a weekly shipment. His doctor banned the prawns and put him on a bland diet. Grace was directed to empty the contents of the refrigerators and freezers, and then restock everything."

"Did anyone else in the household get sick?"

"I don't think so, remember I wasn't there. But somehow when I got back, well, things were different. I do the ordering of the special food items. That's part of my job as concierge. Jill gave me the impression that she held me responsible for Malcolm's illness."

"So your relationship with her started to decline after the trip?"

"Who knows? That's just the feeling I got from her. You have got to understand that the woman is inscrutable. Her nickname around Wudbine Investments is Ms. Spock. Trying to figure out what's going on in her head is always about nuance. I would have been more comfortable if she were yelling and screaming. Then, at least I would have known exactly what she was thinking." Markley stopped and looked down at her hands, then back up at Ray. "But this getting sacked. It had to be Jill. Elliott wouldn't do this to me." She took a deep breath, slowly exhaling. "She insisted that I accompany Elliott on that trip, then sort of acted like I was after her man."

"Any reason she should be worried?"

"Not on account of me. I think he's as much of a cold fish as she is."

Ray slid several pages of paper across the table. "Ms. Markley, I've highlighted your comments from our first interview about the events of Saturday evening. Would you look through those, and see if you have anything that you might want to add or change."

He sat silently and watched her eyes scan the text. When she finally looked up she said, "I wouldn't change anything. This is exactly the way I remember it."

"Jill Wudbine, do you remember seeing her backstage before and during the play?"

"Like I told you, I got there early. I must have seen her in the dressing room or green room, but I don't have any clear memory of that. We were both onstage during the first scene. I exited way before she did. I didn't see her again until I came from the makeup area to see what the hubbub was all about. Jill seemed stunned, just like the rest of us. She was sobbing. I didn't think she was capable of that much emotion."

"But you don't know when she returned to the green room."

"No, I didn't see her." She pushed the pages with the highlighted areas back across the table. "Is there anything else, Sheriff? I have a lot to do."

Ray glanced down at his notes, and then up at her. "No, not at the moment. If possible, I would like you to stay in the area for a few more days. I might have additional questions for you."

"Does this mean I'm a person of interest?"

"No. But you were near the scene of the crime, and you have an intimate understanding of the Wudbine household. I may need to tap your knowledge again. Here is my card. If anything occurs to you that you think might be helpful to solving this crime, please contact me."

Pepper grasped the card with her right hand and carefully scanned the information before dropping it into a shirt pocket. "I see you're not on Facebook, Sheriff." She gave him a mischievous smile before she departed.

40

"I understand that Ms. Markley is no longer employed by Wudbine Investments," said Ray looking across the table at Jill Wudbine.

"That was a long time in coming. Pepper was one of my father-in-law's welfare cases. She started with us as an intern. Although she had her degree from a good place, Malcolm could see that she was far too green to make it in the corporate world. I mean she was from some little burg with a name like Hicksville or Piggott, someplace in Arkansas or Iowa. So he took her on, this Eliza Doolittle, thinking he could turn her into a duchess, or at least a moderately cosmopolitan woman. I advised him against it at the time, but Malcolm was determined. Always the optimist. And I have to admit, this job he created for her, concierge, was brilliant. It exposed her to all the right kind of people and things. But at the end of the day, I'm not sure she learned anything other than a taste for the good life.

"As for her termination, with Malcolm's death, this is the right time for her departure. If she weren't so obtuse, she would have seen it coming months ago. But you didn't drag me over here to discuss human resource problems. I'm pressed for time, so please let's get through this interview as quickly as possible."

"Okay," said Ray, "I have two things that I would like to go over with you. First, you've had a few days to reflect on the events of last Saturday evening. I was wondering if you might have any new thoughts on who might be responsible for Mr. Wudbine's death."

"Your question…don't you think I would have contacted you immediately, Sheriff, if I had anything to add? I have thought of nothing else since…those terrifying moments. I've searched my memory for any detail that might serve as a clue. Nothing. Malcolm Wudbine was an exceptional human being. Whoever killed him was probably a hired assassin or some deranged character who was striking out against the world."

"And who would have hired an assassin?" questioned Ray, wondering what inane response she would next float his way.

"We live in a global economy, Sheriff. We have competitors in distant places, barbarous societies, people who don't play by the same business rules we follow. Perhaps that's where you will find your killer. And then there's the current political climate, all this chatter about the concentration of wealth. This might have been a hate crime precipitated by class envy." Wudbine's answers were delivered in her characteristic monotone.

Without commenting, Ray handed several sheets of paper to her. "There you will find a transcript of our conversation on Sunday. I've highlighted the parts that deal with your recollections of what happened while you were in the theater. Please read your statement and see if there are any additions or changes you would like to make."

Ray sat and watched her read through the transcript, first scanning, and then going over the highlighted areas a second and third time.

"No, Sheriff, I have nothing to add or change. That said, I was thinking about Pepper, just as an example, of course. I saw her early on. She must have been one of the first people there. Then later we were onstage together. And I didn't see her again after her exit, well, until the lights came on. I can remember seeing her wander in from the makeup area when Grubbs was telling us what had happened.

"I'm not trying to suggest that Pepper might have been involved in this crime. But if she had a murderous intent, it would have been so easy to hide somewhere on the far side of the stage waiting for Malcolm to…well you know the rest. And again, I'm not trying to implicate Pepper in any way. What I'm trying to tell you is that you're asking questions that are impossible to answer. People were constantly moving about. At best, they might remember where they were, but to give you reliable information on anyone else, impossible. You are wasting your time. And now to an important issue, when will my father-in-law's body be released for burial?"

"Soon," Ray responded.

"Patchouli oil, do you know what patchouli oil smells like?" asked Sue as she came into the library building, the screen door slamming behind her.

Ray looked up from his screen. "Patch…what? I don't know what you're talking about."

"You sound sort of crabby. What's going on?"

"Jill Wudbine."

"Oh, I just saw her. Remarkable woman. I don't know how you can pass someone on a narrow sand trail without making eye contact. Do you remember what she smelled like?"

Ray gave Sue a long look, "What's going on?"

"Patchouli. It's a scent, or more correctly, an aromatic oil."

"I'm totally lost. So put all this together for me."

"I was just interviewing Tom Lea."

"How did it go?"

"Couldn't have been better. When Tom is on his meds, he mostly makes sense. And fortunately, there were no interrupting cell calls from the great beyond."

"So tell me about this Patch…?"

"Patchouli. We know that Tom was lurking around the auditorium trying to get in to see the play with his personally created ticket. When that didn't work, he watched through an open window until the rain got so heavy that he took refuge under the picnic shelter. From there he had a perfect view of the back of the building. He said he saw someone open the doors on the electrical cabinet, and then the light on the side of the building went out. He's sure it was a woman because of the shape of her raincoat. As this person was leaving the area, she stopped briefly under the shelter to light a cigarette. Tom says the scent of patchouli oil was in the air after she came through."

"He's sure?"

"He claims to have some expertise in aromatherapy, something his mother verified."

"Where do we get some of …?"

"Patchouli oil. I imagine we can find some in Traverse City. That's a good assignment for our summer intern. But there's something more. Before the patchouli-scented woman passed through, there were two others who used the shelter. The first arrived just after Tom got there, a woman driving a golf cart. A few minutes later a man arrived. Tom said there was a lot of kissing going on. Hollywood-style kissing, that's what he called it. The kind you see in movies. Then they disappeared."

"Did someone come back for the cart?"

"He didn't know. Said he left shortly after the patchouli lady came through."

"So where does this leave us?" asked Ray.

"We know that Alyson Mickels parked a cart under the picnic shelter. She told us that. So who was the man? Elliott Wudbine? And if it were the two of them, where did they go next? Were they involved in the murder or were they going off to find a place that offered greater privacy?"

"So we need to talk to Elliott and Alyson again," responded Ray. "And the woman wearing patchouli, your nose is better than mine. I don't remember coming in contact with anyone wearing excessive amounts of perfume the last few days. You know it usually gets me sneezing."

"How about when we were talking to Brenda Wudbine?"

"Roses, carnations, and gin. I didn't sense anything else. Did you?"

"No. But you know I'm Ms. Wash and Wear. I don't own any perfume. I'll get our intern, Barbara Sinclair, headed over to TC. I bet there's someone at central dispatch who can guide her to a source for patchouli oil. When she returns, we'll see if…."

"But what if Tom Lea is wrong about the scent?" asked Ray, standing, putting his hand on the small of his back, and stretching from side to side.

"Then we look for Hollywood-type kissers."

"How much faith do we put in Tom Lea?"

"We use the information carefully and see if some truth follows."

"I like that. Elliott should be here next. Stick around, I may need your help."

41

"Fast trip to Chicago," Ray observed, looking across the table at Elliott Wudbine.

"Too fast. But my employees deserved to know exactly what happened. They heard lots of rumors. We must begin planning what to tell our clients. This will be a very difficult period. Our customers have to believe that we can manage their investments with greater skill than our competitors. While my father has not been involved in the day-to-day operations of the firm for years, our client base believed that his legendary knowledge of the industry still guided our investment strategies. Now we have to reassure them that nothing will change, that we will handle their money in the same competent manner.

"And I should tell you, Sheriff, from this point forward for the foreseeable future I will have to be in Chicago. So if there are any bits of information that you still need from me, better try to get them now. I probably won't be back in the area again for several weeks, depending of course, on where we decide to have the memorial service."

"Just a few things, Mr. Wudbine. First, now that some time has passed, and you've had an opportunity to think about the events of last Saturday, I was wondering if you had some new speculations on who might have killed your father?"

"No. I have no idea. Like I told you, my father was an outstanding human being. His murder is beyond comprehension. Although it seems

213

quite improbable, I somehow think that this was a random act. Anyone who really knew my father wouldn't have done something like this."

"We are trying to establish where everyone was near the time of your father's murder." Ray placed several sheets of paper in front of Elliott. "This is a transcript of our conversation on Sunday. Feel free to read the whole document, but I especially want to call your attention to the highlighted material. You said that you were in the theater until the end of the scene."

Elliott pulled a pair of reading glasses from his shirt pocket and looked through the pages, paying special attention to the lines that Ray had marked with a yellow highlighter. After a few minutes Elliott looked up.

"Is the highlighted material consistent with your memory of the events?" asked Ray.

"Yes, I think that's the way it happened. But so much occurred that evening, it's hard to remember exactly…and I was exhausted and probably had too much scotch on an empty stomach. I think I had a bit of a buzz on. But for the most part, that's what happened."

"Mr. Wudbine, we have a witness who seems to think they saw you under the picnic shelter before the first scene ended. Is that possible?"

Wudbine looked down at the typed copy on the desk, nervously moving pages around. Finally he looked up at Ray. "Like I was telling you, I had a bit of a buzz on, and my back was killing me. I needed to get up and out of there. Maybe some of what I remember was based on things Jill told me. You know how memories sometimes get fused together."

"Alyson Mickels told us that she moved the golf cart down to the picnic shelter. Our witness says soon after that she was joined by a man. Any chance that was you?" asked Ray.

Wudbine was slow to answer. "I think that's possible. Given the rain and thunder and all, I was probably worried and went to check on her."

Sue caught Wudbine's eye. "Our witness said that it was quite the romantic encounter."

Wudbine reddened. "We're friends. I'm sure I only hugged her to show my concern."

"And the two of you left immediately, heading back into the colony. Where were you going?" she pursued.

"Does this make me a suspect?"

"Quite the opposite," said Sue. "It takes you out of the area at the time of the crime."

"I was walking Alyson back to her cottage. She uses the one we keep for flight crews. I had brought an umbrella with me. She was soaking wet. So we got under my umbrella and went over to her place so she could change into some dry clothing. Not too long after we got there, Jill called, asking me to come backstage and get her."

"Why didn't you tell us this the first time?" pressed Sue.

Elliott stammered a bit. "Ah, well, I was afraid you'd get the wrong impression."

"New Topic," said Ray. "I understand that Pepper Markley is no longer with the firm."

"That's an HR matter. I don't know anything about it."

"Nothing?"

"Jill mentioned it in passing. With my father's death, we no longer needed her services. Pepper was probably the highest paid barista in America," he added. "My father was generous, perhaps foolishly so. Is she a suspect?"

"When are you going back to Chicago? We may need to talk with you again," said Ray.

"I'd like to be there in time for the business day on Friday. My father's body, when will it be released? We need to finalize our plans for a funeral or memorial service. I'm losing patience with your bureaucratic bumbling."

Ray stood. "Thank you for coming in. We will be in touch."

Wudbine pulled himself out of his chair, looked as if he was going say something, then hastily turned and pushed his way through the screen door. He stopped on the porch, lit a cigarette, looked back at Ray, then marched up the path away from the building.

"If looks could kill, you'd be dead," said Sue. "We gave him just enough rope for the proverbial hanging."

"How about his account of his encounter at the picnic shelter?"

"Chivalry runs in the family, distressed maidens are a Wudbine specialty. I wonder if he was good enough to help Alyson out of her wet things," scoffed Sue.

"So where are we?"

"You can take Elliott and Alyson off the list of possible perpetrators. Whether they were part of a broader conspiracy is another question."

"When you look at the transcript of the Pepper Markley interview, you will note she suggested that Jill Wudbine insisted that she accompany Elliott on a long business trip abroad in June. When they returned, Pepper felt her relationship with Jill had changed. There was the suggestion Jill thought Pepper might have designs on her husband."

"Does she?" asked Sue.

"I don't think so. And now it looks like he's taken with Ashley."

"Oh, Ray," said Sue, "Elliott is probably like the source of his seed, smitten with anything that wears a dress. They are both very attractive women. Does Pepper stay on the list?"

"For now, but I don't see a motive."

42

Ray washed the tomatoes, removing the last bits of earth from multicolored fruits. Carefully slicing through the flesh, he arranged the slabs by size, the largest on the bottom, the smallest on the top, a medley of colors, shapes, and textures. After sprinkling course gray Mediterranean salt over the top, he added a dusting of freshly ground pepper. He picked through some fresh basil leaves, selecting only the most perfect ones, and arranged them at the center. Turning his attention to the smoked whitefish, he peeled off the blackened skin, and separated the meat from the spine, taking care to remove all the bones. He laid the fish out on a bed of thinly sliced lemon. Next Ray pulled a baguette from a low oven and started cutting pieces at an oblique angle.

"Did you read this?" asked Hanna, her back to him, papers spread in front of her on the table.

"I made a hard copy and glanced through the first few pages. Then I turned my attention to dinner. I wanted to have things on the table when you got here so we'd have the maximum hours of daylight on the water."

"Tell me how far you read."

"In layman's terms, I know Wudbine died from a severed spinal cord. I also know the insertion point and the dimensions of the part of the blade that penetrated beyond the skin. That gives me a good sense of what we should be looking for. Although, by this point, I think the weapon is long gone." Ray made several trips from the counter to the table with the bread, fish, and tomatoes. "Ice water?"

"Yup," she responded, her attention glued to the report. "Did you read the toxicology?"

"Didn't get that far."

"You didn't see the note on the pressure marks and the anterior bruising to the neck?"

"No. Anything else there?"

"Yes, but not definitive. The pathologist speculates, based on the pattern of bruising and fingernail marks, that the victim's neck was held from the front by a right hand, helping pull the posterior part of the neck and spine into the penetrating object. The pathologist further speculates that the perpetrator was left-handed."

Ray walked behind Hanna. He reached around with his right hand, gently grabbing her neck. Then he put his knuckles of his left hand against her spine just below her head.

"You got it," said Hanna.

"Feels awkward," Ray commented. "I'd want it the other way. But it makes sense."

And the arsenic, you don't know about the arsenic?"

"Arsenic, you're putting me on. His blood was loaded with…."

"No, not a trace. His exposure happened a few months ago. Traces were found in an analysis of the hair. The time frame isn't too precise, six or eight weeks ago. And the exposure was short term, but at a fairly high level. There's a note that they can order some more sophisticated tests to better estimate the duration and level of exposure. You should have the complete analysis done. Also, they can do a similar study on the fingernails to verify the hair data."

"Note those things in the margin. I'll make sure they are done." Ray dropped into his chair. "What would that mean, medically? What would be the symptoms of arsenic poisoning? If you wanted to poison him, where would you put the arsenic? Mashed potatoes, oatmeal? Refresh my memory."

"Ray, this is way outside my area, I can only speculate. And there are lots of ways he could have been exposed. The fact that it's present in his hair doesn't mean someone was trying to poison him. For example, if he was downwind from an orchard that was being sprayed with an arsenic-based insecticide, if that is still done, he could have inhaled it. Arsenic is a common chemical in the environment. There are often trace amounts in water supplies and food."

"How about coffee?"

"Depends where it's grown, how much might have collected in the soil...."

"I mean, could you give it to someone in coffee. How does it taste?"

"Get me your laptop. I'll do some background reading while I eat."

Ray ate in silence, watching Hanna handle a fork with her left hand and keyboard with her right. Finally she looked up and said, "Okay, I know just enough to be dangerous. So don't take anything I say as the final word. What were your questions?"

"Given a very discriminating coffee drinker, could you slip some arsenic in his brew without him noticing it?"

"Yes, especially if you were only lightly lacing the brew. Arsenic is odorless and tasteless."

"Would a physician be able to diagnose the poisoning based on symptoms?"

"Well, that depends on how the patient presents. They would have some moderate to severe gastrointestinal symptoms, depending on the dosage. If blood work were done, an usually high level of arsenic would show up. But, I don't think most physicians would start there. At a fairly low dosage, the symptoms would look like an intestinal virus or food poisoning, the kinds of things that usually resolve themselves in a few days on a bland diet. No one is going to order blood work for a common ailment unless there are extenuating circumstances."

"How about shrimp and prawns?" asked Ray.

"Give me a few minutes?" Hanna set down her fork, both hands flying across the keyboard. Then she stopped, her eyes scanning the text as she scrolled down the page. "Naturally occurring. Subject to inspection. No reports of arsenic-related illness." She looked across the table at Ray. "Seafood is usually a leading suspect in cases of food poisoning. I don't know if it is more fragile than other meat sources, or if it is a problem with shipping, storage, and handling.

"So what's going on here?" she asked. "This time you talk while I eat. Give me the back story."

"One of the people I interviewed this afternoon told me that Wudbine had been very ill sometime in June. She said that shrimp or prawns were thought to be the source of the food poisoning. The arsenic finding changes everything."

"How does the coffee fit into this?"

"My speculation. The person who usually prepared his coffee was out of the country. There's a lot here I still don't understand, but I think the pieces are starting to fall together. I need to call Sue. We need some search warrants."

"Tonight?"

"No, just starting the process. Hopefully we can serve them tomorrow morning. I like to start early, keeps people off balance."

Hanna remained silent for several moments.

"What's going on?" asked Ray.

"I think the data just indicates the presence of arsenic in his system at a greater than expected level for a number of days. You would need to study hair samples from other household members and employees to prove that he was an outlier."

Ray nodded his agreement as his mind whirled with the language of the proposed search warrant.

43

"Everything go okay with the judge?" asked Ray, as he climbed into the passenger seat and buckled the seatbelt.

"He was running late and had just recessed for lunch. He wasn't happy to see me," Sue reversed out of the parking place and then headed for the highway. "I had carefully laid out the information from the autopsy report, focusing on the part dealing with the arsenic poisoning. I'm not sure he was completely convinced, but he signed it. I did lay out all the brand names for the household and garden products containing arsenic that we would be looking for, so it didn't look like we were just on a fishing trip. I think we got this one by based on our positive history."

"How much time did you spend on the document?"

"Most of the evening."

"I imagine Harry was thrilled by that. A nice romantic evening in the north woods."

"It worked out, Ray. It worked out. We were on dueling laptops researching arsenic. When I had absorbed enough information, I drafted the affidavit. He helped with the rewrites, anticipating the questions and concerns the judge might have. We had a really good evening, sharing our expertise, strategizing back and forth. We're both too mature and type A to spend a lot of time pitching woo. I did a final draft this morning when I came in. Then it was just a waiting game. There's a copy in the folder tucked next to your seat. Tell me what you think."

Ray carefully read through the search warrant affidavit, looking up occasionally to take in the passing scene. "I'm convinced," he said, returning the affidavit to the folder. "So our search is basically limited to the food and coffee preparation area at Gull House and Brenda Wudbine's greenhouse." He looked over at Sue, "The place will probably be clean. They would be less than bright to leave that kind of evidence around. But nothing ventured…"

Ray started to check his e-mail on his phone. His attention was pulled back to the present moment when Sue turned onto the long drive that ran up to Gull House.

"I wonder what's happened?" she said, motioning toward the ambulance parked near the greenhouse. She pulled in across the drive and they got out of the Jeep just as three EMTs rolled a gurney to the back of their unit and quickly loaded it. Ray could see Brenda Wudbine's motionless body secured to the stretcher. "How is she?" he asked just before the doors were closed. The last paramedic to climb aboard, a young woman, didn't respond verbally, her dispirited expression said it all. As soon as the rear doors swung shut, the heavy unit, its diesel engine laboring under the sudden acceleration, rolled down the drive, lights flashing, siren silent.

Richard Grubbs was standing outside the greenhouse.

"What happened?" asked Ray

"Brenda, it must have been her heart. I know her health has been declining. I put her on my calendar today. I wanted to spend some time with her. That poor woman has been marginalized by everyone."

"Was she alone?"

"Yes. She came down here every morning to cut and arrange the fresh flowers. This was her mission in life. I'd try to stop in and see her occasionally. Brenda, I don't think anyone in the household even bothered to talk to her. She always seemed starved for conversation." Grubbs stopped for a minute and took several long breaths before continuing. "Doing the flowers, that's all that was left for her. She'd prepare the flowers and do the arrangements. Then Pat Eibler, he's the handyman, would carry them up to the house.

"I knew I'd find her here. Like always, the door was open. I walked in and didn't see her right away. I usually stand over there out of her way on the other side of her work area," Grubbs pointed. "So I walked around, and there she was on the floor. I got down next to her. She wasn't breathing. I called 911. They were here in just a few minutes."

"And you've been alone the whole time?"

"Yes. As I was walking down here I saw Pat in his pickup with Grace, the cook. I think he was taking her grocery shopping. And just before you arrived, I got Elliott on the phone. He's on his way over."

Grubbs was silent. Ray watched as a wave of sadness swept across his countenance. "Brenda died alone."

Ray and Sue stood by silently, leaving Grubbs to his thoughts. Finally, Ray said, "Please show us where you found her."

They followed Grubbs into the greenhouse, stopping short of the large worktable still covered with roses. "Brenda was right there on the floor. I imagine she was working and just collapsed."

"Should I get my camera?" asked Sue.

"Yes."

"What was her position?" asked Ray.

"She was on her back. Her eyes were open, like she was looking at the ceiling."

Ray surveyed the table. Two piles of roses were separated by an open space. A pair of gardening gloves, several thick rags, and pruning shears lay on the near side of the table along with a large coffee mug, a crystal ashtray, a pack of cigarettes, and a lighter. A brandy bottle stood near the coffee mug. A toppled-over stool laid at an oblique angle.

"The flowers," said Ray, "tell me exactly what she did."

Grubbs went to the far side of the table, looking across at Ray. "It depended on the type of flowers. More often than not, she was working with roses. That was Malcolm's preference. And what you see here, it looks like she was in the middle of her normal, what should I call it, pattern. If she was working on roses, she'd pile them to her left. One stem at a time, she would take off the thorns using those rags, trim up the stem with the shears, and move it to the right. It was almost automatic. She could talk to me and just continue working away. After, she would arrange them in vases and, like I said, they'd get carried up to the house. You can see that she was about halfway through."

"Was she wearing gloves when you found her?" asked Ray.

Grubbs looked at the gloves on the table, then back at Ray. "I don't think so, let me think."

"You didn't pull them off."

"No. I'm…a bit squeamish. I was almost afraid to touch her."

Sue arrived with her camera and started to shoot the scene. Grubbs joined Ray on the far side of the table. Ray pointed to the brandy bottle. "Tell me about her drinking? Did she always start early."

"I wouldn't know, Sheriff. That said, I think there was usually a bottle around. I imagine you've heard about her drinking. I guess the doctors told her it was killing her. But she didn't seem to care."

"Perfume," said Sue. "Do you know if Mrs. Wudbine was partial to a specific fragrance?"

"Perfume, I wouldn't know about that, either. She did have a certain smell about her. It was sort of musky. I always attributed it to the roses, but now that I think of it, the scent wasn't rose-like. "

44

Elliott Wudbine rushed into the greenhouse. "Where is she, where is Brenda?" He directed his question to Richard Grubbs, taking no note of Ray and Sue.

"In an ambulance. They left five minutes ago."

"How is she?" Again, his question was directed to Grubbs.

"She wasn't breathing when I found her. I don't think they could do anything."

Wudbine's focus shifted to Ray. "What are you doing here?" he demanded, his tone hostile.

"There have been some developments in your father's case. I have a warrant to search this building and part of Gull House."

Sue slipped out of the building to retrieve the warrant.

"Well, you will have to talk to my wife about that. She takes care of the legal affairs. And at the moment she is indisposed. I know she won't be happy having you poking around."

"You won't have to bother her, sir," responded Ray, stalling briefly. Moments later Sue returned to the greenhouse with the folder. Ray passed Wudbine the search warrant. "As soon as you've read this, we can get started."

Wudbine held the document, one hand on each side, pushing it away from his body, squinting as he struggled to bring the print into focus. He remained silent, slowly scanning the words. Then he looked at Ray.

"What's this about arsenic? My father was stabbed for Christ's sake, and you're looking for arsenic. How will the poor man ever find justice with your ship-of-fools approach to the investigation?"

"Did you read the warrant, sir?" probed Ray.

"I need my reading glasses, but I've got the gist of it. I don't understand about the arsenic."

"Some of the tissue from your father's body showed high levels of arsenic. It appears that he had ingested a significant quantity of that element. We are wondering if there was an earlier attempt on his life. As you can see in the document, our search is limited."

"That's the silliest goddamn thing I've ever heard. I'm going to find Jill. We're going to get this shithead, so-called judge on the phone and have your sorry ass ordered off our property." Elliott spun on his heels and bolted for the door.

"Mr. Conviviality," declared Sue.

Ray turned to Richard Grubbs. "Is there anything else you can tell us?"

"I don't think so. You know where to find me."

"Let's get this done," said Ray as soon as Grubbs was out of earshot, "just in case…well…the ship starts taking water."

"You do want to treat this like a possible crime scene, don't you? Until we know otherwise, this is a case of unexplained death."

"Absolutely. It's your scene, and we will secure it until you're finished. I'll disappear for a few minutes. I want to call Dr. Dyskin, tell him where he'll find the body, and ask him to order a forensic autopsy."

"Is Hanna at the hospital today?"

"Yes."

"You should give her a call, too. Brenda's departure is…."

Ray cut her off, "Just too convenient."

"Right. See if you can get the curmudgeonly Dr. Dyskin to consult with Hanna."

Ray looked over at her. "I thought you had softened a bit on him since he's given up cigars."

"I have. But given Brenda's history of heart trouble, if Dyskin will listen, Hanna can probably give him some useful counsel."

"Are you done with the camera work?" asked Ray returning to the greenhouse a few minutes later.

"Yes. Let's get the search done before we have any more interruptions. Here are some rubber gloves. First, I want to call your attention to this smock." She carefully lifted the light gray, cotton garment from a hook and held it in Ray's direction.

"What am I suppose to do with it?"

"Your nose, Ray. Smell it."

Sue watched his tentative moves. "Ray, not little sniffs. Put your nose into the material and inhale."

"Okay."

She pulled a small glass bottle from her pocket and removed its top. "Okay, take a whiff of this." She passed the bottle under his nose. "What do you think?"

"Very close. What's the difference?"

"The bottle has patchouli oil. It's quite unique. If one were in the know about aromas and scents, I don't think they would confuse it with anything else."

"Agreed," said Ray. "So Tom Lea has helped us make a connection between the shadowy woman at the picnic shelter and Brenda Wudbine."

"Yes."

"What does arsenic look like?" he asked, impatient to get the search completed.

"Arsenic, the mineral, is described as a silver-gray crystal. It will be a powder or in granules. Until it was banned in most consumer applications about a dozen years ago, arsenic was commonly found in insecticides, herbicides, and on flypaper. Our most likely suspect will be pesticides that contain arsenic, probably as a main ingredient."

Ray pointed to a tall, metal shelving unit along a wall at the far end of the building.

"Yup," Sue responded. "That's a good starting point."

Twenty minutes of careful label reading had yielded four cartons of insecticide—cardboard cylinders with pry-off metal lids. Three had a tape seal across the top; the fourth had been opened. Ray found a screwdriver in a near-by drawer and removed the lid. They peered in at the grayish powder of the half empty container.

"So what have we proved?" asked Sue.

"That the means for poisoning Malcolm was present and easily accessible. The autopsy suggested that the poisoning was of short duration, probably talking place over a few days. Did you listen to Pepper Markley's interview from yesterday?"

"Yes, before I started to work on the affidavit. There were things I didn't understand. Why didn't they just teach the cook to do the cappuccino?"

"Remember Pepper said Jill was…and these are her words…trying to rehabilitate Brenda. So the question is why?"

"I see where you are going. Was this something Jill did occasionally, or was it part of a larger scheme. Did Brenda start poisoning her husband, or was Jill pulling the strings. And if this is the scenario, why did Brenda, or Brenda with Jill's assistance, stop?" asked Sue.

"I don't know how well Brenda was functioning. But Jill is a very bright woman. If she was behind the poisoning, she wanted to make sure Brenda would take the rap. In fact, it would have ended like this, with Brenda dead. But someone got spooked. Pulled back before the poisoning was correctly diagnosed."

"The problem is," started Sue, "all we have so far is the arsenic in Malcolm's hair, the report of his illness, and a partially depleted container with a compound containing arsenic found in the greenhouse." She gave Ray a mocking smile. "A substance you can probably find in most of the garages, sheds, and barns in this county. Do you want to take our evidence to the prosecutor or should I?"

"Maybe you will find some prints on the container. While we're here, let's give the rest of the place a quick look," said Ray.

He reopened the drawer where he found the screwdriver and looked over the contents. Then he moved over to the next drawer. He surveyed the neatly arranged contents: spools of wire with bright coverings, green tape, florist scissors, pruners, craft knives, and three box cutters next to two containers of extra blades. His eyes swept over the contents a second time. In a back corner of the drawer, partially hidden under rolls of tape, was a rosewood handle with two brass rivets. He pushed the tape aside. The handle was attached to a triangular black leather sheath. With a gloved hand, Ray carefully removed the object and set it on the bench. Sue came to his side. He released the snap on the leather strap that secured the blade and carefully pulled a weapon from its scabbard.

"Nice piece of cutlery you've got there. Looks like the type of implement Dyskin was talking about. He called it a push dagger. Time for a little dusting," said Sue.

Ray stood back and watched, knowing that Sue didn't like chatter as she worked. Finally she looked up at him. "Some very nice prints. The blade looks clean. I wonder if the scabbard absorbed any blood or other residue?"

"We should get this to the State Police lab. Today. Have someone drive it to Grayling."

"I should do that," said Sue. "Maybe I can use the old girl network to get them to give this a quick look. If they find blood, maybe I can get the type and start the process to see if there is a DNA match with Malcolm."

"Take the brandy bottle and the coffee container. Check the contents and get prints. And get her phone added to the search warrant." Ray inhaled deeply. "So where are we? We have Tom Lea's eyewitness account, backed by the scent of patchouli oil. Could Brenda have offed Wudbine alone?"

"What you are asking is could Brenda have switched off the power, gone backstage and killed Wudbine in what, less than a minute, and then passed Tom Lea?"

"Yes."

"I don't think so. Highly improbable."

"Agreed," said Ray. "Someone has cleverly been stacking the evidence against Brenda. Who? And how did they get her to conveniently die? Get over to Grayling and see what you can find out. I'll see if Hanna has anything that will help. I also want to make contact with Pepper."

"Grubbs is always at the scene of the crime," said Sue.

"Yes, I'm noodling around with that."

45

Ray heard a vehicle braking to a stop in his drive, then one door slamming, followed 15 or 20 seconds later by the second door being slammed. Hanna came through his front door, releasing the latch, then shouldering her way into the room, her arms full of packages.

"No paddling clothes?" asked Ray.

"Tonight I am the consummate hunter and gatherer, the chef, too. We will have a leisurely dinner. It's all fresh. It's all local. No growth hormones, no MSG. And you're going to love it."

"But I thought we were heading for the big lake."

"Ray, something rather amazing is going on. I'm not frantic. I don't need to go out and paddle my butt off to feel okay. I'm feeling very relaxed. I want to have a good meal and a slow evening. It's payback time. For better or worse, I'm the cook this evening, and you will love it."

"So what's the menu?"

"Fresh lake trout from Leland, salad and green beans from Meadowlark, local raspberries to put on a salad, a baguette that even you will find acceptable, and at the end a small glass of sherry with Stilton and biscuits. And, along the way, I'll serve tall glasses of ice water, still my safest beverage."

"How about Brenda Wudbine?" asked Ray.

Hanna embraced him warmly, pulling him close, waiting as he enfolded her in his arms, then kissed him passionately. Eventually she pushed away. "Careful," she said playfully, "or you won't get dinner."

"That's not all bad," said Ray.

"True. But at 3 A.M. when you wake up blissfully satiated but starving, you will remember that you didn't have dinner."

"How about Brenda Wudbine?"

"You keep repeating yourself. Here are the rules of engagement for this evening. There will be no shoptalk until after we have had dessert. Agreed?"

"Agreed," said Ray. "What can I help with?"

"Go read your New Yorker. In 20 minutes I'll have dinner on the table."

"Can I ask about Brenda Wudbine now?" said Ray as he sipped from the small glass of sherry Hanna had served him.

She handed him a folder. "There's blood work and the prints you requested in there. Your medical examiner is a real character. I guess he's had serious heart problems recently. He wanted to pick my brain."

"And Brenda Wudbine?"

"Not wanting to violate any protocols before the body was sent to Grand Rapids for a forensic autopsy, I only did a few things, and those were with Dyskin's permission. First, I interrogated the defibrillator pacemaker."

"Voices from the dead."

"You could say that. There was nothing remarkable. The device appeared to be operating normally. You can see where the heart stopped beating and the defibrillator fired. It cycled through a number of times. Then you can see the use of the second defibrillator. This would've been the EMTs. They obviously noted her Medalert bracelet. When the patient has this kind of pacemaker, the EMTs have to take care to position the paddles so the energy they deliver won't destroy the pacemaker. It appears the EMTs did everything right. This was a woman with cardiomyopathy, with alcohol probably being a contributing factor."

"Anything else?" asked Ray.

"Yes, two things. First, we did a blood alcohol. Brenda's was .26. That's a lot for early in the day. Probably had a residue from the night before, too."

"And the second thing?"

"It looked like she had had a fall. The back of her head showed signs of significant trauma. How did you find her?"

"We didn't. She was being loaded into an ambulance. But the person who found her said she was lying on her back in her greenhouse. And yes, there was a brandy bottle and a coffee mug that smelled of alcohol."

"How about the floor?"

"Concrete."

"She might have blacked out from the alcohol or had some sort of cardiac incident, hitting her head on the floor as she collapsed. That injury might or might not have been a contributing factor to her death. We'll know that after the autopsy."

Hanna pointed, "Ray, your phone."

"Rules of engagement? Phone calls?"

"Take it."

Hanna cleared away the dishes as Ray talked. After a short conversation, he rejoined her.

"What's going on?"

"That was Pepper Markley. She served as a concierge to Malcolm Wudbine. You saw her onstage. She played the young wife of the Vicar."

"Yes, I remember her, one very pretty woman. Vivacious."

"That's the one. She told me earlier today she had something to tell me. The circumstances prevented that from happening. I gave her my card."

"And she just called with some information that will turn your investigation on its head?"

"I wish. No. She said she has sent me lots of documents. If I connect the dots, I might have the motive. I asked her to tell me more, but she just hung up."

"I love a good mystery. Where's your laptop?"

Hanna settled next to him at the table.

"And here's her e-mail. Her note reads, No one is clean."

"I see that, what are the attachments?"

"PDFs, dozens and dozens." Ray opened one, then another, then a third. "They seem to be confirmations of hotel reservations. I wonder what this is all about."

"Why don't you print them out, and I'll make some tea," said Hanna.

By the time Hanna brought the tea to the table, Ray was laying out the printed pages. "It looks like three years of reservations. Which would make sense," said Ray. "Pepper had been with Wudbine for that period. There seems to be two kinds of room arrangements. About half of them are for suites, the other for adjoining rooms. The early ones all list Jill Wudbine as the other occupant. Pepper shows up in the later ones. Then Alyson Mickels makes an appearance. She was Wudbine's pilot and security person. What do you notice?" he asked.

"The first reservations are always for two people, Wudbine and one of those three women, never a combination. Give me a minute, I want to rearrange things."

Ray watched as she moved the sheets around. Hanna looked through the stacks a second time, making a few changes.

"I'm feeling a bit like a voyeur."

"How's that?" asked Ray.

"Don't you see it? Look. Early on it's just Jill and Wudbine. That's true for the first year. The second year it's mostly Jill, especially true for the multi-day trips. Occasionally Pepper appears, mostly one-night stays, or should I say, stands. That pattern holds true into the last year, then suddenly everything changes. Jill's out, Pepper's out. For the last six months he's only traveled with Alyson Mickels."

"It's not a practically new plot line, is it?" said Ray

"Nope. Rich and powerful older man, beautiful young women. That one has been around since…the dawn of man and woman."

"You know Jill Wudbine is Malcom Wudbine's daughter-in-law?" asked Ray.

"That makes the story suddenly a lot darker, doesn't it," observed Hanna.

Ray gestured toward neatly arranged pages. "So you really think…."

"Look at this e-mail. All she says is No one is clean. Perhaps Pepper is projecting her behavior…."

"I wondered about that, too." Ray picked up his phone and touched the top of the recents screen. A moment later he spoke into the phone, "How do you know the same is true of Jill?" He listened. "Thank you. That's what I need to know."

"Well?" asked Hanna.

"In flagrante delicto. And on more than one occasion."

"Well, the message is clear." She paused, her tone changed. "This thing with Jill, it's not incest, but it's pathological behavior of the worst sort. Perhaps the ultimate hostility a father can commit toward a son. I think you have lots of people with a motive. Now I need the beach, Ray. A long walk on the beach."

"Ditto."

46

"What did you learn in Grayling?" asked Ray as Sue entered his office early the next morning.

"I've got a good set of prints off the handle of the knife, but the evidence tech—Andy Goodhue, a new guy that I've never worked with before—alerted me to something very interesting."

"Which is?"

"The position of the fingers on the handle of the push dagger. The prints were good, almost too good. The fingers had been positioned in such a way to get the maximum area of the fingertips against the wide area of the handle. After we were done lifting prints, he showed me that it would be unlikely for the fingers to fall on the handle in that way if the perp was gripping it tightly to make a kill. In short, Ray, they looked staged."

"So you're suggesting that the prints were obtained from the dying or dead Brenda."

"It appears that way."

"So who was with Brenda? We know Grubbs was there. Did he do this? Or was it Jill, or Alyson, or Elliott?"

"Or perhaps someone else?"

"I was hoping to find a print or two on the scabbard that would help us answer that question. No such luck. After we established there were no prints on the leather, Andy cut open the seams. We could see traces of dried blood on the interior. He seemed confident that there was enough material to get a DNA profile. We should have the results in about five business days. Assuming a match, sometime next week, we can say this was the likely murder weapon. One more thing, the blade closely matches the dimensions cited in Malcolm Wudbine's autopsy."

"The pieces of the puzzle are falling together," said Ray. "Here are Brenda Wudbine's fingerprints. Dr. Dyskin was good enough to get us this set before the body was shipped to Grand Rapids." Ray removed a standardized fingerprint card from a folder and handed it to Sue.

"So let me do a quick comparison." She placed the cards side-by-side and examined them closely. "Something's wrong here." She studied them a second time. "I see the problem. My mistake. I assumed the prints on the push knife were from the right hand. They are a perfect match with the left hand prints from Brenda's body."

"The pathologists on Malcolm Wudbine's autopsy said the murderer was probably left handed," said Ray. "Did you find prints on the brandy bottle and coffee mug?"

Sue added two more fingerprint cards. She studied them carefully. "They are not of the same quality, but clearly from the right hand. See for yourself."

"Agreed. We need to verify this, but it appears that Brenda was right-handed. How about the contents of the brandy bottle and coffee mug?" asked Ray.

"Andy did a quick and dirty. He'll send a more complete analysis in a few days. Just brandy and coffee with brandy, no adulterations."

"According to Hanna, Brenda's blood alcohol was .26. Another thing she and Dr. Dyskin noted during their preliminary exam was that Brenda had sustained a blow to the back of the head, consistent with hitting a hard, flat surface, like a concrete floor. Let's look at the greenhouse photos, I want see the position of the stool."

Sue opened the laptop, "Is this what you're looking for?"

"Perfect."

"The EMTs probably would have pushed it out of their way," said Sue.

"Yes," agreed Ray. "But would they have changed the orientation? What I'm thinking is that Brenda had an early morning visitor, Grubbs or someone before him. Let's say they were standing on the opposite side of the table. To get at Brenda they would take the shortest route, moving clockwise around the table." Ray ran his finger over the screen to show the path. "And if they gave her a fairly forceful push, she would have ended up about where Grubbs said he found her. So tossing in another assumption, if this was the person who planted the knife and put Brenda's prints on the handle...."

"They were probably moving fast. A mirror image grab of the hand, a simple mistake."

"Or not," said Ray.

"I see where you are going. My head is starting to hurt. I think we've only encountered one southpaw, Alyson Mickels."

"Yes, that's my memory."

"Hold onto that," said Ray. He laid out the copies of the room reservations, following Hanna's organizational pattern. "I'll get a pot of fresh coffee while you look those over. I'm interested in your interpretation."

Five minutes later he returned with the coffee and clean mugs.

Sue gave him a Cheshire Cat grin.

"Okay, let me have it."

"Based on these documents. Looks like Jill was, to put it in the vernacular, Malcolm's main squeeze. There were occasional segues for a little spice with Pepper, but after Alyson happened on the scene, everything changed. She's quite the babe."

"Let's go through our top suspects again." Ray pulled down the whiteboard. "Starting with Richard Grubbs. He's got motive...."

"Lots of motives," interrupted Sue, "motive and opportunity."

"And we've already talked about the fact that he's been at the scene of both deaths. And three months ago, when I first encountered Wudbine, Grubbs jokingly said that if Malcolm ever ended up dead, we'd have an almost endless list of suspects."

"Grubbs seems to be a kind, rational man," said Sue. "But he's only human. There's got to be rage lurking below the surface. Could he have encouraged Brenda to put a little arsenic in Malcolm's coffee?"

"Probably, he seems to be one of her few friends here. How about Pepper? And why did she send me all those documents?"

"She's pissed. She wants revenge. So she's breaking the code of silence and tossing out the dirty linen," said Sue.

"Or maybe she thinks she is under suspicion. She's trying to build some cover. But is she a killer?"

"Pepper was backstage, so she had opportunity. And there probably are multiple motives. She would have needed an accomplice. Could she have maneuvered Brenda into handling the power switch?"

"How about Alyson?" asked Ray. "Again, she's the only southpaw in the group that I've noticed."

"I'm impressed that you picked up on that particular characteristic."

As was his custom, Ray let her comment pass. "I don't know what her motive would be. She seemed to be Wudbine's…."

"Femme du jour. Both Wudbine men seemed quite taken with her. Tom Lea puts her with Elliott. But could he be confused about the sequence of events?"

"A possibility. And then there's Jill," offered Ray.

"We just don't know much about her. Could she manipulate Brenda into handling the power? Pepper said something about Jill trying to rehabilitate Brenda. That seems to be more hostile than friendly."

"So," said Ray, "a key element is how did the killer communicate with the person who turned off the lights. It had to be a cell phone."

"I'll do the paperwork on Brenda's phone right now. The murder weapon should pave the way for the search warrant."

"We need to keep the pressure on these people. Let's try to be there by early afternoon."

47

P epper Markley met Ray at the door of Gull House.

"I thought you might be gone by now," he said.

"Things change incredibly fast. Jill has decreed that the memorial service will be up here. There will be hundreds of the right kind of people coming in from out of state and various foreign locations. Lots of hotel arrangements and catering need to be looked after. Suddenly, I'm a greatly respected, exceedingly competent queen of logistics and once again a highly paid employee of Wudbine Investments."

Ray noted the playfully wicked smile that accompanied her sarcastic tone. "When is this going to happen?"

"Right after Labor Day. We need to get the summer people out of town first. Then there will be adequate lodging available at the proper kind of places and adequate airline seats for those who must fly commercial. I trust you will want a seat close to the family at the memorial service. I can arrange that, Sheriff."

"Right now I'll settle for a brief conversation with Elliott Wudbine."

"He's down at his cottage. I expect him within the next fifteen minutes. They have a planning meeting scheduled here at 2:00. All of the stakeholders have been asked to help orchestrate the memorial service. And I do love that term, stakeholders. Sounds like they're intending to kill Dracula. But, hey, someone already got Drac." She giggled at her own joke. "Forgive my digression. Would you like to wait for Mr. Wudbine in the great room? I've already got coffee set up there."

"That will be fine," responded Ray.

Pepper escorted him, offering coffee, and then disappearing. Ray carefully surveyed the room. Sunlight flooded in the massive windows that faced the water. The doors were open, allowing the sound of wind and waves to enter the room. It struck him that the space was even more dramatic than he remembered. He walked to the piano, opened the lid, and gently, one at a time, pushed a few keys. The sound reverberated through the room.

He closed the lid and moved to the upright string bass. He walked around the instrument, studying the wooden stand that securely held it vertically.

"Do you play, Sheriff?" asked Richard Grubbs, walking across the thick white carpet.

"I wish. There was a beat-up old bass in the band room when I was in high school. The teacher showed me a couple of jazz progressions that I had fun experimenting with. That's as far as it went. But I heard that your daughter is an excellent jazz musician."

"I don't know if that's true these days. I'm not sure she's played much in recent years. But there was a time when she was quite remarkable."

"The bass is set up for a left-hand musician. I don't think I noticed that your daughter was a southpaw."

"That's an interesting story, Sheriff. When Jill was just an infant she showed a preference for using her left hand. For some reason that bothered my late wife enormously. She was constantly moving Jill's spoon or rattle to her right hand. The whole thing became a bone of contention between the two of us. I thought the child should be allowed to do what she wanted to do. But eventually my wife won out.

"My wife, she was a violinist, a very accomplished one. I imagine that's where Jill gets her musical side. It sure doesn't come from me. She started Jill in Suzuki when she was about four. It was a really fine school. They allowed the kids to experiment with different instruments before they settled on one to play. Jill quickly moved toward the violin, which pleased her mother. But the instrument she picked up and insisted on playing was this beautiful little quarter-size violin, setup for the left hand. They tried to move her to a right-hand instrument, and she absolutely refused. So Jill and her mother reached a compromise of sorts. Jill would play the violin, which her mother desperately wanted her to do, but she would play on the left-hand instrument.

"By the time she got to junior high, she had moved on to the string bass, leaving the violin behind. And in high school she started playing jazz exclusively. Not a popular move on the home front."

"When did you and Jill become estranged?"

"Long ago, when she was in college. Her mother died of cancer. For some reason, she seemed to hold me accountable. It's something I still don't understand. Probably never will."

Their attention was drawn to the sound of voices as people flooded through the double doors into the room.

Sterling Shevlin joined their group. Ray noted Shevlin's flushed complexion and the smell of alcohol.

"We've all been pressed into service again, haven't we?"

"This will be an easy one for you, Sterling. No casting involved. They just want you to get things organized. Elliot wants this service to have a very professional look," explained Grubbs.

"Revenge from the grave. Malcolm's last laugh."

"You will cooperate?"

"Oh, absolutely, Grubby. I can be as disingenuous as the best of them."

"Who's attending this meeting?" asked Ray.

"Usual suspects. Isn't that what you police say?" Grubbs laughed at his joke. "Sterling, here, and our summer minister of music, Dick Fulton. Hope enough people are staying on so we can put together a little choir. I think I have to find an organist. First I heard about this whole thing was late yesterday, and now we're hurrying to get everything in place in less than three weeks."

"Who invited you?" Jill Wudbine asked, her question directed at Ray. Elliott Wudbine was at her side, looking abashed.

"Actually, dear, it's good that he's here. We're going to need extra security for this event, and we're going to need the Sheriff's assistance in handling the traffic, too."

Ray opened the folder and handed Elliott a search warrant. Elliott quickly scanned it and handed it back.

"Sheriff, can I hold you off on this for about an hour? As soon as this meeting is completed, I promise to be totally at your disposal. In the meantime, I'd like you to join us. We need to know what resources your agency can provide."

Ray nodded his assent. He moved away from the group and quietly observed as the room filled, extra chairs being carried in by Pepper, Alyson Mickels, and Grubbs. Most of the faces were familiar to Ray: members of the family, including Verity; Wudbine employees; and members of the cast and crew of Murder at the Vicarage. There were a few others he had no memory of ever seeing before.

Elliott stood at a lectern. "Ladies and Gentlemen. Thank you being here on such short notice. As you no doubt have heard, the purpose of this meeting is to begin planning my father's memorial service. We are looking toward the week after Labor Day. That gives us about three weeks. An enormous amount of work has to be accomplished in a very short time. And each of you will be called upon to play an important role in this event.

"The Mission Point Summer Colony was an important part of my father's life. Many of his happiest days were spent on these beaches, in the colony, at his cottage, and, of course, on his beloved sailboat plying the waters of Lake Michigan. It is most appropriate that we celebrate his life here at Mission Point."

Ray, sitting off to the side, watched the faces of the audience as Elliott continued his remarks. Ray's phone vibrated, and he looked at the text message on the screen. B.W. Cause of death: Cranial Bleed, blunt force trauma to skull. Ray thought about the scene in the greenhouse; Elliott rattled on in the background.

Did she fall or was she pushed? If she was pushed, is the assailant here in the room?" Ray wondered as he looked around. Pepper Markley was sitting near him, carefully inspecting her manicure. Jill Wudbine was in a swivel chair, one brought in from an adjoining office. She was slowly rotating from side to side, her gaze fixed on the carpet just beyond her sandals. Alyson Mickels' stared off through the window in the direction of Lake Michigan. Verity Wudbine-Merone was focused on her knitting. She would look up toward her son, then back at her needles.

"With the help of my good wife, Jill, and our resourceful concierge, Pepper Markley, we are currently developing a task analysis for the event. Multiple venues will be required. As soon as the task analysis is done, we will be providing each of you with job descriptions and a calendar of events. Needless to say, you will be generously compensated for your time. Pepper will be looking after the HR responsibilities for the event. Alyson

Mickels will be handling the transportation arrangements. If you have any questions, they should be directed to these women.

Elliott looked in Ray's direction.

"We are going to have many important people in attendance. And we live in a time when we have to be aware of every possible threat. Ms. Mickels will be heading our security team, and we will bring in more personnel from Chicago. But we are grateful that Sheriff Elkins is here, and I know his assistance will be invaluable." Elliott gestured in Ray's direction.

"Are there any questions?" He scanned the room.

"Elliott, we've had two deaths," noted Sterling Shevlin. "Is this service for Brenda Wudbine, too? Surely there needs to be a way of remembering your stepmother."

Elliott was not quick to answer. He looked at Jill, holding her in his gaze for many seconds. Finally, Jill responded. "Brenda's sudden death is most tragic. We will celebrate her life in a family ceremony as soon as her body is returned to us. Brenda was a very private person, and we will honor her passing in a manner consistent with the way she lived."

"So your logic is if you're private you get private, and if you're public you get public?"

"Sterling, we can have this conversation at another time," said Elliott.

Ray watched as Shevlin came to his feet. "This question is for the Sheriff. The events of the last few days have been horrendous for all of us. And now we are dealing with a second death. Brenda—initially we were told that she died of natural causes, but there are reports to the contrary. Would you put the rumors to rest?" Shevlin dropped back into his seat.

Ray stood so he could see all the faces in the room.

"We are aware of the fact that Brenda Wudbine had some major health issues. However, at this time we are still treating it as an unexplained death. We are looking at every possibility. I will be able to tell you more when we have the complete results from the forensic autopsy." Ray studied the faces carefully.

"Sheriff, before you sit down, I have another question." Shevlin was on his feet again. "Malcolm's death. It just happened a few days ago. I know that you and your people have been working on this with great diligence. But there have been no arrests. True?"

"True."

"So let me voice the concerns of many in this room. There's a killer loose. He or she might even be in this room. None of us has ever confronted this kind of violence. Quite frankly, I'm frightened to even go into the theater. Our colony, it's not the same place. Sheriff, can you provide any assurance that this crime will be solved in the near future?"

"That's a good question, Mr. Shevlin, a question that the public has a right to ask. I can tell you that we are making progress. This was a complex, carefully planned and executed crime. The pieces are starting to fall together."

"Sterling, can we get back to the task at hand?" pleaded Elliott.

"This is the business at hand. How can you consider bringing all these very important people here when a killer is running lose?"

"Maybe the Sheriff should have started with you," said Elliott. "This play, casting my father in the role of the most hated man in the village… was all your idea. You put him in that chair. Defenseless. A sitting duck."

"Why, Elliott, why?" shouted Shevlin. "I had nothing to gain. Your wife, your minions, they were all in the theater. Was this a team building exercise for the Wudbine Group? You'd free yourselves from that SOB. Become fabulously rich in the process."

"Can we all just settle down? There's work to be done," pleaded Grubbs in a conciliatory tone.

"If you killed him, Grubby," roared Shevlin, "we'd all be supporting you. Justifiable homicide. Why didn't you do it years ago?" He paused, dropping his voice. "And then there's Brenda. Battered wife? And her dying, just too convenient. Like I was saying, Elliott, how can we go forward with this memorial service when the killer is still at large?"

"If you'd like to confess, we'd get this all behind us." Jill's tone was shrill and hostile.

"The only thing I have to confess to is allowing that bastard to run over me."

"Sterling, enough," scolded Verity.

"Enough, my ass. We all remember those bad old days."

"We don't need to do this in front of…."

Shevlin cut her off. "Yes, I know. We need to protect the children. And that's what we've done for decades, protect, been cowed. Or perhaps been cowards."

"Are you done, Sterling?" asked Elliott.

"Actually, I'm just warming to the topic. But maybe we should throw this back to the Sheriff." He stopped and made a slow, dramatic gesture with his right arm toward Ray. "You've been snooping around for days. We've all been interrogated several times. I imagine a lot of dirty linen has been aired. I'm sure you've heard every titillating rumor that's circulated around here for the last 50 years. The Mission Point Summer Colony is hardly a Peyton Place. That said, we're not totally boring. What can you tell us, Sheriff? Do you think I'm the guilty party? Is a murderer sitting next to me?"

Ray sat silently and considered if this might be an opportunity to flush out the killer. Then he stood. Before starting to speak he carefully regarded the crowd. Every face was turned in his direction. One by one, he gazed at each individual. He was tapping his foot, thinking Largo. Slowly inhaling and exhaling, observing the tension in the room.

"While none of you were ever identified as persons of interest, almost everyone in the room had access to Malcolm Wudbine. And from the beginning we believed that more than one person was involved.

"Verity, Mrs. Wudbine-Merone," he looked in her direction, "made an impassioned case for the killers coming from the outside, foreigners wanting revenge for some alleged misdeeds on Malcolm's part.

"Mr. Shevlin, you certainly had the means and opportunity. No one else knows the theater, the play, or the timing better than you. You cast the play and put Wudbine in a defenseless position. And just in giving him that part, there was hostility and malice. You were having a joke, one that many of your friends here shared.

"And David Johnson, you're still angry about the loss of much of your retirement. From your perch in the light booth you were in an excellent position to orchestrate and participate in this crime. You had means, motive, and opportunity."

Ray started to pick up the pace. "There are a number of women here who have grievances against Wudbine, some ancient, some ongoing.

"And, Elliott, I don't know what motive you might have had, but your whereabouts at the time of the crime has yet to be firmly established.

"But let me return to the sudden death of Brenda Wudbine. Like I indicated earlier, this is still officially an unexplained death. However, things have changed. It's now a suspicious death, very suspicious indeed. So let me take a few steps back. I mentioned earlier that we always suspected two people were involved. We now have evidence that suggests that

Brenda Wudbine was near the electrical boxes on the Assembly Building at the time the lights went out. We strongly suspect that she's the one who pulled the switch and put the place in darkness for close to two minutes, the power finally being restored by David Johnson."

"So who's the other half of the team?" demanded Shevlin.

"That's an interesting question. The person on the inside had to communicate with Brenda, telling her when to put the place in darkness. The assailant had to be a member of the cast or crew, someone who could move about backstage without drawing suspicion. Through careful planning, the killer found a place where they could hide before the attack. On the assailant's signal, the power was switched off. I think a cell phone was used to cue Brenda. We are now in possession of key pieces of evidence and have search warrants for the cell phone records that we think will lead us to the killer. Arrests are pending."

Ray's gaze was fixed on Jill Wudbine. She stared back. Then he saw her left arm come up, a pistol gripped tightly in her left hand, pointing in his direction. Then she swept the gun back toward Elliott. Screams and confusion followed the crack of the pistol. People dove for the floor. Ray saw Jill stepping over them as she sprinted for the door. He followed her, his own weapon now drawn, pausing at the door long enough to see her disappearing over the dune grass toward the water.

48

～

"We've hardly seen you since Independence Day," said Lisa, "and now it's almost Labor Day."

"She's been dying to talk to you," said Marc. "All she knows about the Wudbine case is what's she read in the paper. Lisa always wants the whole story. I've told her this is a social occasion, that you won't want to talk shop."

"We took this pledge at the beginning of the summer," said Sue, coming to the table. "We were going to totally separate our professional and private lives. That included working normal business hours, and taking weekends off. I even scheduled a week of vacation time to show Harry the area."

"And how did that work out for you?" teased Lisa.

"I got to spend a week away from the office providing doggie daycare," said Harry Hawkins.

"So how did you break the case?" Lisa continued her questioning.

"Do you want me to lock her in the car?" asked Marc.

"Just the end, Ray," pressed Lisa.

"We have this pattern," said Sue, taking the question. "We just pursue every promising lead, and slowly the pieces start to fall together. Ray keeps covering his whiteboard with maps and charts, organizers of sorts, searching for connections. And several times, Hanna," Sue looked in her direction, "provided invaluable assistance.

"We're being very careful what we say about the investigation. Jill Wudbine has retained one of the best criminal attorneys in the country. We don't want jeopardize the case."

"Well, why did Jill shoot her husband? What's his name?"

"Elliott. I think we're both clueless on that one," said Ray looking over at Sue. "Fortunately, it was a non-fatal wound."

"And her father-in-law? Why?"

Ray looked at Lisa, "Heaven has no rage like love to hatred turned, Nor hell a fury like a woman scorned."

"With her father-in-law? Oh my God."

"There are elements of Greek tragedy here," said Ray.

"How about the other woman?" Lisa continued her questioning.

"I've been up to see Elliott at the hospital. The woman in question appears to be constantly at his side. She seems quite smitten."

"So what really happened, what's the backstory?"

"I'll let the journalists and writers dig that out. I'm sure there's a book here, or at least a made-for-TV movie. End of story, Lisa. I'll take the whitefish off the grill in a minute or two. Marc, pour some sparkling wine, please. Let's drink to summer."

Author's Note:

I am greatly indebted to Heather Shaw for her story editing skills, cover design, and interior layout. I am in awe of her artistic skills and literary sensibilities. Her friendship, sage advice, and diplomatic prodding keep me on task.

Special thanks to Jim and Tammy Royle, Deb Kline, and other early readers of this manuscript, and to Amié Merzion for her careful final proofing.

None of this would be possible without the support and friendship of the independent local booksellers in northern Michigan who have been stocking my novels and inviting me for signings and book talks for more than a decade.

Also, I am grateful to so many people in law enforcement and medicine who have patiently shared their expertise and time.

And, finally, Mary K, who provides support, friendship, and wise counsel as the book moves from a few random notes to a final draft.

Books in the Ray Elkins Series:

Summer People
Color Tour
Deer Season
Shelf Ice
Medieval Murders
Cruelest Month

Made in the USA
Lexington, KY
27 June 2014